THE RUSHING OF THE
BROOK

Kansas Bradbury

TO MUNA

THANK YOU FOR THE
SUPPORT. I HOPE YOU
ENJOY HAYWARD'S JOURNEY.

NOV 4/2017

ALL THE
BEST

Kansas Bradbury

 FriesenPress

Suite 300 - 990 Fort St
Victoria, BC, V8V 3K2
Canada

www.friesenpress.com

Copyright © 2017 by Kansas Bradbury
First Edition — 2017

ISBN
978-1-5255-0194-4 (Hardcover)
978-1-5255-0195-1 (Paperback)
978-1-5255-0196-8 (eBook)

1. FICTION, THRILLERS

Distributed to the trade by The Ingram Book Company

Dedication

This novel is dedicated to my biggest supporters in writing and in life, my wife Colleen, and my parents, Madonna and Harold.

Chapter 1

We're Just Boys

"Did you see the *Money Movie* last night?" Joe asked as he sipped a juice box.

"Nah," Hayward replied. He had seen it, but wasn't in the mood to talk about it.

"The word was 'gulch!'"

Hayward didn't respond; he was fixated on the girl and boy at the end of the pavement playing hopscotch.

"I called, but got a busy signal," Joe said before sipping noisily.

Hayward stood where the edge of the playground meets the tree line. What was she doing with him? He watched Beth toss a rock along the pavement and hop toward it, her ponytail bouncing wildly with every jump.

"I was gonna try again, but Dad yelled that I would never get through."

Daniel Green. Of all the guys in elementary school. My Beth, playing with . . . him, Hayward thought, then pushed his foot down on a small stump.

"I'll never get through if I don't try," Joe went on before trying to suck the last molecule of juice from the box.

Hayward pushed his foot down harder. It felt as though the stump was about to bust through the rubber of his sneaker and plunge into the sole of his foot. He welcomed the pain and kept pushing.

"Do ya think I'll ever get through?"

Hayward watched in disbelief as Daniel produced a pack of gum from his pocket and gave it to Beth—not a piece, but a *pack*. Hayward realized that, even at only eleven years old, the girls in his grade five class at Lady Madonna Elementary School were already impressed by money—something that Daniel Green's parents were free with, especially when it came to their son. He'd seen Daniel coming back from the corner store with piles of candy and showing it around like he was some sort of elementary school tycoon. Not just pieces of candy but *boxes*, displaying them on his desk for the whole eleven-year-old world to see. *His showboating can't be working on Beth. . . my Beth.*

"Hayward!"

Hayward ignored Joe and pushed his foot harder into the stump; he imagined he must be bleeding by now, his sock soaked with blood.

"Hayward!"

Hayward looked up at Joe.

"Aren't you listening?"

Hayward stared at him without saying a word, still thinking about the hopscotch players.

"Do you think I'll ever get through on the phone to the *Money Movie* people—you know, if I keep tryin'?"

Hayward just stared. Joe began to look distressed. Finally, Hayward responded.

"You gotta be in to win."

Joe's eyes widened as Hayward continued.

"Your dad—he's never going to win because he's not in."

Joe's smile got so big that Hayward thought the corners of his mouth would fall right off his face.

"That's what I keep telling him," Joe replied, pointing at himself. "If I don't call, I don't even have a shot."

Hayward looked back in Beth's direction, but she and Daniel were gone. "Great!" he said suddenly. No longer paying attention to the pain, he took his foot off the stump.

"What's great?"

"Nothing." Hayward changed the subject. "Are we going to go with Davey and Pete to the junkyard this afternoon?"

"I want to, if they're still going."

Hayward, Joe, Davey, and Pete lived on the same street. Davey and Pete were a year older, and in the sixth grade. The four boys were great friends and did almost everything together. Most of the time they all got along, but the older two occasionally gave Hayward a hard time because he was smaller. As a bigger kid, Joe fit in a bit better.

Joe finally accepted that the juice box was empty and tossed it into the trees. "Do you want to go over to the grade six area and ask them?" he asked.

"Nah, lunch is almost over. We'll see them after school. Let's head over to our door."

Joe nodded in agreement, and they walked toward the side of the school with the grade five entrance. As they rounded the side of the building, Hayward saw Beth and Daniel standing by the door. They were standing very close together—too close. Heat built up in Hayward's belly, and his head felt like he was wearing a helmet that was too small. He had to do something. *Daniel can't be on school grounds, in front of everyone, standing that close to Beth. . . my Beth*, he decided.

"I gotta do something!"

Hayward marched up and stopped in front of Daniel and Beth, leaving Joe looking completely confused. They halted their conversation and looked at him, obviously waiting to hear what he wanted. Suddenly, Hayward was overcome with nervousness and unable to speak. His body froze and his mind went blank. Seconds passed, and he watched both of their faces begin to reflect the awkwardness. He was just about to turn and walk away when he felt his mouth open. He had no idea what would come out.

"Are you guys going to Kevin's birthday party on Friday?"

They both looked relieved.

"I think so," Daniel said.

Beth looked at her feet, and then at Hayward. Her face was bathed in sunlight. Her eyes were so blue, and Hayward thought that she was the most beautiful thing he'd ever seen.

"Yeah, I'm going," Beth said, shyly looking down again.

"Great!" Hayward exclaimed, "I guess I'll see you there, then." He turned and walked away with Joe in tow.

"What the hell was that?" Joe asked.

"What was what?"

"What you just did there."

"Nothing."

"You did something. You looked nuts."

"No, I didn't!"

"Okay, okay, you didn't," Joe said, his voice dripping with sarcasm.

"I didn't!" Hayward insisted, and then looked over his shoulder. Beth was looking in his direction. He quickly looked down.

***

"Why won't you trade with me?" Pete asked.

"Because, I want this one," Davey replied.

"I really think you should trade with me."

"I don't."

Pete didn't understand what was going on; he could normally get Davey to do practically anything. What he wanted now was the topic of the ruffed grouse Davey was assigned for their latest school project. Pete's father was a hunter and sometimes brought home a ruffed grouse after a hunting trip. If he had the ruffed grouse instead of the squirrel, his father would be eager to help him and they would get to spend time together.

But none of that would happen, though, because of Davey. He glared at him. Davey was oblivious to his anger, intent on drawing a picture on the last page of his notebook—a picture of a ruffed grouse. Pete felt his body temperature rise.

"Are we still going to the junkyard after school?" Davey asked, without looking up from his drawing.

Pete said sternly, "Trade projects with me."

Davey stopped drawing and looked up at him. Pete saw a frightened look on his friend's face as their eyes locked. Suddenly, Davey's frightened look turned to one of determination, as if he had just been injected with a syringe of courage.

"No!" Davey snapped.

Pete looked away in frustration, not only because he couldn't get the topic he wanted, but also because Davey had never stood up to him like that before. Their relationship had just changed. Suddenly he didn't have Davey under his thumb anymore. Pete felt wounded.

***

Hayward sat at his table with Joe in their grade five classroom. His mind kept replaying what had happened with Beth. *What did she think of it?* He wondered. *You know what she thought. You looked like an idiot in front of her and Daniel. . . and Joe.* Joe was his oldest friend. They had met when they were four years old, and they used to make mud pies in his backyard. He knew Joe was not really concerned with girls yet; his focus was on going to the junkyard after school with Pete and Davey. He still liked hanging out with those guys more than girls. *He's lucky. He just looks forward to the next time he can be with his idols. He's not thinking about Beth Cooper and what she's doing now . . . or now . . . or now.* He turned to Joe.

"Okay, I guess I looked stupid in front of Beth earlier."

"I guess you did," Joe replied.

"Did you see this coming?" Hayward asked, wanting to blame someone else for his problem.

"See what coming?"

"This thing with Beth and Daniel."

"No!"

"No?" Hayward's tone was accusatory.

"Look, if you like Beth, do something about it."

"What do you suggest I do?"

"I don't know."

"I don't know, either."

"I think you're too young to worry about this. Davey and Pete don't have girlfriends, and they're a year older than us. What's your rush with this girl stuff? What is so special about Beth?"

What isn't special about Beth? "I just have a gut feeling about this," Hayward replied.

"About what?"

"About this Daniel and Beth thing. I think it's very bad, and I feel like I need to stop it."

Joe turned to Hayward and looked him in the eyes. "Look, Hay," he began. "We've been friends for a long time, and this is how I see things. You are making this situation into something it doesn't have to be. We're in grade five! We have the rest of this year—and *another* whole year—before junior high, which will be three full years of girl drama. After that, there's the soap opera of high school, where everyone dates everyone."

"How do you know that?"

"TV."

Hayward nodded in approval.

"Hay, you are way too young to be thinking about this right now. We're just boys. Yes, we are mature boys, but still boys. Let's enjoy it."

Hayward stared at him, amazed at how dead-on Joe's analysis was. It was the smartest thing he had ever heard Joe say.

"You're right," he said to Joe. "You're totally right. And thank you."

Joe nodded firmly, ending the conversation now that he'd finally gotten through to his friend. Hayward turned around at his desk, more determined than ever to stop this Beth-and-Daniel relationship—or whatever it was.

Chapter 2

The Plan

Writing in his notebook, Pete pressed the pencil so hard it broke. He looked over at Davey, who had turned sideways to engage in a debate about wrestling with Bill at the next table. Pete thought back to when they were in grade four. They had been playing catch in their own area of the schoolyard when three grade six boys came over to them. The older boys took the ball and wouldn't give it back. Davey tried to get the ball back, and after several failed attempts, he called them a bunch of idiots. They quickly surrounded him and pushed him to the ground. Pete had intervened and basically talked them out of giving Davey—and possibly himself—the beating of their lives. Did Davey remember that?

Another time, his parents allowed him to take one friend to the cottage for a week filled with canoeing, fishing, barbeques, and board games. He could have taken any one of the kids from the neighbourhood. He chose Davey. Had Davey forgotten that? And then there were the days that Davey had come knocking on his door to ask him to come out to play or to walk to school, and Pete had gone with him. Had Davey forgotten about that? Maybe he'd spend more time with Hayward and Joe. They really looked up to him. Maybe he'd start hanging out with some of the other kids on the street. How would Davey feel if he went to the door and Pete had already left for school with the other boys? He looked over at the slip of paper on Davey's side of the table and read the words again: "ruffed grouse." He clenched his teeth. How would Davey feel about doing things without his best friend?

***

Hayward copied math problems from the chalkboard—his homework for the evening. It wouldn't be easy to concentrate on math tonight. He knew what and whom he'd be thinking about. How did it come to this? When did this happen? How did he become so wrapped up in a girl—not just a girl, *that* girl . . . *his* girl? Things would be so much easier if he could just forget about her and pretend she didn't even exist.

Joe was right. There would be years of dating—probably many different girls—and then marriage someday. Certainly marriage, in about fifteen or twenty years, wouldn't involve a girl from his fifth-grade class. If he asked everyone he knew if they had heard of any couple that got together in grade five, he knew what their answer would be. He had seen countless shows on TV about married people and how they met, and he couldn't remember any of them being about a couple that had got together in grade five. A high school sweetheart story was about as far back as they go. But the fifth grade? Never. *Maybe you'll be the first*, he mused. Why, then, was this feeling so strong? What was this feeling of *jealousy*—a word Hayward had just learned the meaning of, and probably couldn't even spell?

Hayward stopped copying the math problems and looked at Beth, who sat a row over and up two. Her hair was pulled back in a ponytail and he could see the side of her face. Her skin looked so soft. Her ear looked so perfect. It was cute that her head was tilted slightly as she copied the math homework. *This feeling, so strong.* He sighed.

Hayward turned to his right and looked back a seat. Daniel was also copying the homework problems. What did she see in him? He looked like someone who would have a hell of a time with acne during puberty, because the babies of the acne mother lode were already starting to show. He would probably end up as an adult with a deeply pockmarked and scarred face. Hayward smiled. The smile quickly faded as he envisioned his own face looking that way. Suddenly, Daniel glanced back at him. Hayward quickly looked away.

Great! After that stupid walk-up-and-make-an-idiot-of-yourself episode at lunch, now he catches you staring at him. He must know something is up, Hayward concluded. He wondered if all girls in the future would complicate his life this much. *She's your future.*

What about Kevin McLeod's party? Both Beth and Daniel said they were going. He pictured the basement of Kevin's house, his classmates slow dancing to the last couple of songs of the night. Who would pair up with whom? He knew, from previous parties, that Jamie Williams and Dorothy Stevens would dance together. Since they started having dance parties two months ago, those two always danced the last dances together. The other kids expected it; they were kind of a couple. How could he get that with Beth? How did that start? Did Jamie ask Dorothy to be his girlfriend? He probably would have heard about that. Had Jamie asked her to only slow dance with him, or had she asked him? Were they actually boyfriend and girlfriend, and just keeping it a secret? If so, why wouldn't they tell anyone?

Hayward pictured Jamie and Dorothy dancing together. He wanted to be dancing next to them with Beth. He wanted the others to look at him and Beth and think the same thing they thought when they saw Jamie and Dorothy: *When the slow dances come on, don't ask either of them to dance, because they're a couple.* On the playground today, it had looked more like Daniel would be the person that Beth would be slow dancing with. A shiver went up Hayward's spine. How could this be prevented? How could he speed up this coupling-up process, and ensure it went in his favour? Unable to come up with any answers, he started to sketch a robot in his notebook.

The teacher wiped away the problems she'd written on the board. Those who hadn't finished copying them down sighed. The teacher shrugged her shoulders as if to say, "Get it from someone who cares."

Hayward noted how loud the sigh was. How many people had not written down the math problems? Why? What were they thinking about? Were they thinking about Kevin's party? Were they thinking about whom they'd be slow dancing with? He was suddenly horrified. Did he have other competition for Beth besides Daniel? The muscles in his chest started to tighten. He had to act fast. He flipped his pencil back and forth. Okay, what did older kids do? A lot of older kids were boyfriend and girlfriend. He didn't have an older brother or sister, so he didn't know much about how they acted, except from what he saw on TV. On TV, older boys and girls went on dates, and that's how they became boyfriend and girlfriend.

How could that apply to this situation? He scribbled the word "date" on the page. None of the parents of the kids in his class would allow them to go on a date, and there were no school dances for grade fives. He and his classmates only went to birthday parties, where they danced with each other. He scribbled the word "parties" on the page. He looked down at the words he had written. That was it! Date parties! A guy could ask a girl, "Would you like to go on a date to Kevin's party?" and then if she said "Yes," that guy and girl would hang close to each other and dance together the whole evening. This was brilliant, but he had to get some people on board for the idea to work. He felt sure everyone would go for it—and why not? It was dating without your parents knowing a thing. Most of the girls wouldn't be allowed to officially date for quite a few more years.

He picked up his notebook, flipped the page, and started to craft a note to pass around the class, outlining the plan. He remembered from TV that this was called "floating an idea." He hoped it wouldn't sink.

***

Pete stared at the small piece of paper in front of Davey. He wanted that topic bad, and was having a lot of trouble understanding the situation he was in. He was used to getting what he wanted. Why wouldn't Davey trade with him? Did he want it for the same reason as Pete? He didn't think Davey's dad hunted; he was more of a fisherman, and even owned a boat. If he had gotten a topic better than a stupid squirrel, then maybe there could have been some sort of deal.

He opened his piece of paper again, hoping as he unfolded it that it would say something else, but there it was: stupid "squirrel." Pete sighed. Maybe he could do his project on something else, and just pay no attention to his piece of paper. Could that work? He pictured the day the teacher called for him to do his presentation. He would get up and start to present his project on something cool, like a bat. Would the other kids and the teacher be so impressed with his killer project they would forget all about his original topic? Or would someone put up his hand and say, "Hey, I thought his project was on the squirrel"? He knew someone would do that. *Probably Davey*, he reasoned. *After all, he's different now.* He looked at the piece of paper again like it was some sort of punishment.

Pete looked around the classroom. Maybe someone else in the class might want to trade. *Hey, you want to trade? Not sure, what you got?* The thought of answering "squirrel" made him clench his teeth. Nope. The only way he would get out of this was to get Davey to trade with him—Davey, his oldest friend, his buddy, his pal. They were virtually inseparable. How could Davey turn his back on him? Maybe Davey didn't realize how much trading topics meant to him. If he let him know how important it was, and pulled on the heartstrings a little—or a lot—Davey would understand. He would explain to Davey why he really wanted it, the excitement of spending time with his dad. Surely his best friend would trade project topics with him then. Pete turned to Davey.

"Hey, man."

Davey turned in his chair to face him.

"Listen, you know my dad's a hunter, right?"

"Yeah," Davey said hesitantly.

"So, you know that he hunts partridge, which are the ruffed grouse." Pete pointed at the piece of paper on the desk as he said it. "Yeah, well if that was my project, my dad would help me with it, and it would be so cool to spend that time with him. A lot of his interests are things that I'm not old enough to do, like drinking with his buddies and going to the horse races. This project could be something special. If you traded your topic, it would mean so much to me."

There it was; he had put it all out there. He had shown Davey a softer side that he had never shown before, and he wouldn't regret any of it—if it worked. Davey stared at him blankly while Pete felt like he had finished talking yesterday.

Finally, his friend replied, "My dad hunts sometimes too, and he spends a lot of time on his boat, so this project would be great for me and my dad."

"Your dad doesn't hunt!" Pete said, raising his voice.

"Yes he does!" Davey barked back.

"When?"

"What do you mean, 'when?' I don't know, I didn't write it down on my calendar. He just does."

And there it was—Pete had shown his weak side. His mother had taught him to never show another person weakness . . . never. He had shown it to Davey . . . for nothing. Pete felt a wave of heat rise from his genitals and move up toward his head. That damn piece of paper was still Davey's. He stared into Davey's eyes and saw fear there.

I tried to avoid this, but you had to be stupid and let it come down to this. All you had to do was trade.

Pete felt the heat in his head; it felt like his ears would burst into flames. He reached out and grabbed Davey by the front of his shirt and pulled his face up to meet his own. Pete started to breathe through his teeth as Davey's expression turned to horror and tears welled in his eyes.

***

Hayward watched as each student read the note and passed it on. Some smiled, some glanced at him, and some acted as if they hadn't read it. A sudden rush came over him: an embarrassing feeling that this had been a mistake, a feeling that everyone would think the things he wrote in the note were absurd, and that he would become the laughing stock of the fifth grade. His chest felt tight again. He watched intently as each student read it. He studied their reactions, trying to read their minds.

"Hey," Joe said.

Thankfully, it was something to stop the horrible roller coaster in Hayward's mind. "What's up?" he replied.

"If Pete and Davey are going to the junkyard after school, are you coming?"

It would be fun to go to the junkyard even if he was a lovesick fifth grader, but if this note worked, he would need time after school to begin the next phase of his plan. As the other students went home to mull over this new and exciting element in their lives, he would hopefully have already sewn up his date for the party. He would ask Beth right after school and get the jump on Daniel or any other would-be suitor. He planned to meet up with her where she got on the bus and pop the question. Then he would be free to dream about the last dances at the party, while the others worried about who they would ask, or who would ask them. *What if she says no?*

"I don't know yet," Hayward said to Joe.

"What the hell else you got to do?" Joe asked, stunned.

"I just have some stuff I have to do," Hayward said, not wanting to tell Joe what was up.

He knew Joe would have enough questions later when the note reached him. The main one would be, "Why can't the boys be together?" Himself, Joe, Pete, and Davey: the "Cornflakes," as one of the neighbours once quipped. The name had stuck.

"I have to see the teacher about something," Hayward said.

"About what?" Joe asked.

Damn! What a dumb thing to say; this would fire up Joe's interest even more. Now he had to come up with another lie. His father once told him, "Son, if you lie, you better have the time and energy to plan out all the lies that you'll have to tell to back up that one." He had no time to waste coming up with new lies or new plans. His main plan was still being passed around the room.

"I have to see her about some days off later in the year. My family is planning a trip."

"Where?" Joe asked. Of course.

Maybe if you just stop talking, you won't dig yourself a deeper hole, Hayward thought angrily, then said, "It's a surprise."

Even Hayward was having trouble believing what he was saying. *You're asking for the time off, for a surprise. Boy, you're a bad liar.* He had to end this even if he looked like a jerk.

"Look, my parents said they want to go somewhere south this winter. They didn't say where! They told me to ask the teacher when would be a good time depending on tests and assignments! Okay?"

Joe was shocked by his demeanour. "Okay!" he said and turned back to face the front of the classroom, offended.

Hayward, feeling bad about snapping at Joe, looked around to see his note just as it was passed to Beth. She gently unfolded it underneath the table to shield it from the teacher. Hayward felt as if he would explode with anticipation; he would give anything to read her mind. She stared at the note for about thirty seconds. She should be done reading it by now. He started to panic. Did he write it clearly enough? Were there some embarrassing grammar and spelling mistakes? Finally, she folded the paper and pulled it up from under the desk. Gently tapping Darren Wilkie's shoulder, she passed it on. She nodded her head as Darren took it, her ponytail waggling around, and then, to Hayward's surprise, she turned around and looked right at him. Hayward's eyes widened. Beth smiled before turning back.

Chapter 3

Like a Bull

The man looked around the trailer home and wondered how it had come to this. His infant son was crying in the back bedroom. Taking a drag from his cigarette, he blew the smoke up in O shapes, then raised his bottle of beer and took three large gulps, the last spilling a little down the corners of his mouth. The baby continued to cry. He heard Jill calling him from the other room but ignored her. Instead, he looked out the window where his truck sat idle; the transmission had died a week ago. Jill came out of the bedroom and stood in the hallway, staring at him.

"Can you hear that, or are you friggin' retarded?" she barked.

He calmly pulled his cigarette up to his lips and took another drag. She stared at him without moving. He blew smoke rings and listened as the volume of the baby's cries grew. Jill continued to stare at him. He looked out the window again. It was getting dark quickly. He wished he could go to the bar and have a few drinks with the boys, but he didn't have the money. He hadn't gone to work since last week; he couldn't, with his truck broken down. He looked at it, just sitting there. There's nothing more useless than a truck that won't run.

He took a swig from his bottle and turned his head to see Jill in the hallway, skinny with matted, unclean hair, wearing a long T-shirt and pyjama bottoms, her hands on her hips. Her silhouette made him think of stick people. He was wrong about the truck; the most useless thing is a mother that doesn't stop her baby from crying. He looked at her with disdain, wondering how long she would stay there, staring at him with nothing coming out of her stinkin' mouth, while their son lay wanting his mother. He took another drag from his cigarette and this time blew the smoke out his nose like a bull. She didn't move. Was she going to stand there until he did something? *Well, she better not push it, or the move she is waiting for is something she is gonna regret*, he thought hatefully.

At this moment, if he got up, he'd walk over and sink his beer bottle into her skull. He looked back out the window, trying to shake those thoughts. He couldn't. He turned back and looked at her, made a giant hocking sound as he sucked some phlegm up from his throat, and spit a large gob of mucus on the floor about halfway to where she stood. She froze. He waited, ready to welcome any confrontation, and actually hoping it would come. He liked it, had liked it all his life: the rush of having someone trying to harm him, and the thrill of hurting them. He wondered if "thrill" was the right word. It was.

Finally, she spoke. "Get out!"

He took a drag from his cigarette, not taking his eyes off her.

"Get out!" she yelled louder.

He laughed, knowing it would only fuel her anger. He couldn't hear the baby crying anymore. He suspected that the baby was listening to see how this would play out.

"Get out, you half-man!" she yelled.

He squinted his eyes in anger as the smoke rolled around them.

"Yeah, that's what you are. Half-man. You got a dick, but you ain't no man."

Pressure started on the back of his neck and shoulder blades, as if something was trying to push him down. He knew this feeling. This was the start. He had always been told that he had a "bad temper" as a youngster, and "anger management issues" as an adult. He never described to those who told him these things what "the Push" was, for fear they would lock him up in one of those nut houses or something. He knew right from wrong, but not after *the push* started. After the Push started, he didn't know anything except rage—an incredible rage that had no thought process, no consequences, and no mercy. He wasn't a bad guy until the Push started.

"A man looks after his family," she barked. "A half-man sits on the couch all day blamin' everyone else."

His lower body and arms started to push up against the pressure that was pushing down.

"That's why your truck is broke down, it's everyone else's fault."

The upward and downward forces were pushing so hard he felt like he had no choice but to implode or explode. He jumped up off the couch. Jill screamed and turned as he started toward her. She ran down the hall. He cocked his arm in a fluid motion, and without even realizing he was going to do it, threw the bottle, continuing after her so quickly he thought he would pass the bottle in flight. Jill grabbed the door handle and turned it, but she was too late. The bottle met her ear with a sound like a brick hitting wet sand and then shattered. She staggered for a second, her knees buckling, eyes rolling up into her head, and started falling to the floor. He grabbed her hair, caught it between his fingers just before her head hit the floor. He yanked her up and held her face in front of his. Her eyes were still rolled back. He pushed his jaws together so hard they cracked. He knew she was in there. He was going to get her out.

***

"What is this stuff?" Joe asked.

"Dates!" Hayward replied defensively.

"This is not a good time to start this stuff," Joe said.

"Stuff! It's a lot more than stuff!"

"What if some of the parents find out about this?" asked Joe.

"Are you going to tell them?" Hayward snapped.

"I'm not going to tell anyone, because I think this is nuts," Joe barked back.

"I happen to think there are a lot of people in this class who think it's a great idea," Hayward replied.

"Hay, you shouldn't rush nature. Leave young people to let their feelings grow." Hayward had thought Joe was miles behind him in maturity. Now Joe suddenly sounded like some kind of wise man with years of experience. Joe continued, "If any of the parents over-hear any of the girls talking about this as a dating-type of party, do you think they will be allowed to go?"

Hayward was stunned. Joe was making perfect sense. This could jeopardize everything. One loose set of lips—say, those of a little brother or older sister—overheard by parents could crush this whole party scene. It could set the scene back a whole year, maybe even two. Holy shit! The feelings would grow with no interaction allowed because of him. When dating finally did start to happen, there sure as hell wouldn't be a date for him—the kid who ruined everything. How had he missed this? How could he have not thought this through? He suddenly felt complete terror, and it was more frighten-ing then anything he'd ever felt before.

There was only one thing to do—one thing *left* to do. He would run away. Start new. Find another grade five class, one in which he hadn't passed a note around. One where he wasn't responsible for bottling up everyone's hormones and making sure they were kept in check for a long time. Where would he run? Where could he go? Where would he stay? Would someone adopt him? He looked at Joe, who was still staring at him, and snapped back to reality. He couldn't leave; this was it, there was no running away. Any kid he'd ever heard of that ran away ended up being returned to their parents, usually that evening, or at the latest, the next day. Each time the runaway was in so much trouble when they got back that their lives were worse than they were before they ran away.

Hayward would have to take this on; there was no turning back. Even though he had not thought this through, and despite how much sense Joe made, this was his baby. He had made the note, and it had gone around the room to each and every classmate: this was his idea, and whether it worked or not, it would always be attached to him. He turned to Joe. The only thing he could do was stick to the plan and defend his idea.

"I think you should start thinking about who you're gonna ask."

Joe looked stunned. Hayward smirked. Joe stared at him for another couple of seconds and then turned back to face forward. Hayward felt bad. He knew Joe didn't want to ask anyone. He hadn't even shown a remote interest in girls yet. *You never know*, he thought, *maybe this is the kick in the pants Joe needs. Maybe this will force him to grow up.* Joe might even thank him someday. Why wasn't Joe consumed by mushy feelings?

It would be easy to abandon his plan, leave immediately after school and go with the boys to the junkyard, and ask Beth to the party tomorrow. Maybe that was the right thing to do. Then, in bed that night, he could go over what he would say and how to say it.

Someone walked by Hayward's desk and knocked a paper off the side, sending it floating across the room. He or she didn't even stop, as if they hadn't even noticed what they'd done, or didn't care. Hayward looked up to see who could be such a jerk. Daniel! Gritting his teeth, he made a fist underneath his desk. Daniel continued to walk up to the teacher's desk. She was writing in her planner, and Daniel leaned over to speak to her. The teacher nodded, and Daniel headed toward the door. Bathroom break. Hayward couldn't take his eyes off Daniel. He saw his nemesis smile at Beth. Was Beth smiling back? The palm of his clenched fist *felt* wet. This wasn't good, not good at all. There would be no waiting until tomorrow; there would be no rehearsal. He had to act fast. He needed to strike early, immediately after school. The whole purpose of this plan was for he and Beth to be together. If he couldn't go to this party with her, he didn't care if every friggin' parent knew about it. Beth going to that party with Daniel would be far worse than setting the adolescent clock back. If that happened, he would have to blow it up and ruin it for everyone. If Beth planned on going with anyone but him, he would have to turn this into a kamikaze mission. He'd ask Beth today; it was the only way.

***

Pete, still clenching Davey's shirt, stared into his eyes as a tear leapt out and rolled down his left cheek. Seeing Davey cry made Pete realize he'd lost his temper. He let go of Davey's shirt, which was wrinkled where he had gripped it. Davey didn't bother to fix it. Why not? Davey didn't seem too worried about his shirt; he was still staring at Pete, either waiting for whatever was coming next, or simply stunned at what had just happened. Pete knew he had to say something; he had to back up what he'd done. Here was his oldest and dearest friend in the world sitting across from him, wondering why he'd been attacked. Pete turned to him and was surprised to see Davey's expression changing. He was looking angry and breathing heavily. Was Davey going to stand up to him? He decided he better take this head-on.

"Look," Pete said. "I really think you should trade with me, if you know what's good for you."

He turned away. He could feel Davey's stare, but it didn't worry him. He knew that if it came down to it, he could take Davey in a fight, and if Davey wasn't a complete idiot, he knew it, too. Was he that stupid? He'd know soon.

"I am never going to trade with you, so whatever you have to do to deal with that, do it." Davey's voice was full of determination, but cracking with terror.

Whoa, Davey! Pete mused to himself. *I'm kind of proud of you for standing up for yourself, but unfortunately it was to the wrong person. You shouldn't betray your friends like that—the friends who have been with you your whole life.* Pete thought of the many times they had traded hockey stickers. Davey would trade anything Pete suggested. He wasn't focused on filling his sticker album; he was just content to be trading the stickers and making Pete happy.

Those days have passed. Davey is maturing, Pete thought. He would have to elevate his game. His grin turned into a smile. *Level two. This one will be harder, Davey, old bud.* He looked at Davey, with his flushed cheeks and his hair, on the side, wet from sweat; he looked weak. *That's good. Really good.*

***

Beth wrote her full name over and over again on a page in her notebook. She kept an eye on the classroom door, waiting for Daniel to return. He had smiled at her as he left the room, which had given her butterflies. She didn't know why she was so anxious for him to come back; he was just coming back from the bathroom. *He might smile again*, she secretly hoped. She flipped the page of her notebook to reveal a new blank one, thought for a minute, and then wrote her full name over again. She wondered about the date party, and how it would work. There was an exciting feel to it, going on a date with a boy. If any parents found out, they would probably load the lot of them up and take them all to counselling or something. She thought of the asking process. Who would ask her? She knew Daniel liked her; he'd been hanging around her a lot, giving her gifts of candy, gum, and stickers. She liked the gifts. Sometimes she showed them to the other girls, even though she knew they'd get jealous—that was the whole point of showing them, wasn't it? She thought Daniel would ask her for sure, but would anyone else? Probably not, especially if she said yes to Daniel quickly.

She thought about how she had always envisioned her first date. She turned and looked at Hayward. She'd had a crush on him for a long time and thought he would be her first date. She heard he once had a crush on her, but that was a while ago. As far as she could tell, the date party was his idea, so he must have someone in mind to ask. Had she seen him with any other girls over the last part of the school year? No. If Hayward Barry had been paying attention to any other girls at Lady Madonna Elementary School, she would have realized it. She watched as Hayward chatted with Joe; they were always together. He'd probably go to the party with Joe as his date. She turned back around, laughing to herself. The classroom door opened and Daniel came in, walking to his desk with his head down. A feeling of dread crept over her as she visualized everyone going to the party with a date except her. Just as she was starting to feel nauseated, Daniel raised his head and gave her a big smile. She smiled back. *Probably a little too big. Play it cool, girl,* she told herself.

As Daniel passed her desk, her eyes followed him, but it was Hayward they landed on when she turned around. *He's so cute.* Who would he ask? This was his idea. She envisioned Hayward and Joe holding hands and walking into the party and laughed again. Would Daniel ask her—and what would she wear? Those were the only questions that concerned her. She wrote her name in her notebook again—"Beth Joan Cooper"—then paused and wrote "Beth Joan Green." Then "Beth Joan Barry." She stared at the last one, then scratched out all three names and closed her notebook.

Chapter 4

The Wrong Side

He looked down at her lifeless body. Her eyes were wide. Blood was streaming from numerous places. He wondered if anybody had heard her screaming; but when he thought about it, he couldn't remember her screaming at all. Maybe she hadn't. The baby was crying again. He thought about how lucky the baby was that the Push had stopped. He needed to get out of here, go somewhere, start fresh, like the other times, every few years running, always at the mercy of the Push. Always having to run away from the carnage when the Push was over. Looking at Jill, he felt sad, remembering the good times they'd had.

What should he take? The man looked around the dirty trailer. *I don't want anything in this dump. Better to just start fresh.* He flung the door opened and stumbled down the steps of the trailer, his shirt covered in blood. *She shouldn't have said those things; she shouldn't have started the Push.* He grimaced, looking at his useless truck. Not going to get very far in that. He needed a vehicle. A flicker of blue light could be seen in the window of the next trailer as the TV belted out some show. The neighbours, Jed and Tammy, always looked at him with turned-up noses like they were so much better than him.

He laughed, and then asked silently, *You live in a fucking trailer park, and you walk around with turned-up noses?*

A Ford Focus was parked in Jed and Tammy's driveway. He smiled and walked around to the front of the trailer and looked around. Everything was dark. He looked up and down the street and saw no one.

Turn up your noses.

He walked up the steps and banged on the door. Inside, Tammy asked Jed who that could be at this time of night, and Jed said he didn't know. The light came on above his head and suddenly he noticed his bloodstained shirt. Maybe he should get out of here! Too late. He folded his arms over the bloodstain, but it did little to hide anything. The curtain on the door window opened and Jed peered out, his hand above his eyes, straining to see. He shifted his position on the step nervously as he heard Tammy yelling, "Who is it?" from somewhere in the trailer. He could tell by the look on Jed's face that he had recognized him. Then it happened.

That's the last time you'll turn up your fuckin' nose at me.

His fist exploded through the glass and caught Jed right in the face. Jed dropped to the floor. Tammy screamed. He pulled his hand back out of the window to inspect the damage. Tammy continued to scream. Pretty good—only one deep cut was bleeding significantly. He had punched a lot of windows in his day, and knew this was minimal damage. He jammed his hand back through the hole in the window, found the lock, and opened the door. Tammy began to scream louder and yell for help. He turned the door handle and pushed it open. Stopping the screaming would have to be the first order of business. The door only opened partially because Jed was writhing on the floor behind it. He slipped through and started after Tammy. She screamed and started to run for the bedroom, but tripped on her nightgown and fell to the floor. "Please!" she screamed, over and over.

Please what? Please kill me and take my car? Because that is what is going to happen.

He put his foot on her shoulder blades to prevent her from getting up and looked around. Jed was still in the fetal position, hands on his face, moaning. He spotted a pot on the stove. He pushed his foot down hard on her back and sprung over to the stove, grabbed the pot, and was back before she could get up. She kept screaming as he pushed his knee down on her back and cocked his arm with the pot. "Please," she yelled, her head facing the other way. *Is she talking to me?* He smirked. His arm began its forward motion. She screamed. The pot struck her in the side of the head in mid-scream, and her head dropped to the floor. That seemed pretty easy. He hadn't even thought he'd hit her that hard. He looked at the pot still in his grip. The handle was bent back, and he felt pride at the sight.

He could hear Jed moaning as he got off Tammy's body. Not sure if she was dead yet, he went to the kitchen, opened some drawers, and found a knife. He knelt down beside Tammy, raised the knife, and thought he heard a "please" as the knife dug into her calf. She didn't even flinch. He must have imagined it. He took his hand off the knife and it stayed erect. *Wow*, he thought, *I'm pretty good at this.* Must be all the practice he'd gotten after the Push had started.

Fuck that, this is all me. The Push hasn't even started. He had killed that old bitch with one shot from that pot. He got up and looked at Jed, still moaning in the same position. He hadn't even noticed what had just happened to his wife of a billion years.

Was Jed thinking this strength and violence of his wasn't all him? The man jumped up from his kneeling position. He had to show Jed that this was all him, baby, this was all him. He grabbed Jed's arm and yanked. His body rolled over, exposing his face. He looked at Jed's nose. Fucker! He raised his foot and brought the heel right down into his nose. He heard several cracks as he pumped his heel over and over into the nose area of Jed's face so many times that he lost count. *One for every time you turned it up at me.* Finally, he stopped and looked around the trailer. He saw a small wooden key-holder hanging on the wall, grabbed the keys with the Ford keychain, and walked out into the night.

***

Hayward looked at his watch: 2:30. The final school bell would ring at 2:45, and he knew what he had to do. Beth had watched that idiot Daniel leave the room. His dumb charm may be working, but this was Hayward's plan, his game, and it was time to get ready to play. Hayward knew that Beth would be waiting at the south entrance to the school until her bus came. He would leave the school the way he usually did on the west side, and go around to meet her there. He played his perfect plan out it in his head. He would smoothly ask her to the party, and she would smile and say, "Yes." How good it would feel afterward! He could see himself floating home, feet gliding, heart pounding. Maybe he would be able to catch up to the guys at the junkyard! A date with Beth and a trip to the junkyard? Now, that's a day, a day for the ages, a day to mark on the calendar . . . *a day to forget.* He suddenly felt a shiver go through his body.

Have to focus, Hayward thought, *put on the game face, check out the situation, scout out the major players and the major obstacles.* He scanned the room. Joe was talking to Jeff at the table next to theirs, talking about trucks and whose family members drove the biggest ones. Hayward looked back at Daniel, who was writing or drawing in his notebook. He began to feel envious; he couldn't draw—he could barely keep his colouring between the lines. If that nimrod Daniel gave a picture or portrait to Beth, how could he compete with that? She would think Daniel was so sweet and so talented and so artistic, and what would he do? Stand in the background with a stack of hockey cards? *Uhh, Beth, you can have whatever player you want.*

Hayward looked over at Beth, who was drawing in her notebook. This plan had to work.

Joe interrupted him. "So listen, how long you gonna be talking to the teacher? Should I try to get the boys to wait for you?"

"Yeah, man, I won't be too long. I really want to go, so tell them to wait."

"Alright, but you better not take too long, 'cause I gotta be home for supper," Joe replied.

"If I'm not there twenty minutes after the bell rings, leave without me."

Joe turned back toward the front of the classroom and began to assemble his things to leave for the day. Hayward reviewed his plan, and checked on the main players one more time. He looked at his watch: 2:40. "Showtime" was a word his father always used when it was time to do something. He started to pack up his things. It was almost showtime.

***

Pete was feeling better; the anger had begun to subside. He would do a kick-ass project on the squirrel, and throw in some funny habits and a joke or two. He'd entertain the class as usual. His confidence was very reassuring, but he still couldn't shake the feeling of betrayal. Davey had some nerve, standing up to him—the gall to treat his best friend like he had. Pete had to establish some rules again—had to re-establish himself as the physical dominator—but the time had to be right. He would have to create a situation that led to a physical confrontation between he and Davey—something that would get Davey mad enough that he'd want to fight him. He had no doubt in his mind that he would win a fight against Davey. He would come up with some scenarios later. First, he had to make peace; he had to ensure that Davey thought things were normal between them. He turned to his friend.

"Hey, man, the bell's going to ring. Are we cool? Are we still going to the junkyard?"

Davey looked puzzled. Pete knew he had to do more convincing.

"Look, I'm sorry. I just really wanted that ruffed grouse project for my dad, alright? I've already forgotten about it. Listen, we're cool, man." He put his arm around Davey and gave him a friendly shake.

A smile came over Davey's face as Pete continued. "Yeah alright, that's it, buddy. We're going to get Joe and Hayward after school, and we're all going to the junkyard. I bet after all the rain we've had over the last few days, the waterhole with the snakes will be overflowing."

Davey looked up at him adoringly and nodded. Pete continued to sell. "Let's get our stuff together, man. When that bell rings, we got to hightail it home and get on our scrubbies. We got some snakes to catch today."

Davey, still smiling, began to pack up his stuff.

"You up for this or what, bro?" Pete asked.

"Yeah, yeah," Davey replied.

Back to normal, Pete thought. *Perfect.*

***

The final school bell rang, giving Hayward the same feeling as a starter pistol did. He grabbed his bag, jumped up from his chair, and headed for the door. Joe was expecting him to talk to the teacher— a minor detail that he could explain later. He fell behind a couple of other students, but was the third one out the door. He grabbed his jacket off the hanger outside the classroom, gave the exit door a hearty push, and bounced out into the cool afternoon air. Hayward didn't break stride as he pulled on his jacket and headed toward the south entrance. He could see the buses parked there, awaiting their passengers. He was walking so fast that the backs of his calves began to hurt. Everything was running smoothly. He would make it there well before Beth, and would have enough time to go over what he would say—and to stop sweating.

Hayward parked himself in a good position between the buses and the school exit. He wasn't sure which bus Beth would be getting on, so he had to be ready to cover some ground. The air was so chilly his nose started to run. One of the supervisor ladies—who made sure all the students got on the buses safely—started walking toward him. He shifted uncomfortably on his feet. She was looking at him strangely. Hayward could tell the supervisor knew he wasn't one of the students that usually got on the buses. *Should I say I'm waiting for a friend?* he wondered. Of course, she would ask who the friend was.

Just then, the south exit doors flew open and students began to stream out. The supervisor turned and looked back towards the students. Hayward felt relieved. *Yeah! Go do your job, lady, don't worry about me.* Once Beth passed the supervisor, he would be able to talk to her before she got on the bus. The students flowed out of the door until finally, there she was: Beth. His heart skipped. She came down the steps and started to walk his way; as she did, the supervisor looked back at him again, squinted, and started to walk toward him, as well. Hayward's heart began to race. This wasn't good. She was going to ruin everything by coming over. She would start asking him a lot of questions. *I have to get to Beth before she gets on her bus*, he thought desperately. Hayward, trying to avoid the supervisor, quickly started to go around the front of the bus to the blind side when he heard her yell.

"Hey, where are you going?"

Hayward felt the pressure on the sides of his head when he realized what he'd just done. They weren't allowed to walk on that side of the buses. The supervisors referred to the side without the door as the "blind side" because they could not see kids who were over there. He could hear every teacher grinding it into all the students' heads over and over at the beginning of every year. It was a cardinal rule of the school, and he had just broken it. This was bad. The supervisor came after him on the blind side of the bus.

"Get back here, Mister!" she bellowed.

Hayward reached the space between the parked buses where he planned to squeeze back between them. He stopped. He knew that if he kept going he would meet Beth with this yelling supervisor on his ass. It would be quite an embarrassing situation. The supervisor lady grabbed him by the arm.

"Hey!" she yelled again, even though he was right in front of her. "You're not allowed on this side of the bus."

"Yeah, I forgot," Hayward replied guiltily. From his viewpoint between the parked buses, he saw Beth walk by. His heart sank even further.

"What are you doing here? You're not a bus student."

Hayward had to come up with something good to get this mole-nosed supervisor to release his arm before Beth looked out the bus window and saw him. He began to try to explain, even though he hadn't decided on what he would say yet.

"I couldn't go the way I usually go home because—" his heart pounded,

"—because there was somebody who was going to beat me up."

Her face changed from sternness to compassion in about a millisecond.

"You poor dear," she said. "You must be very frightened."

"Yes, yes I am," Hayward continued in a whiny voice. "I couldn't go home."

"What's the name of this bully?"

Hayward knew this was coming. "I don't want to be a snitch," he replied.

"If this person is causing you to break school rules and go on the wrong side of the buses, I need his name. This is very serious."

Hayward knew the only way out of this situation was to give her the name of a student that went to this school, or his excuse meant nothing.

"Davey Arcal," he blurted out.

She looked up and started to recite his name. "Davey Arcal . . . Davey Arcal, isn't that a grade six boy?"

Hayward dropped his head and said nothing.

"I know who that boy is. We'll just have to talk with him and Principal Crewe tomorrow," she said emphatically.

Hayward wondered how he would explain this to Davey later. He figured he really would get beaten up. Right now, though, he still had some work to do.

"Listen, Miss, he's probably not waiting for me anymore. Can I go? My mom's going to get worried."

She looked down with even more compassion than before and let go of his arm. "Yes, of course, dear, but you and I and Principal Crewe are going to have a meeting first thing in the morning."

Hayward nodded and started to run back around the bus. The supervisor lady yelled after him.

"And stay away from the blind side of the bus, no matter what!"

Her voice trailed off as he began running at top speed. He headed toward home and didn't look back. Tomorrow he would have to figure out a new plan to ask Beth to the party. And now he had to deal with the Davey thing. He wondered how life could get so hectic and dramatic for an eleven-year-old. Beth in the morning, Davey today—*How mad is he going to be? This may be painful.* He hoped they could work something out. Hoped.

***

The bell rang and Pete started for the door. Davey was directly in front of him. Pete had the urge to kick his feet out from under him, making him fall. The thought of Davey lying there as the class

35

laughed made him smile. Would he have the gall to stand up to him then? He followed Davey out of the classroom, and they both grabbed their coats and headed down the hall to their exit. As they stepped outside, Davey finally turned to him.

"Hey, are we going to wait for Hayward and Joe?"

"Yeah, sure," Pete replied.

He liked Hayward and Joe and hoped they came with them today. They respected him, and never gave him any gall. He and Davey stopped at the edge of the path through the woods that led to their street.

"Do you think the brook is high? Have you been down there lately?" Davey asked.

"Haven't been, but probably high. But nowhere near how high it is in the spring."

Every spring thaw, the brook would run at its highest. The boys would build a bridge of rocks across it, which would last the whole summer. During the fall and winter, the bridge would usually get destroyed by the current and ice, ensuring construction was an annual project. But their hard work in the spring made a great short-cut to the fair that came to town every summer. Adults, girls, and younger kids that lived on their street all used the bridge to get to the fair.

Pete was proud of the bridge. It had been his idea and he organized it every year. His parents and his friends' parents were impressed. Hayward's mom even called the boys "industrious." And why wouldn't she? This was no small brook, and the banks were very high on each side.

Pete was curious to see how it looked now. He hadn't been down to the brook since the last day of the fair. He remembered how amazing it had looked with summer light coming through the trees. *Davey could never organize the bridge build; he isn't a leader like me,* thought Pete. *I have gall.* Davey hadn't started a long-standing tradition that benefited everyone on the street. *He's not even smart enough to trade projects with me.* He looked at Davey with disgust. Davey was looking off in the distance.

"Joe's coming," Davey said.

"Is Hayward with him?"

"Not that I can see," Davey replied.

Where is that little fucker? Pete thought. They watched in silence as Joe advanced.

"Hey guys," Joe said.

"Hey. You coming with us to the junkyard today?" Davey asked.

"Are you kiddin'? I've been thinking about it all day."

"Right on," Davey replied.

"Where's Hayward?" Pete asked Joe.

"I don't know," Joe replied.

"You don't know? Weren't you in class with him?"

"Well, yeah I was. He had to speak with the teacher after class, but after the bell rang he was gone."

"Gone?" Pete asked.

"Gone," Joe replied.

"Gone where?" Pete asked again.

Joe shrugged his shoulders.

"So he didn't talk to the teacher?"

"Nope. He left the room, and I don't know where he went."

"Where the hell did he go?" Pete asked.

Joe shuffled his feet, thinking about his answer. When he spoke, his voice was sheepish.

"I don't know. He had to talk to the teacher after class, but he didn't."

"You said that already," Pete said, extremely frustrated now.

Joe just shrugged his shoulders again.

"Alright boys, let's go!" Pete exclaimed. He turned and started to walk down the path through the woods.

"Don't you want to wait another couple of minutes and see if Hayward comes? He said he wanted to go today," Joe called after him.

"Nope," Pete said.

Davey turned to Joe, shrugged his shoulders, and followed Pete down the path. Joe took one more look around, and then followed the other boys.

***

Beth walked down the hall and saw Samantha—who went by Sam—waiting in her usual spot. Sam was younger, but sat with Beth on the bus; she lived a couple doors down the street from Beth. Sam looked up to Beth and wanted to be just like her when she got to the fifth grade. As they walked, Sam began telling Beth how she wasn't getting the math they were doing. She felt the teacher was maybe teaching it too fast because, like her, some of the other students weren't getting it, either.

Beth was half listening as she wondered about the note in her pocket. Daniel had given it to her as she was leaving class. He asked her to read it later. Curiosity gnawed at her. She knew if she pulled it out of her pocket now, Sam would pester her to read it. They walked out the exit and started toward the bus. Sam continued blabbering on about her teacher. Beth wondered how she would see the note before she got home. Would there be an opportunity? Could she create one? She looked at the parked buses and the space in-between them. Could she slip through to the other side of the bus, out of sight, just for a minute? That would be enough time to read the note. *No one's allowed on that side of the bus*, the voice in her head boomed. Every year, that rule was pounded into their heads. She would just have to get on the bus and wait until she was home and in her room. That thought angered her. Her curiosity was overwhelming; she felt like she would explode.

Sam had started talking to Lisa, who was a year younger. Could this be the opportunity Beth was looking for? She watched as Sam and Lisa climbed the bus steps. It was odd that Mrs. Jackson, the bus supervisor, wasn't waiting where they boarded. She was always there. She suddenly had an uneasy feeling and a shiver went up her back. *Something isn't right here.* She hurried up into the bus.

Beth walked down the bus aisle to her usual seat with Sam, who sat directly across from Lisa. She thought about just plopping down in one of the empty seats along the way, but decided that would probably involve some damage control. Why make waves when the sea is smooth, as her grandpa used to say? She wasn't exactly sure what it meant, but thought it sounded like a good fit for this situation.

She slid into her usual spot. Out the window she could see kids playing on the playground as they waited for their parents to pick them up. *How lucky are they,* she thought, *to get picked up in their own cars and not have to sit every day with the same uninteresting people?* Sam was telling Lisa about some girl in her class named Treena, who would be her new friend. Lisa actually looked like she was interested in what Sam had to say. Beth then noticed something out the window past Lisa: Mrs. Jackson. Sam noticed her too, and pointed.

"What's Mrs. Jackson doing on the wrong side of the buses?"

The other kids all looked to the windows. Sam got up. "I'm gonna go ask her," Sam bellowed, and then started to make her way to the front of the bus.

Beth wasted no time retrieving the note. She had trouble unfolding it; her hands were shaking with excitement.

October 8, 1987

Dear Beth,

I have something important to ask you at lunch tomorrow, meet me behind the school, by the ball field fence.

Daniel

Beth quickly refolded the note and jammed it back into her pocket. She took a deep breath. Sam was making her way back to the seat. Beth looked out the window. *Looks like I'm gonna get asked to the party*, she concluded. *What else could it be?* How would she answer? She felt sad that the excitement of the note was now gone, and all she had were questions and answers to think about.

"Some kid was on the wrong side of the buses," Sam said matter-of-factly to the rest of the passengers.

The bus roared to life as Sam sat down. "Are you okay, Beth?" she asked. "You look kind of, I don't know, blank."

"I'm okay, I just have a lot on my mind," Beth said, and then turned to look out the window as the bus began to pull away from the school.

Chapter 5

Gonna Be One of Those Evenings

The man drove out of the trailer park, stopping where the driveway met the road. The car sat idling as he tried to decide which way to go. It reminded him of "fork in the road of life" scenarios. *Don't really matter,* he thought. *The only way I can't go is back.* He looked in both directions again, knowing this would be the last time he ever pulled out of this trailer park. He felt a sudden sense of sadness. This had been his home for the last three years—except for that ninety-day stint in the county jail. It would become a memory. Time for some new ones.

The boy. Go back and get the boy. And then what? The boy would just be in danger the next time the Push started. His son would be far better off with whomever he ended up with. He'd call from a pay phone when he got far enough away and get someone to go over there and find the child. After the call was placed, he would probably never see his child again.

He looked to the left. Darkness. More darkness to the right. He held his hand up and started swaying it back and forth . . . eeny, meeny, miny-fuckin'-mo. His hand stopped swaying on his right side. He put the car in drive and turned right onto the road. The people on the left would never realize how lucky they were.

***

Davey shuffled his feet as he and Joe waited outside Pete's house. Pete was inside changing from his school clothes to his scrubbies, which they had already done.

"What's wrong with Pete today?" Joe asked.

"Nothing!" Davey snapped back.

"Nothing? He's acting like he's pissed."

Davey shrugged. "Seems fine to me."

Joe shook his head and looked again at Pete's house. The wind blew a chill that went up Joe's spine. Something in the air seemed off.

"So, how's your teacher this year? She okay?" Davey asked.

"Fine," Joe said.

"Who is she?"

Joe didn't want to let this lame-ass conversation carry on.

"Mrs. Shut Your Mouth."

Davey looked at him in disbelief. "What did you say?" he bellowed.

"Relax. I was only joking."

Davey glared at him. "Well, it ain't funny, and you say it again, you ain't gonna think it's very funny either. Got it?"

"Alright, alright," Joe said.

Joe looked back at the front of the house, thinking he could probably take Davey in a fight, anyway. No, not probably—he *knew* he could. Just then, Pete came out the side door and bounded down the steps.

"You losers ready?" he shouted.

The boys faked laughter and looked at each other, waiting for the other one to say something back. Neither did. Pete walked the length of the driveway to meet them.

"Are you ready, or what?" he asked.

"Yeah," Davey said suddenly.

Joe felt the chill again as the wind practically blew his head around. He spotted Hayward coming out of the woods.

"Look!" he shouted, pointing.

Davey and Pete both turned to look.

"Yeah, so?" Davey said. "He still has to go home and change into his scrubbies, and we're ready to go now."

"Just wait," Joe said, waving his arms to get Hayward's attention. Hayward started to jog up the hill toward them.

"We're not actually going to wait for him," Davey snarled.

"If he wants to go right now the way he is, in his school clothes, then he can come," Pete replied.

"We might as well just go," Davey muttered.

"Would you shut up?" Joe snapped. Joe waved again at Hayward in a hurry-up motion.

"What did you just say to me?" Davey said to Joe.

Before Joe could reply, Pete stepped in front of Davey. "He told you to shut up, and you better, because Hayward is one of us, and we're gonna see if he wants to go," Pete said.

Davey shuffled his feet and began to pout. Pete stepped away from Davey and patted Joe on the back reassuringly.

Hayward was huffing and out of breath. "Hey guys, what's up?" he asked between gasps.

"We're goin' to the junkyard right now if you want to come, but you gotta wear your school clothes. We don't have time to wait for you to change," Joe said.

Hayward scanned each of the boys' faces. He could tell he wouldn't be able to change their minds. He considered how mad his parents would be if he got real dirty, but this was too good an opportunity to pass up. He would lie and say it had happened at school recess if he had to.

"Okay," he said, finally able to catch his breath a little.

Joe clapped his hands in delight and swung an arm around Hayward's neck.

"Right on! Let's go, man."

The boys began to walk to the top of the street, where there was a path that would take them through the woods, over the brook, up along the high banks, and then across the field to the junkyard.

"I'll go as long as you don't do that gay clap again Joe," said Hayward.

The boys all chuckled. The wind grew stronger.

***

The bus wound its way along the road towards Beth's house. The chatter had gotten louder, but she didn't notice. She was looking out the window, daydreaming of standing at the ball field fence and watching Daniel and Hayward talking off in the distance. She wondered what they were talking about as they repeatedly looked in her direction. She watched as they shook hands and Daniel began to walk toward her. She saw Hayward's despair as he headed in the other direction, his shoulders slumped. She smiled at Daniel.

"I have something to ask you . . ."

Suddenly the bus lurched forward. Beth put her hand out and grabbed the seat in front of her to stop the forward motion of her body. The bus came to a complete stop and the bus driver yelled something at the car in front of him. Beth looked over at Sam, who was still jawing away a mile a minute to the other girls. How could someone talk so much? She looked back out the window and saw the old gas station; her stop wasn't far off.

Soon she would be home to see her mom. She wondered how her mom would be feeling; she hoped it was good. She liked the "good mom." There were a couple of other sides of her mother that weren't so fun. And there was the mom when her father was home—that was the worst one of all. That was the "cranky mom." That was the mom she'd seen the most of, lately.

Her mom had been happier when she was younger, but that had changed the last few years. Her mom used to work as a bookkeeper at the lumberyard, but the business had closed down a few years back and she had been home ever since. At first she seemed happy to be off, keeping the house in top shape. There were always the smells of lemon cleaner and baked goods from the kitchen, and usually the sounds of the TV blaring and the laundry machine or dishwasher going. Her mom used to run to give her a hug. Beth used to love the feeling when she opened the door. Now this was rare, especially in the past year. Lately, she often came home to find her mother sitting in front of the television and not even batting an eyelash at her presence. She wondered if her mom would even notice if she didn't come home one day. Over the past few months, there were times when Beth felt alone even though her mom was home.

The bus pulled up in front of Beth's house. She got off and noticed that her mother's car was gone. The front door was locked. She reached in the side pocket of her school bag and produced a key, opened the door, and went inside, dropping her school bag on the floor and walking through the living room and into the kitchen. It was odd that her mother wasn't home. Even though she seemed really unhappy, she was still there every day. She looked around the kitchen and spotted a wine bottle with about a quarter of its contents left. *Gonna be one of those evenings when she gets home, I guess,* Beth surmised.

Beth was starving; she needed a snack before supper. She opened the freezer, pulled out a pack of pizza pockets, and popped one in the microwave. She and her father usually ate frozen dinners for supper, or he would grab takeout on his way home from work. Her mother had decided about six months ago that she wasn't going to cook anymore, and she had kept her promise.

The buzzer on the microwave let her know the food was ready. She grabbed her plate and a fork and headed into the living room to eat and watch TV. As she ate she thought about the note and the meeting with Daniel. Should she set aside some time tonight to pick out something good to wear? Excitement came over her as she thought about the date party. *At least I have that.* She flipped through the channels, and then yelled the thought sarcastically to the empty house.

"At least I have that!"

***

Pete was leading the way down the path toward the brook. Davey was behind Pete with Joe, and Hayward was at the rear. The path went down a very steep bank so each of the boys had to go backwards, grabbing on to trees to keep their balance. The boys followed Pete's lead, grabbing the same trees as they descended the steep hill. The soft ground was very slippery. *Always your leader,* Pete thought as he navigated down the hill.

Something shot out of the underbrush, scaring him. Pete felt his heart skip a beat. When he realized it was only a squirrel, he quickly looked to the other boys to see if they had noticed him jump with fright. They were all busy descending, with their backs to him. *Can't let anyone see weakness.* He could hear his mom saying these words to him, as she had for as long as he could remember. Pete stopped and watched the squirrel. It stood about five feet away, rubbing its little paws together, seemingly watching him with one eye. *Why don't you do something interesting so my project won't be so boring?* The squirrel just stood there on its hind legs, rubbing its hands together.

There's nothing you can do? Nothing? Pete's anger was beginning to surface. Davey had just about caught up to him with the other boys close in tow. Pete reached out and cracked a stick off the tree beside him and tossed it at the squirrel. The squirrel ran into the underbrush at lightning speed. *You did somethin' now, didn't ya?*

Davey, who was just catching up to Pete, slipped. His legs shot out and kicked Pete's feet out from underneath him. The cold mud welcomed the side of Pete's body and left its mark from his knee to his neck. He quickly jumped up, fuming.

"Sorry, man, sorry," Davey said as he stumbled to his feet.

For the second time that day, Pete grabbed Davey by the shirt and pulled him up to his face. He looked into Davey's eyes, but this time there was no look of determination, no look of defiance in his friend's eyes, just a look of guilt. Pete let him go.

"Just watch what you're fucking doing," Pete said.

"Yeah man, I'm sorry," Davey repeated.

The other boys had caught up to Pete and Davey. Pete looked at Hayward, who was still wearing his school clothes, which were now mud-covered from his feet to his knees.

Pete started to laugh. "Man, Hay, I wouldn't want to be you when your parents see that shit."

Hayward looked down and said, "Tell me about it. I better make this a good trip to the junkyard, 'cause it's the last adventure that I'm gonna be on for a while."

The boys all laughed.

Pete resumed his descent. Each boy carefully followed the other down the hill. Five minutes later, all four were at the edge of the brook, staring. The bridge of rocks they usually used to get across the water was completely gone.

***

The man looked at the gas gauge: half empty, it read. He would have to get some money soon. He thought about his bank account and laughed. Normal people had bank accounts with money in them, not people who hadn't worked in quite a while and who were on the run. No, those people got money a different way—they took it from someone else. The car blazed along at fifty-five miles an hour. The window was down and the cool night air felt good on his face; it also kept him from smelling the sweat and blood on his clothes. He'd have to get some clean clothes after he solved the money problem. There were probably no shopping areas open this time of night; he'd have to take that from someone too. He grinned.

Need some beer too, and a bottle of Jack maybe. Holy shit! I have to prioritize all this stuff. He laughed. *Here's me, a guy who just killed a few people, here I am taking out a fuckin' pen and making a list of things I gotta do.* He laughed harder. *Holy fuck, I'm bossy. I better watch myself, or I'm gonna kill that bastard that keeps bossin' me around.* He started to howl with laughter. Deliriously, he swerved the car back and forth down the highway, passing a sign that said "Rest stop and gas station twenty-five miles."

"Twenty-five miles to the bank!" he yelled, then screamed into the air, "Did you hear that, Mister Bossy Pants?"

***

Beth began to stir as she heard the front door of the house open. She rubbed her eyes, realizing she must have fallen asleep on the couch. Her dad entered the room with his briefcase in one hand and a takeout pizza in the other. He placed the briefcase on the floor.

"Hi, Bunny." That's what he had called her since she was a baby.

"Hi, Dad."

Beth jumped up and hugged him. He hugged her back with one arm, holding the pizza high. She didn't use to hug him when he got home, but since her mom had started to flake out, she felt they needed each other's support.

"Your mother's not home?" her father asked.

"No, she wasn't here when I got home."

"Really?" her father replied. "Well," he gestured with the pizza, "supper's ready."

Her father went into the kitchen with Beth following, placed the pizza on the counter, opened the box, and took the pizza cutter from a drawer. Beth opened the cupboard and started to get the plates.

"So, Dad, can I ask you something?"

"Sure, Bunny," her father said as he cut the pizza into slices.

"What's wrong with Mom?"

Her father stopped cutting the pizza. "I wish I knew, Beth. I think she's depressed. I've asked her, she says no. I've asked her to go to the doctor, but she won't."

"She can get some medication if she's depressed, can't she?"

Her father put a slice of pizza on each plate and sat down at the table. "If she would go to the doctor, I'm sure he or she could prescribe her something," he said.

Beth opened the fridge, got two sodas, and then sat down at the table with her father. "Well then, why won't she go?"

"I wish I could tell you, I really do, but I've kind of stopped asking her what's wrong. She never answers me, so I'm just hoping it passes and she starts to come around soon."

"Are you going to get a divorce?"

"Beth, that's not something that I think we should be discussing."

"Dad, I think I deserve to know what could be happening here."

Her father took a deep breath and put his slice of pizza down. "Look, Bunny, I'm not sure what your mother is going through, and why she doesn't want help, but if we get divorced or separated, it will be her decision. I will be here for this family, and we—" he pointed at her and himself, "are going to be there for her."

Beth rolled her eyes and asked, "But for how long?"

Her dad pointed at her emphatically. "As long as it takes. Families stick together."

"They're also supposed to love each other," Beth said defensively as she got up and left the table.

Her father called out after her. "Bunny? Bunny, come finish your supper."

Beth ignored him and went into her room. She lay on her bed and stuck her head in her pillow. Why did it have to be like this? Why couldn't it go back to the way it was? How could he let her treat him like this? A relationship took two people. How could he defend her when he was the only one acting like they were a family? *I could never act the way my mother is acting; I could never treat my husband or boyfriend like that.*

She thought about the date party again. Would Daniel be asking her? What about Hayward? She thought about slow dancing with Daniel, his arms holding her, and felt warm inside. She felt loved. Beth pulled herself up from her bed and went back downstairs. Her father was still sitting at the table, eating his pizza. Beth walked over and put her arms around his neck.

"I'm sorry, Dad, you're right. We need to stick together right now."

He patted her hand. "I know it's hard right now, but it will get better. I just need you to not wig out, too." He laughed. Beth laughed too. *Might as well*, she thought. *Beats crying.* "Come on, Bunny, finish your supper and the two of us will watch a movie tonight."

She sat down and picked up the rest of her slice. "Sounds good, Dad."

The conversation stopped at the sound of the front door opening.

Chapter 6

We Can't Back Down Now

"What are we supposed to do now? The bridge is gone!" Joe exclaimed.

"Go back home," Hayward replied. Davey turned to Hayward with a grunt of disgust.

"How can it be gone?" Joe asked.

"Kids from other neighbourhoods probably wrecked it," Pete answered.

"Why the hell would they do that?" Joe asked.

"The same reason we wreck tree forts when we find them," Davey said.

Joe kicked a rock into the water. The brook was high, the water flowing fast because of the rain over the last few weeks.

"Let's check around and see if there's another place we can cross," Pete said. He started walking down the brook, following the flow of the water. The rest of the boys fell in line.

"The brook is flowin' pretty good. Do you really think we're gonna find a place to cross?" Hayward asked Joe.

Joe half turned and shrugged. "We'll find out, I guess."

The boys walked for about ten minutes until Pete stopped. He pointed to a tree root sticking out of the flowing water on the other side of the brook. It was about five feet away.

"How are we gonna cross here?" Hayward asked nervously.

"Jump!" Pete said. "Jump! Man."

"That's way too far," Hayward said.

"Well, let's see if it is," Pete replied confidently.

Pete, who had never been afraid to try anything even if it seemed impossible, backed away from the edge and went up the slope of the high bank to get some running distance. *Here he goes again*, Hayward thought. That was one thing about Pete: he was a daredevil, and for some reason or another always seemed to come out unscathed. Pete would climb trees and jump from one tree top to another and had never fallen. For kicks, he would climb a tree and get someone to cut it down while he was still in it. He would ride the tree as it fell. There was no shortage of stories of Pete and his Evel Knievel shit. Hayward envied Pete's confidence. He was amazed at some of the things his friend could do. And now, they were about to witness another Pete Special. So many things could go wrong; the root might not be able to support his weight, or he might not get enough air and come down in the brook. Did Pete even think about these things? *Or does he just do things because he thinks he can?*

Pete charged down the bank, ran to the edge of the water, pushed off with his right foot, and flew—it literally looked like he was flying. He brought his feet together in the air and landed on the root as if a guardian angel were guiding him. His momentum carried him off the root and up the bank on the other side, where he finally came to a stop, raising his hand in the air in celebration of his victory and screaming, "Yeahh!" He looked back at the other boys. "What a rush!"

Before he could fully grasp what he had just seen, Hayward saw Davey running down the bank toward the brook, flying through the air, hitting the root, and propelling himself up the other side to the hard ground. It wasn't as pretty as Pete's masterpiece, but there was Davey, standing on the other side, looking back at Hayward and Joe.

"Let's go," Davey said, motioning with his arm.

"I don't know if I can do this," Hayward said in a soft voice to Joe, knowing the other boys couldn't hear.

"We can't back down now, Hay. We'll never live it down." Joe went to the spot up the bank where the other boys had started to run. Hayward was sweating. He would have to do this if Joe made it across.

Not the most athletic of the four, Joe came chugging down the hill. He lumbered up to the edge of the brook and jumped, getting a lot less air than Pete or Davey did. He landed with one foot on the root, the other crashing into the water, but his momentum carried his foot back out and he hit the bank. He used his arms to pull himself the rest of the way up. Joe stood on the hard ground examining his pant leg and sneaker, which were completely soaked.

Hayward turned and looked at the spot the other boys had started their approach from. He took a deep breath and started walking toward it.

***

He passed a sign that said "Gas station and rest area one mile ahead." The man opened the glove box and began pulling out the contents. There were a few bingo dabbers, which he threw out the window. He pulled out a book. There was a cross on the front and the title simply read "Church Hymns." He pretended it was burning his hand, screaming mockingly in pain, and fired it out the window, laughing. He reached in farther and came across some change. He put it on the passenger seat and added it up. Four dollars and fifty cents. He laughed. That wouldn't get him what he needed. He scooped up the change and jammed it into his front pocket. He reached back in the box and pulled out the last thing that was in there: a pair of reading glasses. The style reminded him of pictures from twenty years ago when he was a kid. He threw them out the window.

"Fuckin' old people," he muttered.

The trunk! He slammed on the brakes and the car came to a screeching halt. He pulled on to the shoulder of the road, jumped out, and went around to the back. He opened the trunk and peered in. Just what he thought he'd find: one of Jed's cardigan sweaters. Old people always have lots of sweaters close at hand, *'cause those fuckers are always gettin' cold.* He pulled his blood-soaked shirt over his head, tossed it in the ditch, put the cardigan on, and buttoned it up. *It probably looks nuts,* he thought, *but I'd rather look nuts than look like I just killed three people.* He chuckled as he got back in the car and headed toward the gas station, its lights twinkling up ahead. He started to sing "Sharp Dressed Man" by ZZ Top, getting only about half the lyrics right.

He rolled into the parking lot, happy to see only one other car in customer parking. He pulled in and waited. A young couple emerged with a bag. The guy got in the driver side and the girl went around to the passenger side. He stared at her ass as she opened the door and she slipped into the car. *Pretty hot. Better hope your pretty little ass don't break down in my path or we's gonna have some fun.* He laughed, watching them back out of the parking lot and drive off into the night. He sat there for a few minutes, grinning. *Wow! This is the best I've felt in months, maybe even years.*

"What a fuckin' rush," he said aloud. Then he got out of the car. He looked around to make sure there weren't any other cars around or lights approaching from the distance. His grin disappeared. It was time do some business. The door of the store gave off one of those annoying *ding-dongs* as it swung closed behind him. The young guy behind the cash was skinny, full of acne, and probably still hung over from turning eighteen. He nodded at the young clerk and headed toward the back of the store. He grabbed a fifteen pack of Budweiser, a bottle of Jack Daniel's, a couple of bagged sandwiches, and some insect repellent. He brought everything to the front of the store. The clerk was looking at him strangely. *Makes sense,* he thought, *in light of the cardigan sweater with nothing underneath it.* He placed the beer,

Jack, and sandwiches on the counter. The cashier started to scan the items. He dug into his pocket and brought out the change, keeping it in a cupped hand close to his chest. He counted it, stopped, and shook his head. He glanced up at the clerk and mumbled.

"What?" The clerk leaned forward to hear him better.

"This looks like a Bermudian dollar," he said. "What do you think?"

He moved his cupped hand with the change about six inches from his chest. The clerk leaned forward to look at the coins in his hand. The man brought up his other hand and sprayed the insect repellent directly into the clerk's eyes. The young clerk screamed in pain and fell behind the counter to the floor. He jumped up on the counter, reached over to the register buttons, typed $50.00, and hit the cash button. The register drawer popped open. He quickly grabbed all the bills, shoving them into his pockets, then grabbed the beer, Jack, and sandwiches and headed for the door, the clerk screaming behind him. He jumped into the car and tore out of the parking lot.

Driving on the highway, he laughed, feeling proud of himself. That went exactly as he had planned it. He cracked open a can of Budweiser, downed it, and threw the empty can out the window. He cracked open another and sped off into the night.

***

"Jump."

Why do they always have to be so pushy? Hayward wondered as he looked at the root on the other side of the brook and once again sized up the distance.

"Come on, Hay, hurry up."

Pete can be such a jerk sometimes. Don't they realize that . . . I'm scared?

They were all older and bigger than Hayward; the jump was easier for them. He looked at the brook. At that moment, it was the highest he'd ever seen it.

"Let's go, guys. I think I hear the wussy's mommy calling him."

Thanks, Davey, Pete's right-hand asshole. "Shut up, I'm comin'," Hayward told them. He looked at the water. It appeared to be waist-deep, and was flowing very quickly. He tried to figure out the amount of push he would need to make it. *What if I don't make it? Will they be able to pull me out? Will I be swept down the brook? Will I drown?*

Pete, Davey, and Joe were becoming more impatient by the second. "Would you just fuckin' jump over here so we can go?" Davey barked.

Hayward took a deep breath and adjusted his feet; he was so excited to be going to the junkyard. If he didn't jump now, they would go on without him. He couldn't bear the thought of that; there was no turning back now. He took another deep breath—but this only made him realize how fast his heart was thudding in his chest, like it would bust right through his ribcage at any moment. He felt numb from his bum up to the back of his neck, and his body felt a lot heavier than it really was. Sweat trickled down his ear from his soaked and matted hair. The guys began to move about and look up the other side of the embankment. They were going to leave. His heart began to sink.

"Okay, here I go."

Why did I just say that? I'm not ready just yet. Suddenly Hayward could feel the heat of all six eyes. This was it; he had about ten seconds before they gave up on him. *Make sure you have good traction.* Four seconds passed. *Just look at the root where you want to land and push with all your might.*

Three more seconds. *Don't look down.*

Three . . . two. . . one . . .

Holy shit!

The world went silent as he ran down the embankment and pushed off the edge as hard as he could with his right foot, never taking his eye off the root. The air over the rushing water was so cold; he got the feeling that if he didn't make it he would freeze to death. A wave of panic went through him as his foot started to come down; it would be the first part of him to feel the cold as he plunged into the icy water. Then his foot hit the root and momentum carried him forward, he pushed off the root and caught his other foot on the ledge, and surged up onto the embankment. He pumped his fist over and over, yelling.

"Yes! Yes! Yes!"

"Alright, let's go," Pete said as he headed up the hill with Davey and Joe in tow.

As Hayward followed, Joe turned and smiled at him. Hayward had never felt more a part of the group, like he belonged. This was one of the highest points in his life. This would be one of those days that he would always remember.

***

Beth continued eating her pizza as her mother came through the door, singing, "*Three rounds of José Cuervo*."

Beth listened as her mother stumbled around in the porch and knew she was drunk. Her father put his pizza down and went to meet her in the doorway. Beth chewed more slowly so she could eavesdrop.

"Are you alright?" her father asked.

"Of course I'm alright," her mother barked back at him. She started to sing again, "*Three rounds of José Cuervo*."

She heard her mother brush past her father and fall against the wall. Pictures clattered as her mom stumbled along, knocking them down. Beth's mom entered the kitchen and placed her hand on the counter for balance.

"Peesa, tha's nice. How was yer day, 'Liz'bif?" she slurred.

Her father was standing in the kitchen doorway, holding the pictures he'd picked up from the floor.

"Maybe you should go up to your room, Bunny."

Her mother looked over at her father. "Wishhh you wouldn't call her tha', I hate tha', I really hate tha'. Her name is E. . . liz. . . a. . . Beth." She said it again, "E . . . liz . . . a . . . Beth." She threw her arms up in the air, almost losing her balance.

"It's a beautiful name."

She grabbed onto the counter again to balance herself. Beth found it odd that her mom still had her purse over her shoulder. It seemed amazing that she could barely stand but still had her purse.

"And you call her a 'bunny.' Tha's not a name, Jim. It's a fucking rabbit."

She yawned. Beth and her father waited to hear what would come out of her mouth next. After what seemed like a week, Beth decided to speak.

"I don't mind when he calls me Bunny, Mom."

Her mother glared at her. "Of course you don't. You don't mind not making anything for supper, either."

"That's not fair, Sharon," her father said.

Her mother pushed him aside, almost falling. "Don't you tell me about fair."

Her mother went into the living room. Beth and her father could hear the channels of the TV being rapidly switched. Beth got up from the table and started to clean up. Her father looked like he would cry.

"I'm sorry, Beth."

"It's not your fault, Dad."

Beth put the dishes in the sink. Her father, fighting tears, went upstairs. Beth closed the box with the remaining pizza and put it in the fridge. She heard her mother scream.

"Who gives a shit what she's wearing!"

There was a *bang*—probably the remote control crashing off the wall. Beth started to wash the dishes and thought about what her mother had said—about Beth not making anything for supper. Should she have? She had never been expected, or asked, to prepare supper for the family before. She supposed she had enough time after school and she was old enough to use the stove; she had used the stove many times when her parents were home. Was that why her mother was acting like this? Could this be her fault? Was she not helping around the house enough? If that was the problem, she could surely fix it. She would help out with everything she could to help her mother get better. She finished the dishes and dried her hands. She would ask her mother what she needed help with first.

She walked into the living room and came around in front of her mother, who sat upright with her head back and eyes closed, snoring. Beth fetched a blanket from the hall closet. She was spreading the blanket over her mother when she saw her mother's purse sitting on the couch next to her. It was open, with a pack of cigarettes sitting on top of the other contents.

Beth looked at her mother; she was still out. She picked up the pack of cigarettes. She had never seen her mother smoke a cigarette in her life, and wondered why she had a pack in her purse. Opening the pack, she saw that there were a few missing and a pack of matches was jammed in with the cigarettes. She pulled the matches out and read the jacket cover: "The Redwood Inn." A hotel close to the airport. She had seen it a few times when they had travelled or picked other people up from the airport. Her mother let out a cough and a moan. Beth jumped, threw the cigarettes and matches back into the purse, and backed away. She quietly left the living room and went up to her bedroom and sat on her bed. What was her mother doing smoking and possibly at a hotel? It didn't make any sense. *She must be holding them for someone else. That must be it.*

Tomorrow she would come home from school and make something for supper. That would make her mother happy and get the family back to normal. Tomorrow would be a big day, making supper for the family and that meeting. Meeting with Daniel! She had forgotten. Beth jumped up and went to her closet. What to wear? She started looking through her sweaters then stopped. She suddenly felt like her life was swirling. Dating, looking after a family meal: yesterday life had seemed simple, but now . . .

Wow, she thought. *Wow!*

Chapter 7

Tough Guys Don't Throw Up

The man yawned and threw another empty beer can out the window. It was light now, and he'd been driving all night. He'd drunk a lot and was ready to get some shuteye. Should he get a hotel, or just pull over and sleep in the car? He wondered if anyone had found the bodies yet. It was pretty early, but there were always those nosy pricks—those people who got up early and weren't really out walking for exercise. They were out there to snoop, to check out scenes from the previous night that people hadn't been able to clean up or rectify. Those nosy pricks would see things, shake their heads, and make their own conclusions. Exercise: it was all a fuckin' ruse to make those pricks feel superior to the people who liked to party and enjoy life. There definitely would be a couple of those people who would find those old fuckers next door. That would lead them to Jill and the baby. He actually hoped they found them soon; he hadn't called anyone and thought the baby might be hungry. He felt a sense of responsibility that quickly faded. What was he going to do?

Go back. Go back for the baby. He thought about it, shook his head, and smacked himself in the face. The slap seemed to wake him up a bit, as he must have been starting to doze off.

Have to get rid of this car, too. After the nosy fuckers report the old fuckers, the cop fuckers will be looking for the car and this fucker, he pointed at himself and laughed. *Got to get some new clothes and a place to rest my head. Start another fuckin' list.* He laughed. It was good to laugh. As long as he was laughing and kept his mood light, the Push couldn't start. He felt in control. He could see buildings coming up on his right side. There was a sign: "Welcome to Sifton Factory Outlets."

"Bingo," he said aloud. Then he laughed. Did other tough guys like him say "bingo" when they were alone? He guessed not. He took the next exit and turned into the empty parking lot. The stores weren't open yet. He'd park at the back of the parking lot and have a snooze; he was pretty sure he had a couple of hours before the cops started looking for the car. He picked up a parking spot in a deserted area. A maintenance man was sweeping and collecting garbage along the front of the stores.

The man tilted the seat back and closed his eyes, his mind wandering, thinking about Jill. He knew they had some good times, but he was having a hard time remembering any. *Do you really want to?* He remembered the nagging and the fights—the way she didn't understand how hard it was for him. How difficult it was, having this thing living inside of him, always trying to keep it in check. At one point, he had tried to explain it to her, but she told him that he was full of shit, trying to pass the blame as always, and that he was just lazy. *Stupid bitch, she didn't understand.* Why couldn't she get it? She'd probably still be alive if she had just listened to him—just tried to understand. *Doesn't matter now. Why the fuck am I not sleeping?* He reached over to grab the unopened bottle of Jack, unscrewed the cap, and guzzled about a quarter of the bottle. He stuck his head out the window, gagging, but didn't throw up. Tough guys don't throw up. He put his head back and closed his eyes. Sleep engulfed him.

***

Hayward looked up to see that Pete was already quite a way up the steep embankment, and started to climb. The bank was muddy, but a cakewalk compared to that jump he had just nailed. And he really had nailed it. He thought his jump was probably better than any of the others, but he would never say it to them because he knew they would never agree. He carefully watched Joe to see each shrub and rock he was using for leverage as he climbed the hill. Hayward used the same ones, comforted by the fact that Joe outweighed him by about thirty pounds, so anything that supported Joe would work just fine for Hayward. He really had to watch his footing, though, as he was the last of the four boys to be using the same spot in the soft mud for traction. He wasn't having too much trouble—*not yet.*

He started to think about how he would explain the state of his school clothes to his parents. They would be majorly pissed. Changing your clothes after school was a steadfast rule all their parents had. The boys always had to change into their scrubbies before they went out to play. What the hell was he going to say? His original plan of using the school recess excuse seemed like it would be a little far-fetched with the mud stains he was covered in now. Maybe the truth, then—there was no time, the boys were going to leave. "So let them leave," his mother would say. "Are they not going to play tomorrow or the next day? They live here on this street, Hayward. Were they wearing their school clothes? How come they had time to change, and you didn't?" What was he supposed to say to that? He slipped and his knee dug into the mud. *This keeps getting worse.* Maybe he'd just tell the truth: that he wasn't able to change because he was chasing some girl around the school to ask her out on a date. That would go over well. They would surely understand that, especially knowing that he and the girl were in grade five. His parents would think he was completely insane.

Hayward looked up. Pete was standing on the ledge at the top of the hill and Davey was just reaching it. He put his head down and kept moving. Not much farther. The climb was a workout for his calves. They had started to hurt a few minutes ago; now they felt like they would burn right off his legs. He looked up to see how far he still had to go. About fifteen more feet. Pete was standing there watching him, and Davey was on the ledge walking towards Pete. Maybe he should tell his parents that he had forgotten to change his clothes, but he knew that would really set them off. He had learned it was actually better to lie than to act stupid, because thinking they might have a stupid kid made them even angrier. He could already hear the lecture he would get about the cost of clothes, about how hard his mother and father had to work to buy those clothes. They would say how he should take a lot more care of his things and respect that the things have value. He was lucky to have nice clothes; some kids—even kids at his school—would love to have clothes like his. Those kids would take care of their clothes and respect them a lot more than he did. How did they know that? *Maybe if these kids had my clothes, they would take them for granted, and maybe even treat them worse than I do.* Hayward knew if he said anything like this to his parents, it would be the end of his freedom for a long time. There would be no more junkyard trips or—

Suddenly Hayward heard a scream. "*Aaahhhhhh!*"

There was a loud crack. He turned his head and could not believe what he was seeing. Davey was falling down the hill, flying past Hayward and Joe about ten feet to their left.

"*Aaahhhhhh!*" Davey yelled as he hit another big shrub. His whole body flipped; he hit his back and then flipped again, hitting his head then his feet, and over again. There was another big crack. Hayward didn't know if it was a tree branch or a bone. Davey screamed again as he flipped over and over, crashing through everything and seemingly picking up speed. He was in middle of a scream as he crashed through some shrubs close to the bottom of the hill. Then there was silence.

Holy fuck! *He's all the way to the bottom, he must be pretty beat up, he must have like ten broken bones.* Hayward turned, without looking at the other boys, and started back down the hill. He was moving fast, but not fast enough to lose control, not after what he'd just seen. He could hear Joe muttering behind him.

"Oh my god, oh my god, oh my god."

Joe kept repeating it as they continued down at a swift pace. How many bones had Davey broken? How the hell would they get him out of here? *How the fuck are we going to get him over the brook?* He could still hear Joe muttering. *Oh my god is right.* Hayward couldn't believe how fast Davey had fallen. It was like some kind of bad dream. They all had done so many crazy things and escaped injury, and then something like this, something this horrible happens, right in front of his eyes. Hayward started to panic. *If that could happen to Davey, if he could lose his footing, I could lose it too. That could have been me.* His lungs were having trouble keeping up to his panting. *Got to get a hold of yourself. This is no time to worry about you. Your friend is at the bottom of this hill with a bunch of broken bones and he needs your help.*

They were getting close to the bottom of the hill. He couldn't see Davey through the brush. He couldn't hear Davey. All he could hear was Joe and Pete coming behind him. Maybe Davey wasn't writhing in pain because he wasn't hurt—maybe they'd get down there and he'd just be dusting himself off. After all, they were . . . *invincible.* They had been pretty lucky when it came to their adventures. Hayward's legs carried him the rest of the way down the hill. He ran out onto level ground. There was Davey, lying on his side. He wasn't okay. A cold shiver ran up Hayward's spine.

"Davey! Davey!" Hayward yelled as he ran up and knelt down beside him. "Davey, are you okay?" Davey's eyes were wide and empty-looking. He didn't even look at Hayward. Joe came up beside him.

"Oh my god," Joe said. He started crying.

What's he crying for? We gotta help him. Hayward was about to reach out, but something kept his hands back. Joe cried louder and buried his head in his hands. Finally, Hayward realized what his brain didn't want to admit. Davey was dead. Hayward could hear Pete running up to them.

"Get out of the fuckin' way!" Pete yelled.

Hayward and Joe didn't move. Pete practically bowled them over as he threw himself down by Davey's side. "Davey! Davey. Davey, are you okay, buddy?"

Pete reached over Davey's body and pulled him onto his back. His arm flopped over like a ragdoll. Hayward couldn't believe what he was seeing. The side of Davey's head was covered in the darkest blood he had ever seen, and the rock that his head had been resting on was covered in blood. Pete grabbed Davey's wrist and held it, feeling for a pulse. Hayward couldn't stop himself; his body lurched and he threw up violently just below Davey's feet. Joe was still sobbing. Pete dropped Davey's arm and looked up at the sky.

"Fuuuuccccckkkk! Fuck! Fuck! Fuck!"

Hayward wiped his mouth. "We've got to get help!" he yelled.

"He's dead!" Pete yelled back.

"No, no," Hayward said. "They can revive him. The paramedics, they have those machines. They can revive him. They got to. We got to get him some help."

"Can they do that, Pete? Can they revive him?" Joe asked, sobbing.

Pete screamed at the two of them. "His fucking head is bashed in! He can't be revived from that!"

"I gotta go get some help, I gotta go call the paramedics, I gotta go," Hayward said. He ran back toward the brook.

Chapter 8

I Won't Let Them Take Your Seat

There was the sound of knocking. He opened his eyes. *Where the fuck am I?* He heard the knocking again, turned, and looked at the driver's side window. A security guard. *You're so lucky I don't have a gun right now.* He reached over and rolled the window down.

"Are you alright, mister?"

The man looked around the parking lot. *Ah yes, the factory outlets.* "Yes, I'm fine," he replied, "just got here early and had a nap until the stores open. They open now?"

"Yes, yes they are, sir. Do you plan on shopping in them this morning?"

"Well yes, that's why I'm here."

"Great, sir, that's all I need to know."

He stretched and rubbed his hand over his face. The security guard hadn't moved. "Did you want something else?"

The security guard leaned down and asked, "Well, sir, do you think I could have a swig of that?" He pointed to the bottle of Jack Daniel's sitting on the passenger seat. He laughed. "I have to walk around this fucking parking lot all day, and it's pretty boring, as you can imagine." He laughed again.

"That does sound boring. I think I'd get bored to death just imagining it," the man replied, then handed the bottle to the guard. "Giv'er, man. You keep it."

"You sure, sir?" the guard asked excitedly.

"Yeah, no problem."

The security guard shifted his gaze right then left, and then shoved the bottle into his jacket.

"Well, you have yourself a good day, sir, and thank you."

The guard walked away. *Poor fucker.* He pushed open the door. The stores were pretty far away. Fuck it, the walk would help him wake up. Pain shot through the muscles in his legs and arms as he climbed from the car.

"Fuck!" he yelled. That made him laugh again. *I guess you use muscles you never knew you had when you're killing people.* His mother used to say that about swimming. His mother, old Mom. He rubbed his fingers over the cigarette scar burns on his wrist. *Hope you're in Hell, oh mother dear.*

He flashed back to the dirty shack of his boyhood, where he had once tossed and turned in bed with a bad earache. It was like he was there again. The smell of cigarette smoke was coming through the cracks in the bedroom door. It hurt so much, with the pain shooting from his ear right down to the bottom of his jaw. He got out of his bed and tramped over his dirty clothes that were strewn all over the floor, pulled open the door, and walked into the living room. The coffee table was full of beer bottles and a large ashtray was overflowing with cigarette butts. There was another smell, too. His mother was seated on the couch with her head back and a grin on her face. She looked as though she was going to fall asleep. Sitting next to her was her latest boyfriend, J.P., who was rolling up some type of cigarette. J.P. looked at him.

"What do you want?" J.P. said in rough voice.

His mother didn't even realize he was there.

"I have an earache," he said timidly.

"Just go back to bed. It will go away," J.P. said as he waved a dismissive hand.

"Mom," he said.

His mother lowered her head and looked at him. It looked like she was asleep with her eyes half closed.

"Wh-Wh- . . . What are you doing up, Tommy?"

"I've got an earache."

She laughed. How could she think that his pain was funny? He could not remember ever having this much pain and his mother was . . . laughing. J.P. got up off the couch, grabbed him by the arm, and almost yanked it out of its socket as he pulled him back toward his bedroom.

"I told you to go to sleep, and it will go away," he growled in his rough voice.

J.P. whipped him through the bedroom doorway so hard he fell and slid across the floor. The door was slammed closed. Tommy got to his feet. He knows his arm is hurt, but couldn't feel it because of the explosions of pain coming from his jaw. His mother didn't even care. His anger grew. They didn't give a shit. He clenched his fist, his jaw exploding in pain. He grabbed it with the other hand. He swung his clenched fist into the air. His jaw exploded again as he walked over to the wall. *If I can cause different pain, my brain won't be able to concentrate on this so much*, he figured. Another explosion in the jaw. He pulled back his fist and punched the wall with a *thud*. The pain in his fist momentarily took over from the pain in his jaw. *It's working*. Then came another explosion in the jaw. He thrust his fist against the wall again, this time harder. He welcomed the pain in his fist. It hurt so much less than his ear and jaw. He punched the wall again, this time before his jaw exploded, trying to time it. He was shaking off the pain in his hand when the pain exploded again in his jaw, even worse. The competition was making his jaw pain grow stronger. He pulled his hand back even further and threw it as hard as he possibly could against the wall. His fist hit the wall, but this time it didn't stop—it just kept going as a piece of the wall disappeared and his arm crashed wrist-deep into it. The door flew open.

"What the fuck are you doing in here?" His mother was furious.

He was standing with one hand still gripping his jaw and the other still in the hole in the wall. His mother, eyes half closed, a cigarette hanging from her mouth, stood in the doorway. He could see the rage building. Then her eyes popped wide open and she was on him. She yanked him from the wall, dragged him over, and threw him on the bed. She didn't have J.P.'s strength, but close. She leaned over him, screaming. "A hole in the wall! A fucking hole in the wall! I don't own this place! I don't own this place, you stupid little fucker!"

She grabbed his wrist and sat on the bed, pinning the rest of his body. He tried to pull his wrist away, but her grip was too tight.

"The next time you want to do something that fucking stupid, you think about this." She took her cigarette out of her mouth and pushed it into his wrist. He screamed in pain. "And think about this." She did it over and over until he couldn't feel the pain in his jaw.

***

Pete was kneeling over Davey with his eyes closed. He would open them every thirty seconds to make sure this was really happening. Joe was pacing a few feet from Davey's lifeless body, his loud sobbing now replaced by a constant whimper.

"How did this happen?" he asked Pete. "How did he fall?"

Pete raised his head and looked straight ahead for a few seconds and then turned to Joe. "Man, I don't know," he answered. "He was walking towards me. I turned to see which way would be the best route to take after you guys got to the ledge, and then I heard a scream. When I turned, he wasn't on the ledge. He was falling down the hill. One second he was right there, and the next he wasn't." Pete sounded confused.

"He lost his footing?"

"I guess," Pete replied. "I wasn't looking at him, he was just there, then gone. He must have been walking too close to the edge."

"You were too close to the edge, you stupid fucker!" Joe yelled at Davey's body. He started to cry. In between sobs, he apologized. "I'm sorry, Davey. I'm sorry, buddy."

Pete lowered his head again and closed his eyes. He could still hear Joe's sobs as he pictured Davey, his lanky walk, his big feet, his upturned nose that always made Pete think of a little pig. He saw himself and Davey in their sleeping bags in front of the television having a sleepover, up until the early morning watching scary shows, fighting sleep as long as they could. He thought of him and Davey coasting down the road on their bikes, the two of them side by side, the wind whooshing in their ears. He thought of each of them taking turns throwing rocks at a large wasp nest hanging from a tree, Davey nailing it with a direct hit and the nest falling to the ground. He had done so much with Davey, his best friend for as long as he could remember. He burst into tears. How could this be real? How could Davey be dead? Young boys didn't die. Old people died—his grandfather had died last year, he was old. His friend shouldn't die, he was young. He had never understood when people said that someone had their whole life in front of them. He understood now. He thought about school; Davey sat at a table with him. Davey wouldn't be there anymore. Davey wouldn't be there ever. Would they just leave it empty? Would they assign someone else to sit with him? How could they? That was Davey's seat. Anybody else sitting there wouldn't be right. Would he have to tell the teacher that? Would he have to tell the teacher that he would like to keep Davey's seat empty? Would the teacher think he was having problems with it? Would the teacher give him a talk about how that's not Davey's seat anymore, and that he had to move on? Would she try and send him to a shrink because that was Davey's seat? He opened his eyes and a tear dropped on Davey's jacket.

"I won't let them take your seat, buddy," Pete sobbed. "I won't let them take your seat."

***

Beth opened her eyes and looked at the buzzing alarm clock. 6:30 a.m. She reached over, turned it off, rubbed her eyes, and hurled herself up to a sitting position. Big day ahead. She had a meeting, and there was probably going to be some date party drama in class. Things could get interesting. *You're acting like Daniel is going to ask you for sure, like it's already a done deal.* She got out of bed, grabbed her robe from the chair, and put it and her slippers on. A sound outside her room startled her. She stood motionless, trying to figure out what it was. It sounded like a retching throat and it was horrible. It stopped and then started again. She opened her bedroom door and ran in the direction of the sound. Her father stood in the doorway of the bathroom, dressed in his work clothes. Her mother was on her knees with her head over the toilet.

"Good morning, Bunny." He closed the bathroom door and gestured for Beth to walk downstairs. The retching started again. It sounded so painful; it made Beth begin to well up with tears. She shook it off. *Have to be strong. She's okay, she's just throwing up, that's all.* In the kitchen, her father put his arms around her and gave her a big hug.

"Are you okay?" her father asked.

"Am I okay? I'm fine. Is Mom okay?"

"She will be. I think she's just a bit hung over, but just to make sure, I was wondering if you could stay home from school and keep an eye on her."

She looked at her father, stunned. He had never asked her to stay home from school before; he must be really worried about her mother. Her parents had always taught her about the importance of school and of attendance. She couldn't ever remember missing a school day, except when her grandfather had died, and even then she wanted to go but her parents said it wasn't appropriate. It would be easy to say, "Sure, yeah no problem, I'll stay home," but today . . . today was different. This was the day that the party dates would be determined. If she weren't there, would Daniel ask someone else? Probably. He was just like everyone else, and wasn't going to chance being left out in the cold without a date. Her father was still waiting for a reply.

"Today is kind of an important day at school, Dad. We're doing some group projects and I really don't want to miss it."

"I'll phone the school and make sure you can catch up on the work," her father said. "I'll be back in a second, I'm just going to check on your mother."

There had been silence from the bathroom the past few minutes. Beth began to feel guilty. *Mom is really sick; my family needs me.* Her mother's health should be her most important concern . . . *but she does this to herself.* She headed to the bathroom in time to see her dad carrying her mother into their bedroom.

"Is she okay?" Beth asked again, frightened.

She followed them into the bedroom. Her dad placed her mom in bed and covered her up. Her mother mumbled something incoherent. Her father tried to feel her forehead but she smacked his hand away.

"I'm fine!" she barked.

He motioned for Beth to go downstairs again. He closed the bedroom door behind him and they both went into the kitchen. Beth sat at the table.

"I would make dinner tonight when I got home from school, you know, to help out."

"That's great," her father said. "That would be a great help. Thank you. But I really want you to stay home with her today, just today. I know how important school is to you, I'm just worried about her and I really can't miss work." He looked at his watch. "Which I have to get going to, right now. Listen, Bunny, I'll call the school when I get to work. Just do what you want around here, check on her from time to time, make her a sandwich or get her some water if she needs it."

Her father grabbed his jacket and briefcase. "I'll call you later to see how you're doing." He kissed her quickly on the forehead and left the house.

Beth was stunned. She couldn't believe what was happening. She was looking after her mother—her mother, who was supposed to look after her. Stuck at home, missing a major event in her adolescent life because her mom couldn't act like a mom . . . *It's just the beginning*. She hoped this wouldn't become a regular thing.

***

The man was walking across the parking lot wearing a blue sweater and khaki pants—something he would never regularly wear, but he was on the run and thought he might as well look as harmless as possible. The clothes from the Gap did the trick. He wondered if any other murderers shopped at the Gap. He figured he would only have to dress like Nerdy McGeekwad for a few days until he found a new area where he could start fresh. The other clothes he had purchased were jeans and T-shirts, which he would switch to when the heat died down . . . *They are going to keep looking*, he thought.

He arrived at the car from his third trip to the stores, opened the trunk, and put the bags in. It was time to organize. He pulled a new knapsack out of a shopping bag, unzipped it, and tossed the paper stuffing into the air. It blew away. He watched it go for a few seconds and marvelled at how far it travelled in a short amount of time. It didn't seem that windy. He pulled open another shopping bag and took out some Walkmans, cameras, and video cameras that he had "picked up" from the electronics store. *Everybody's good at something, and for me it's the bad things*. He shoved the electronics into the knapsack. Out of another shopping bag, he pulled a neatly folded duffle bag. He pulled off the plastic and tossed it into the air. It hit the ground beside him with a crackle and stayed there. He looked around.

Where the hell did the wind go? He paused. *Who gives a fuck? Jesus, you think about some weird shit.* He looked around again to see if there was wind, as if it were playing games. Nothing. *Wrong person to play with, Wind.* Again, he paused. *What the fuck? Get back to work.*

He unfolded the duffle bag, took the clothes out of the other bags, and put them in it. He crumpled up each shopping bag and put them all in one bag. He zipped up the duffle bag and unzipped its side pocket, dumped the contents of the last shopping bag inside, and zipped it up. He threw the last shopping bag in with the others and placed them on the pavement beside the car, leaving the knapsack and the duffle bag in the trunk. He slammed it closed. *Got to get moving and ditch this car,* he thought. *The nosy fuckers have already started their cat-and-mouse game.* He laughed as he climbed into the car. *Maybe I'm the cat.*

He pulled out of the parking lot and back onto the highway. His new outfit fit pretty good; maybe he'd lost weight. The new clothes didn't mask the smell, though; he needed to shower. Another fucking list. He drove about two kilometres and turned off on a logging road. After three minutes, he found a relatively flat land area and hit the gas, driving the car directly into the woods. The car crashed along for about fifty feet and then came to a stop when it became wedged between some trees. It had travelled a lot farther than he thought it would. *Look at you, Little Ford Focus.* He jumped out, grabbed his duffle bag and knapsack from the trunk, and put them on the ground. He grabbed a tree branch, cracked it off, and leaned it on the car. He grabbed another and did the same thing. He stopped when he realized how many branches it would take to cover the car. Fuck it. He grabbed his bags and started back toward the road. *In your younger days, you'd hide your stolen cars so well it would take years to find them, if they ever did.*

He started to walk up the logging road, heading back to the highway, wishing he would leave himself alone sometimes.

***

Hayward was lying on his bed, unable to shake the feeling that he wanted to throw up, even though he hadn't in about two hours. He looked up at the window. The drapes were drawn, but the head of the bed was right underneath the window so he could see pockets of the outdoors in the fabric ripples. It was totally dark out now. He knew that the cops would have gotten Davey's body out of there by now. Where would Davey go now? To the hospital for after-death tests, cause of death, and that stuff. How would the body get there? An ambulance. When Mr. Chisholm died from up the street, they had wheeled him out on the wheelie stretcher with the sheet covering his whole body. Hayward had watched as they put him in an ambulance and it drove away slowly, no sirens, no speeding. After that, every time he saw an ambulance driving normally, he thought they must have just picked up a guy who was already dead. He once saw an ambulance going through the McDonald's drive-through and wondered how they could eat with a dead guy in the back. He figured that they must just get used to it.

They must have brought Davey up from the brook and put him in one of those slow-moving ambulances. They would drive right by his house. He could not bring himself to look out the window to check the scene on the street. He didn't want to see any of it. He knew if the ambulance were still there, people would be looking out the windows of every house on the street. He didn't want to see it.

There was a knock on Hayward's bedroom door. "Come in," he answered.

His dad came in and walked over to his bedside. "How are you doin', bud?"

"I'm still really confused."

His dad rubbed the back of his hair. "I know, bud, I know. Listen, there is a police officer in the kitchen. He'd like to come in and talk to you. That okay, bud?"

Hayward had already told his story to a number of adults, and to a police officer, who had written it all down. He felt like he was starting to recite lines from the television reruns he liked to watch.

"Yeah, Dad, it's okay."

"Don't be nervous, just tell him what happened."

"Okay," Hayward replied.

His dad left the room. He wasn't nervous at all. *Talking to a cop? How about finding your friend dead at the bottom of a hill? That's something to be nervous about.* He had to cut his dad some slack. He knew that his dad was the one who was nervous. His mother and father were devastated, but he knew they were thanking God that it was Davey and not him. They were nervous because it easily could have been him, and he understood that. The door opened and an officer, dressed in his police uniform, entered his bedroom. He was portly with a dark moustache and dark hair. He held his hat in his hand.

"Hello, Hayward. My name is Officer Scharfe," he said as he pulled the chair out from Hayward's desk and sat down.

Hayward sat up in his bed.

"I was already talking to the other two boys about the accident," the officer said. He placed his police hat on the desk, took a notepad out of his breast pocket, and flipped it open. Hayward noticed a pen in his other hand, but hadn't seen him take it out. It reminded him of those old dudes who pulled silver dollars out of the area around your ear.

"I know the main story, and you've already given your statement, so what I want to do here is just ask you a couple of questions. Is that okay?

What would happen if he said no? He often fantasized about doing disrespectful things, but never actually did them. "Sure," he said to the officer.

"What was Davey doing the last time you saw him alive?"

Hayward had been living this nightmare for the last seven hours, but it still didn't seem real, especially when people were using so many phrases he had heard a million times on TV, but never in real life. "The last time you saw him alive" was on every cop show he'd ever seen.

"Davey was walking along the top ledge of the bank above the brook."

"Was he walking close to the edge?" the officer asked.

"Well, the ledge is pretty narrow. I remember from being on it before, but from where I was climbing up the hill and the ledge being up higher, I couldn't really tell how close he was."

Officer Scharfe adjusted himself in the chair. Hayward noticed that the officer was still wearing his boots. He had never seen anyone in his mother's house with their boots on. *I guess because he's the police*, he figured. *How could you ask the police to remove their boots? They always need them on in case they get a call and have to spring into action. Can't have someone getting away while they're on somebody's porch tying up their boots.* He pictured Officer Scharfe sitting there in full uniform with white tube socks. What an odd sight.

"Hayward." Officer Scharfe was staring at him. He had asked him a question and he hadn't heard it.

"I'm sorry, could you repeat that, please?" Hayward said in as polite a manner as humanly possible.

"Was there anyone else on the ledge?"

"Pete," Hayward said.

"Was he close to Davey?"

"No."

"Where was Pete?"

"He was at the far end of the ledge."

"Did you see Davey fall off the ledge?"

"No."

"Did you see Davey when he was falling?"

"Yes."

"Did Davey reach the far side of the ledge where Pete was?"

"No."

"Are you sure?"

"Yes, he didn't have enough time. I looked up as he was just start-ing to walk across the ledge. A couple of seconds later, he was falling down the hill."

"Was Pete still at the far end of the ledge after Davey fell?"

Hayward was stunned by the question. No one had asked him this one yet. "Yes," he replied.

"Did you see this?"

"No, after I saw Davey falling, I didn't look back up at the ledge."

"Who was the first to find Davey?"

"I was."

"What did you do?"

This was the part of the story that was the hardest to tell. "Nothing," he said to the officer, with a sigh and headshake.

"Did you touch him?"

"No," Hayward replied.

"What did you do then?"

"Nothing. I kind of froze."

"Did you know he was dead then? Is that why you froze?"

Hayward pictured it in his mind.

"No, I didn't know then . . . but you could tell by the way he was lying. I just froze," Hayward said, frustrated. He gathered himself and continued. "I guess I had never been in that situation before, and I really didn't know what to do."

"Where were you? When you froze?"

"On my knees beside him."

"Could you see his face?"

Hayward thought of Davey's face after he had rolled him over. "Part of it, he was on his side."

"Who came to Davey's body next?"

"Joe did."

"What did he do, Hayward?"

He pictured Joe muttering over and over. "Joe was crying."

"Did Joe touch him?"

"No," Hayward replied.

"Then Pete came?" asked the officer.

"Yes. Pete got there, pushed us aside, and rolled him over. I guess I should have done that to see if he needed help . . . *but he was dead.* I just froze," he said, his voice cracking.

"Well, Hayward, that's what's known as shock, and it's the brain's mechanism for helping us deal with situations when emotions are extreme. The brain becomes overwhelmed, and it can't process things properly, prohibiting a person from figuring out what to do," the officer said softly.

"Really?"

That must have been it, that's why I couldn't touch him . . . *he was dead* . . . to see if Davey needed help. I must have been in shock.

"What did Pete do when he came to Davey?"

"Rolled him over."

"Did Davey moan or cough or could you see any breathing?"

"No," Hayward said as he shook his head.

The officer was about to ask another question when Hayward looked him right in the eyes and spoke as if he were an adult.

"He was dead."

The officer looked at him silently for a few seconds, then scribbled in his notebook, closed it, and put it back in his pocket.

"Okay, thanks for your time, Hayward."

The officer got up and walked over to his bedside. Hayward expected him to reach out and shake hands, like adults did, but he gently placed his hand on Hayward's head and rubbed his hair. The officer spoke softly, as if he somehow knew what Hayward was going through. "It may not seem like it now, son, but it will be okay."

Hayward looked at the officer's boots as he left and thought of the tube socks. He was almost going to laugh but then felt guilty. How could he laugh on the day Davey had died?

He looked up under the drapes, into the night sky. *How long after you died did it take to get to heaven?* he pondered to himself. *Davey must be there by now. I wonder if he misses it here.*

Chapter 9

Never a Good Picture

The television was blaring something about a juicer that makes you lose weight. Beth was sitting on the couch with her feet up, looking at it but not watching. She was thinking that she might have to skip the party if she didn't have a date. But everyone would know the reason why she wouldn't be going. She would have to come up with a humdinger of an excuse.

"Humdinger" was a word her father used that her mother didn't like. She wondered if her mother liked anything about her father anymore, or if she'd just be happier without him . . . and her. Beth let out a heavy sigh. She wanted things to be the way they were before, when her mother was happy. When did she start to become unhappy? She couldn't remember when it had begun; her mother just seemed to become more and more distant over time.

Beth could hear her mother walking around upstairs. She placed her feet on the floor and was about to get up and go see her, but then thought she'd better wait. She heard the bedroom door opening, her mother walking down the hall, going into the bathroom, and closing the door. *Just going to the bathroom.* She'd ask her mother if she needed anything when she came out. She heard the shower running.

Shower? Her mother had been pretty out of it just a few hours ago. *Maybe she's feeling better, she may even be happy today.*

Beth looked back at the television. Everything the juicer made, people were gulping down and smiling afterward. Beth smiled. Must be a humdinger. She picked up the remote and switched channels, stopping on a show about some young boys playing baseball. Their uniforms looked a little too pretty for boys' uniforms—soft green with a bright yellow stripe. She wondered if any of the boys had second thoughts about playing for a team with such awful uniforms; surely the other teams made fun of them. She remembered seeing Hayward playing baseball. His uniform was grey and had an orange stripe, and he looked so cute in it. There was a loud crack of the bat from the TV and the boys playing outfield ran for the fence, but the ball kept going right over it for a home run. One of the young boys in the outfield threw down his glove in disgust. Beth laughed as she pictured Hayward doing the same thing. He was super competitive no matter what game they were playing.

She heard the bathroom door open and her mother walk back down the hall and into her bedroom. She looked at the ball field fence on the television and thought about the fence at her school where she was supposed to meet Daniel Green. Daniel would probably be asking someone else to the party today in that very spot—Tammy Gisbourne, or maybe Kimmy Marks. She pictured herself standing by the fence with Hayward. He was dressed in his baseball uniform and asking her to the date party. After she agreed to be his date, he joyfully tossed his baseball glove up in the air.

Her mother's bedroom door opened again and she came down the stairs. Beth could smell her perfume before she even entered the room. She came into the living room and looked at Beth.

"What are you doing home?" she asked.

"Oh, Dad just asked me to stay home in case you needed anything. I could get it for you."

Her mother's expression turned angry. "That man . . . that man should worry about himself sometimes, taking you out of school. What the hell is he thinking?"

Beth didn't say anything. Her mom was wearing a black dress and high heels, and her hair was pulled back on both sides with two clips. Beth had only seen her mom dressed like this a few times in her life, usually when her parents were going out to a party and she was staying home with a babysitter. Her mother grabbed her purse from beside the couch and dug into it. She pulled out a twenty-dollar bill and gave it to her.

"Here, use this, call a cab and get yourself to school."

Beth was astounded.

"But Dad asked me to—"

Her mother cut her off. "I know what he was doing, but I'm going out, so there's no one here for you to worry about. So just go to school, and I'll see you later on."

"I was going to make dinner tonight," Beth exclaimed.

"Whatever, sure dear, whatever you want." Her mother zipped up her purse and started for the door.

"But where are you going?" Beth called after her. Her mom opened the door and left without answering. Beth, still sitting on the couch, heard the car start. Where was she going dressed like that in the daytime? And giving her money for a cab? She had never taken a cab by herself. It was all very strange.

She headed upstairs to get ready for school, thinking about the smokes and the hotel matches she had seen in her mother's purse the evening before. Was that where she was going? Beth looked at the clothes she had picked out the night before for today's school day and started to get excited. She wasn't going to miss all of date-party-drama day after all. She started to dress, hoping it wasn't too late. *What if everybody is already paired up?* Maybe Daniel, noticing she wasn't at school this morning, changed his plan and decided to meet someone else. *Who says it has to be the guy who asks anyway?* She could ask . . . *Hayward.* . . someone. She pictured herself grabbing Hayward's ball glove from him and throwing it into the air. *Better get a move on,* she thought as she pulled on her pants.

***

"Thanks for the ride," he said.

"No problem, have a good trip," the driver said.

The man slammed the truck door and walked down the sidewalk toward the door to the airport. He stopped before the entrance and leaned up against the building. Putting the duffle bag down, he lit a cigarette, sucked the smoke deep into his lungs, and exhaled it out of his nose. He looked out at the parking lot and the sea of cars. He wasn't here to get on a plane, he was here for a new ride. The people that parked here and flew away wouldn't know their car was gone until they came back, giving him at least a week before his new vehicle was even reported stolen. His belly grumbled; he needed to eat before picking out his new car. He knew it would be a family sedan, and why not? He was dressed in his khakis and sweater— "Dad of the Year."

Guilt wrapped around him like a smothering blanket. He hoped the nosy fuckers were looking after his son. They would probably put him in foster care in the next few days—better than that stupid bitch of a mother he had. *Did you a favour, boy.*

He grabbed his duffle bag and walked along the front of the airport. A mother and father were trying to hurry their two kids along into the entrance. The dad had two suitcases and the mother was carrying a diaper bag and a baby, the kids were each dragging a suitcase that was bigger than each of them. *Why the fuck do you need that much stuff? Are you going for a month?* He was envious of the kids, with their suitcases. He'd never been on a trip when he was a kid. And if he had, he would have never needed a suitcase; at any point in his childhood he could have fit all his clothes into a small plastic bag. He felt the back of his neck start to get hot, and his arms started to tremble. He could feel the Push starting. *Holy fuck, not here.*

He walked on past the entrance. He couldn't go in now and sit in the food court with all those families going on exotic vacations. He needed to relax, get a drink, and calm down. At the end of the airport building, there was a hotel called the Redwood Inn and an attached restaurant, the Redwood Bar and Grill. Perfect, a steak and a splash o' Jack: that sounded exotic enough right now.

He headed toward the restaurant, but he couldn't shake the thought of those exotic vacations. People lying on the beach in the sun, hot chicks splashing each other, everyone sipping pina coladas. He would never be able to leave the country with his criminal resume, which had begun when he was thirteen years old and had been added to ever since. *Well, I could at least make my way to Florida. Maybe that's where I'll head, lots of pina coladas there,* he thought. *Half of these exotic travellers are heading to Disneyworld, anyway.* He could do that; he didn't need any khaki-wearin' dad to bring him there, either. *Nah,* he thought, *too hot in the summer, wouldn't want to live there all year 'round. Make up your fuckin' mind.* He pictured himself getting his picture taken with Mickey and then pictured himself in a mug shot, with the numbers underneath. He pictured Mickey the same way, in a mug shot. *Need some Jack for this mind, Holy Jesus. Why does it just keep going on and on sometimes?* He sometimes felt like he was going to go crazy. Maybe he'd sell the electronics, score some dope later. That always calmed him down, nothing like a good puff. He pulled open the restaurant door and went inside.

***

Pete looked at the clock beside his bed: 3:07 a.m., and Davey was still dead. He rolled over and closed his eyes. All he could see was Davey falling down the hill. He squeezed his eyes tighter. Still saw him falling. He rolled onto his belly and buried his face in the pillow, but no matter what, there was Davey, falling. Every time Pete tried to relax, it was all he saw. Each time, all Pete could do was watch from the ledge. He wished he could catch Davey, wished he could go back and stop it from happening. There he was, just standing there, watching as he fell.

Pete sat up. The neck of his shirt was damp from sweat. He thought about how he had grabbed Davey in class over a stupid project. He had grabbed his best friend and physically threatened him over a project, and now he was dead. Dead. All the great times they had spent together, and on Davey's last day alive, Pete was a complete ass to him—a complete jerk. If only he could go back and be nicer yesterday. What was he thinking? If he could go back they would never go to the junkyard. That's what he'd change.

Pete looked around his room and thought of Davey's bedroom, how empty it must be. He pictured Davey's still-made bed and his toys in his closet. Davey's air rifle—he and Davey would never shoot cans or small birds together ever again. He wondered what Davey's parents would do with all his stuff. Probably give it to Davey's little cousins. They would use it, but they wouldn't look after it like Davey did; they wouldn't look after it at all. They should respect it—it was Davey's! He knew they wouldn't, and there was nothing he could do about it.

He thought of Davey's hatchet. How many trees had he cut down over the years, how many forts had they built? He would never swing that hatchet again. Would Davey's father use it to split wood, then leave it out in the backyard to rust? He probably would. He'd never know how much that hatchet meant to Davey. He would never know the power they all felt as they walked into the woods with their hatchets, knowing, even as boys, that they could take down any tree and build something themselves. No one except Pete and the other boys knew how much that hatchet meant to him; the thing should be framed. He pictured it in a frame and decided he would watch

Davey's backyard, and if his dad left it out there, he'd steal it. He didn't steal things, but this would be an exception.

He thought about Davey's bike, remembering the day he got it. It was one of those ones with the plastic motorbike gas tanks, cheap and cheesy, and they all let Davey know it. He defended it for a while, but then one day it wasn't on his bike. The boys figured he had deliberately thrown it away, but he said it must have fallen off at some point and he hadn't noticed, and when he went back and searched for it, he couldn't find it. He thought about the tent Davey had gotten for his eighth birthday, and how many times they had slept in it. Pete's belly clenched in pain. He would never sleep in that tent again. He began to cry.

Of all the shit in this world, of all the assholes, pricks, murderers, and drug dealers out there, Davey has to die, he silently mourned. He saw Davey falling again. He buried his face in his pillow and began to scream.

***

Hayward opened his eyes. It was light out. Surprisingly, he had fallen asleep. Maybe it was a bad dream, and Davey was still alive! Yes, that was it—the whole thing was a dream. He jumped out of bed and headed for the kitchen. His mother was at the counter and his dad was sitting at the table. His mother grabbed him and gave him a hug. His heart sank. No dream.

"I'm so sorry, dear."

"Thanks, Mom." Hayward sat down at the table.

"Would you like some toast?" his mother asked.

He was starving. "Yes, please. Could I have a hard-boiled egg, too?"

"Of course, I can whip you up something before I head to school." Hayward's parents were both teachers who would be leaving for work soon.

"Dad, how long do you think it will be before I go back to school?" Hayward remembered that when his grandfather had died, his parents had him stay home from school for three days.

"Well, Hayward, I think you should probably stay home until next Monday, just to make sure the funeral and burial are finished. When you do go back to school, a lot of people are going to want to talk to you about it. You may not feel up to that just yet, so the time will give you and everyone else a chance to come to grips with this and try to start moving on.

"Okay, Dad."

Hayward hadn't thought about the funeral, mainly because he had never been to one. He was too young to attend his grandfather's funeral. He had only seen them on TV. "When do you think the funeral will be, Dad?"

"With your closeness to Davey, I'm sure his parents will let you know soon."

"His parents will let me know?" Hayward asked, surprised.

"I imagine they will. They'll probably ask you to do something at the wake or the funeral."

"Something?"

"Like a job, Hayward."

"A job," Hayward choked. "What do you mean?"

His dad spoke in a calm voice. "Hayward, you're getting older, and you have to learn that with that, there comes certain responsibilities."

"My friend just died. What does that have to do with responsibilities?"

"Hayward, listen for a minute. When someone dies, the family and close friends are responsible, out of respect for that person, to give them a wake or visitation, a funeral, and a burial. The extended family and friends usually have responsibilities to help the immediate family deal with the loss." Hayward sat in silence. "Do you understand what I'm saying, Hayward?"

"Yes, sir."

"Just be ready if the family asks you to do something. You should consider it an honour, and you should carry yourself well out of respect for Davey and how much Davey meant to you."

"Okay, Dad. Well, what should I do today?"

"The family and close friends, which includes you, are in a time of grieving right now, so you should stay in the house and let yourself go through the many memories you have of Davey, and do things around here you enjoy to take your mind off it for periods of time."

"Okay, Dad. I get it."

"If you're having trouble handling things today, call my school and I'll come home. It's no problem at all. Otherwise, if you have any more questions, I'll answer them when I get home, okay, buddy?"

"Okay, Dad. I should be okay. If I have any questions, I'll write them down so I remember."

His dad chuckled. "Sure, Hayward," his dad said as he rubbed his head. "Look, your mom and I gotta go."

His mother gave him another enormous hug. "You heard your father—just stay in here. Don't go out outside."

"Yeah, Mom, got it." He knew his mother was having a hard time, so he didn't give her a smart remark, as he usually would. He decided he would appreciate some things a little more, one being his mother. He would cut out the smart remarks and show more respect, because Davey's death had shown him that you never know what can happen—one moment someone is there and the next they're gone and you're left reflecting on their life and the role you played in it.

Hayward's mother placed a hard-boiled egg and some toast in front of him. Hayward thanked her as both his parents started to gather their things to leave for work. He began eating his breakfast. *What jobs are there at a funeral?* He thought about jobs at the church, where Joe was an altar boy every Sunday. Handing out programs, being an usher, reading scripture—surely they wouldn't ask him to read aloud. He was too young to speak at a funeral. He pictured a casket with the American flag draped over it. He knew that Davey's

91

wouldn't have a flag on it—that was only for politicians and war heroes—he had seen that many times on TV. Caskets were carried by people in and out of a funeral; he believed the name for those jobs were "pallbearers." Maybe that's a job they might give to him. Was he strong enough to lift his portion of the casket? How far would he have to walk with it?

His parents said goodbye and said they would call to check in on him during the day. Hayward acknowledged them, but his mind was deep into pallbearer analysis. What if he couldn't hold it? Davey was a lot bigger than him and those caskets looked freakin' heavy. What if he dropped it and Davey rolled out and it was his fault? He started to panic. He wasn't big enough for a job like that. They wouldn't give him that job, would they? "You have to do whatever they ask and consider it an honour," is what his father had said. He had to calm down, get a grip. *They haven't even asked you to do anything yet, and you're going on like a fraidy-cat.* That wasn't exactly taking on some "getting older responsibilities," as his dad had called them. He walked over to the window, pulled back the drapes, and looked out into the street. Beside the church was the path they used to get from their street to the school. As if he needed more grief, a feeling of dread hit him like a wrecking ball. Today he was supposed to ask Beth to the date party and beat Daniel Greensnot to the punch.

"Shit!" he said aloud. "Shit! Shit! Shit!"

He thought about getting dressed and going to school anyway, but he knew that was definitely the wrong thing to do. Could things get any worse at this point? His father had said he was not going to school until the beginning of next week, and he wasn't supposed to do anything during this grieving period. The date party was this Friday night. That meant he wouldn't he going to that, either. Oh man!

"Shit!" he yelled again to the empty house. This was horrible. He started to list the things that could realistically happen. Daniel would ask Beth to the date party today, she would say yes, they would go to the party, probably hold hands, and only slow dance with each other. They would then officially be a couple, and he would be on the outside looking in until they broke up. *But what if they don't?* he worried. And who knew how long that could take. Hayward's chest felt like it had bruised muscles, because he had tightened it up so much over the past twenty-four hours. Frustrated, he ran his hand over his face, not taking his eyes off the path. His chest would heal, and he would be there when they broke up. He had to be.

***

Beth thanked the cab driver, closed the car door, and headed into the school. The principal's office was immediately to the left of the entrance. The principal, Mr. Crewe, was a tall, thin man who always wore wrinkled suits. He stood in the doorway talking to another teacher as Beth walked by.

"Beth."

Damn! She really didn't want an interrogation—just wanted to slip into class like she had been there all morning. She turned back towards Principal Crewe. The other teacher turned and walked away. "Your father said you wouldn't be in today because of a family issue," he said.

"Yeah, my mom wasn't feeling well earlier this morning, so Dad asked me to stay home with her in case she needed anything, but she's feeling better now."

Principal Crewe shifted on his feet and rubbed the corners of his mouth. "Well, Beth, even though she's feeling better, maybe you still could have stayed home to make sure she didn't start to feel sick again."

What was with this guy? Why did he even care? Then she remembered that her father played badminton with Principal Crewe on Thursday nights.

"Yes, but she told me that it was okay. She told me I should go to school."

"That being said, I really think if your dad thought it was that serious, you should be home with your mother."

Beth shook her head in frustration. "No, it's okay, my mother's not home. She left. Gave me money for a cab and told me to go to school."

Principal Crewe's eyes opened really wide and he frowned. He again shifted uncomfortably on his feet. He looked right, left, and back to Beth. He took a deep breath.

"Okay, well then, let's just get you to class."

Principal Crewe motioned with his arm for Beth to walk down the hall with him.

"I'll come with you and let Miss Nyers know it's okay that you're coming to school late."

Beth noticed something strange about the way he walked that she had never noticed before. His leg strides were long and steady, but his feet seemed loose at the ankles. It was like his legs threw his feet out there and his ankles were so wobbly they had no control over where each foot landed.

"So Beth. Your grades are very good this year."

"Thank you," Beth said uncomfortably. She couldn't remember ever having a one-on-one conversation with the principal before.

"Miss Nyers is one of our best teachers. She really has a way with the students."

"Yeah, she does," Beth agreed.

What was he talking about? What was her "way with the students?" Beth didn't see much difference from the other teachers she'd had. If anything, Miss Nyers seemed kind of boring. What would he say if she told him that she sometimes felt like Miss Nyers didn't care if the students were doing anything at all? Once she had even snapped at a student, saying she "Didn't give a rat's ass about his excuse." And here Principal Crewe was giving her the Teacher of the Year award.

They arrived at the classroom. Beth watched as Principal Crewe opened the door.

"Miss Nyers, can I see you for a second?" the principal asked.

Beth started to get closer to the door to go into the classroom, but Principal Crewe had his body positioned to block it. He must have noticed her moving that way.

"Just wait here—okay, Beth? The teacher is going to talk to you before you go in."

Miss Nyers came out of the classroom and walked down the hall with the principal until they were out of Beth's earshot. Holy moly! Date party drama or not, if she had have known it would be this type of rigmarole—another word her father used that her mother hated—she would have just stayed home. She watched as Principal Crewe waved his right arm as he spoke to Miss Nyers. He was a hand talker. Beth's mother used to see people on TV and point out that they were hand talkers, back when her mother used to watch TV with the family. Principal Crewe then turned and walked away from Miss Nyers, who came over to Beth, looking uncomfortable.

That's it, I'm never going to come to school halfway through the day again, she decided.

"Beth," Miss Nyers started. She adjusted her collar, licked the corners of her lips, and continued. "We had a terrible tragedy befall our school yesterday. One of our grade six students, Davey Arcal, had an accident and lost his life."

Beth stared at her blankly. She was trying to process what she had just heard, but her mind wouldn't let her. It wouldn't believe.

Miss Nyers continued. "He fell from a high ledge over the brook on Campbell Street and hit his head."

"Oh my god," Beth said as she put her hands up to her face.

"I'm not sure if you knew this boy—"

"No," Beth interrupted. "I mean, I knew who he was, but Hayward and Joe were good friends with him."

"Yes," Miss Nyers said softly. "They won't be in school for the next couple of days."

"Oh my god," Beth said again.

"So, Beth, there are grief counsellors at the school today if you feel you have trouble focusing or dealing with what I have just told you. They will be available here at the school for the next few days for any students who feel they need to talk."

"Okay," Beth said. "I understand."

"Beth, as a class, we are going to try and move on from this and carry on with our regular day. Sometime over the next few days, the school will have an assembly to celebrate Davey's life. So, Beth, do you think you're okay with this right now, to go into class and proceed?"

Beth nodded.

"Are you sure?" Miss Nyers asked, wanting a verbal response.

"Yes," Beth replied.

Miss Nyers put her hand on Beth's shoulder, opened the door, and walked her into the classroom.

***

The man ordered another Bloody Caesar and a Jack Daniel's. The first drinks had gone down perfectly. *Stay double-fisted, that's the way.* He looked around the restaurant. *Pretty nice in here.* The bar, tables, and chairs were made of oak and the tables had a plastic topping so the wood wouldn't get destroyed.

The place was pretty empty for being beside an airport. He hoped the food was good; he had ordered a sirloin and baked potatoes. A guy sat a couple of tables over wearing a shirt and tie and eating a pasta dish. He wondered how shirt-and-tie guys didn't get food on their ties. *Who gives a fuck? Like you'll ever have that problem.* He watched the bartender pour the drinks he'd ordered and put them on the waitress' tray. There was a small breeze and the smell of nice perfume as a lady in a black dress walked past his table and took a seat at the bar. He looked her up and down. *Well, well, well. A table with a view like this. The place just got a whole lot better.*

The waitress placed his drinks on the table and he threw down the Jack, wondering how far the ball had rolled since the nosy fuckers had started rolling it. Was his picture going to be on the news? When they did show a picture, it was never a good picture. It was always a picture that looked like you just had killed a dog—*or three people*—that wouldn't stop barking at night. They never showed a picture of you happy, like at the beach or your high school graduation photo. *You had to graduate first.* He knew they would find a crappy one of him with a sinister look. He laughed. The word "sinister" wasn't used much in regular conversation, but it was used a lot in the cartoons. He wondered why there weren't any wrestlers called the "Minister of Sinister." He laughed again. Maybe it was being saved for him and his wrestling debut. He was still laughing as the waitress placed the steak and potatoes in front of him.

"Is everything okay, sir?"

He looked at her, still smiling, "Not if you're Hulk Hogan."

"I'm sorry?" she said, confused.

"Nothing. Can I get another Jack?" He shook the empty glass.

"Okay," she said with little hesitation.

He picked up his utensils and started to cut into the steak. The lady at the bar was smoking and drinking a martini. She was dressed for the evening, but it was only lunchtime. For a moment he thought she was a hooker, but her hair was pulled back on both sides with clips like a soccer mom would wear—or maybe that was this hooker's angle. If it was, it was brilliant. Whatever her deal, she was lookin' good.

Businessman Johnson had finished his meal and was paying for it with a credit card—an expense account, for sure. *All those fat-cat fuckers have expense accounts*, the man thought. He realized he had an expense account too, at the expense of others, and laughed. He'd get a card that said that, and it would save him the trouble of going out on the streets and earning it. *Expense account*, he snickered. *Boy, you are on today.*

The lady at the bar was looking at him. She smiled. He smiled back. *Must be the khakis*, he figured. She was looking at her own drink when he picked up his Caesar and held it up. It had celery salt on the rim. He continued to hold it up and stare at her. Finally, she looked back over at him. He sloppily licked all around the rim of the glass, as if he were a cow. She laughed, and he gestured to her to join him. She gave him a hesitant shrug as if to say, "Oh, I don't know." He knew then she was no hooker, and this made the game a whole lot more interesting. He took his fingers and made a circular motion above his head, as if to indicate that he had a halo. She laughed again, only this time she began to gather up her things. *Stupid fuckin' bitch.* If there were a professional bastard league he would be the motherfuckin' MVP, but every game he played ended bad for the competition. Real bad.

"Hello," she said as she sat down.

He looked at her and smiled. Batter up!

Chapter 10

Time to Play

Pete was lying on the floor below the window, staring up at the sky. He should have been a better friend to Davey. Davey had idolized him, and for the most part he had taken advantage of that. He felt like he had never given Davey enough respect. Why did it take Davey dying for him to realize it? He always thought of himself as tougher, smarter, and cooler, and that Davey was lucky to have him as a friend, but lying there, he knew that all those things were just to cover up his own insecurities. He had always acted in a way that showed Davey, Joe, and Hayward that he was the one in control, he was the one who could handle anything, he was the one who made the decisions; but on the inside, he constantly second-guessed himself. To him, the most important thing had been the way the guys made him feel: like a leader. He wasn't the coolest in his class, but he was with those guys. He wasn't the toughest in his class, and sometimes even got bullied, but to those boys, he was very tough, even though they had never seen him in a fistfight. He had acted tough, and it had worked. He was constantly putting on an act; he was a phony. Davey was the one who was real. Davey was the one who was himself. He never tried to be someone else, just Davey, and he just wanted to hang around with Pete.

Tears began to stream down Pete's face. He was selfish and he knew it. Pete would get Davey to trade things with him if Davey had something that he liked, and Davey had always obliged . . . *until yesterday.* Hockey cards, dinky cars, and action figures: if Pete wanted it, he would get it. How could he have acted like that with someone he called—and who called him—a best friend? No more. No more phoniness. He wasn't going to act anymore. If he wasn't sure about something, he would say it. And he would never knowingly take advantage of someone who considered him a friend.

Pete looked at the sky. *Sorry, Davey. I should have been a better friend.* Davey's life was over; how the fuck could that be right? He was just a kid; what would he have become? Would he have had a wife? Kids? No one would ever know. *We are trying to make sense of it, but what's the sense? What are we doing here in life? Just doing stuff until one day we die. What's the purpose of this?* Pete felt like he had to do something—had to do something in his life that meant something to him, to others, to Davey. He would use Davey's life as motivation to change aspects of his personal life. He was also going to use it as a motivation for a direction. Which direction? Towards what?

Before I die, I want to look back on my life and think that I made a difference. I did something that I set out to do, and made the world a better place, living the way that I lived, following the path that I had started to follow when my best friend died.

He pulled himself up to a sitting position, his mind flying. It was right there; he just had to grab the thought. He looked at a cloud, trying to see the cloud as the shape of a cop hat, a badge, or a pair of handcuffs, but it was just an oddly shaped cloud. He knew what he would do with his life. He would be a cop, putting bad guys away, and making the world a safer place. He would make a difference. For himself, for Davey.

"Thanks, buddy," Pete said to the sky.

***

Hayward sat on the couch watching television. On the program, two men ripped down some drywall and a bunch of cockroaches began to fall out. Normally, he would be on the edge of his seat, thinking that it was one of the coolest things he'd ever seen, but he just stared. How would those men ever get all those bugs out of that house? He knew the show would end by showing that the bugs were gone and the house was all fixed up. They'd say they rid the house of cockroaches, but he wondered if, in a couple months, he walked up to the house, with the cameras long gone, knocked on the door, and asked if they had seen any bugs since the show, they would have come back.

Hayward put his head down on a throw cushion and stretched out into a lying position. He was feeling very lonely, but didn't feel like talking to just anyone. All most people would do was ask him questions about the accident and how he was dealing with it. He wanted to talk—not answer questions. There were only two other people he could have a conversation with right now, and they were going through the same thing at the moment. He wanted to call Joe, but felt it might be too early. Everything was still fresh. Joe was more emotional and was probably taking Davey's death harder than he was. There would be no phone calls, no conversation until they saw each other at the visitation. After that first meeting, the phone calls would resume between them. How would this affect their friendship in the future? Would they hang out like they did before? Obviously, things could never be the same, but how would they change? In what ways? Would Pete hang around with them anymore, with him being a year older and Davey gone? Would he feel too much like an older guy hanging with some younger kids?

Hayward realized that the first change had already happened, and they didn't even have to all be together to notice it. The group dynamic had changed: one older boy and two younger ones. Everything with the group from here on would be totally different. How each of them dealt with this new group dynamic would answer the question of what changes there would be. This was some deep shit. Along with the enormous amount of sadness that he was feeling for Davey, there was a great sadness for the loss of their childhood, their innocence. The changes that would come would be a reminder of Davey's death for the rest of their lives. Each of them would look back and see that this event in time was the beginning of their adult lives.

Hayward was very observant, even for a young boy. Most young people wanted to get older, and he had noticed that adults didn't really seem that happy. They seemed stressed. They had bills. They went to jobs they didn't like. Most kids thought that adults had the freedom to do whatever they wanted, but when you really looked at it, it was the kids who had the freedom. And that recognition was part of Hayward's sadness. They would never again go on any adventures with a carefree, boyish attitude. Everything from now on would be planned and analyzed for safety. They'd probably scrap every adventure as being too dangerous. The woods and the brook had been their adventure land, and it was now tainted. Even if he, Joe, and Pete wanted to get together and go for a walk into those areas, it would be too painful. They wouldn't enjoy themselves with all that had changed. Not only had they lost one of their best friends, but a part of their boyhood life was gone, as well, and they could never get it back. So that was that. He felt like a baseball player who didn't want to retire but wasn't good enough to make the team. He wasn't walking away; he was being forced out.

Well, bring on the next part: the zits, the clothes, and the dates. Beth. She was supposed to be his first date; he had gone over and over it in his head, it was the whole reason he had planned the whole date party thing. The kids in his class would have their first dates under their belts. He was being forced out of childhood, but still going to miss slow dancing with Beth, his Beth. Hayward began to feel the tightness in his chest. He was tired of it, tired of hurting, tired of crying, tired of life. *When the fuck is this gonna get better?*

Maybe Davey was the lucky one. He quickly pushed that thought away, and then got mad at himself for even thinking it. He had to keep his mind on the great things in life, such as getting presents at Christmas, swimming on a hot summer day, and Beth.

***

Beth sat at her desk replaying Miss Nyers' words in her head. Holy. How? How could this have happened? Kids fall every day, everywhere, but they don't die. She looked over her shoulder at Hayward's desk. Both his and Joe's seats were empty, and it gave her an eerie feeling. As soon as the teacher left the room, she asked Kimmy Marks—the gossip queen of the fifth grade at Lady Madonna Elementary—what had happened. Had she heard anything? Kim looked at her with eyes beaming and leaned forward.

"Well," she said, "Joe and Hayward were with Davey and Pete Lyons. They crossed the brook down behind Campbell Street and were up on the high bank on the other side. Davey lost his balance and fell. He just missed Hayward and Joe on the way down. When Davey got to the bottom, his head landed right on a rock and it killed him."

"Holy shit!" Beth didn't usually swear, but she felt that this certain situation warranted it. "Just missed Joe and Hayward?" she repeated.

"Yeah, they almost were killed, too."

"How did you hear this?" Beth asked.

"Well, you know Stephanie Lewis in the fourth grade?"

"Yes," Beth nodded.

"Her dad was one of the cops that got Davey's body up from the brook."

"Wow! How are the boys doing?"

"Well," she said, eyes still beaming, "her dad said they were a mess, and I can understand it. They did watch their friend die and almost died themselves."

"Almost died," Beth repeated. She turned back and faced forward. Poor Hayward. Almost died. The words felt like a sword poking at her heart. She looked over her shoulder at Hayward's empty seat and felt like a part of her was missing.

Beth began to doodle the shape of a horse on her notebook. She always seemed to draw horses when she was nervous; the picture of a horse just seemed to calm her. She was drawing the horse's mane when someone walked up and stood beside her. Beth looked up from her notebook to see Daniel.

"Hello," Daniel said.

"Hi," Beth replied.

"Are you gonna meet me at lunchtime?"

Beth hadn't thought about it after learning about the accident. Meet him? Were they still going to have this party? She remembered she wasn't even sure if that was what this meeting was about.

"Yeah," she said. "The ball field fences, right?"

"Yes. I'll see you there," Daniel said and left as quickly as he had appeared.

She wasn't excited about their meeting now. It seemed so insignificant. But then again, she didn't want to be dateless for a date party. *Almost died. Davey did.* She thought of Davey, tall with black hair, kind of cute; she knew some of the other girls in her grade found him cute, too. *It's so horrible. That easily could have been Hayward.* A shiver went up her back and she looked over her shoulder at his empty seat again. She turned back around and started to draw another horse. She had to get her mind off this.

Beth started to relax—until her thoughts turned to her mother. Why was she acting so strangely? Where was she going dressed like that? Had she started smoking, or were they someone else's cigarettes? Was she going to come home drunk again tonight? Beth hoped not; she really didn't like seeing that side of her mother. But Beth was making dinner tonight, and that should make things a little better. She hoped her mother would appreciate that.

And her dad—how amazing was he to keep strong while her mother was going through this? *He's a good man*, she thought. She hoped she was lucky enough to be with someone like that someday. "A good man is hard to find," she had heard on TV. She knew if she had a husband like her father, she would never, in a million years, treat him the way her mother was treating him right now. She had a feeling her mother would come around soon, and realize how she was treating her family. She didn't know why, she just felt it. She tapped her pencil on her desk. She didn't feel like drawing a horse; she felt like drawing a house. She started drawing and the lunch bell rang. *Well, let's go solve the Daniel note mystery.* She packed up her books, grabbed her coat, and headed out to the ball field fence.

***

"So," he said, as he chewed his steak, "what's your deal?"

She giggled. "Deal? What do you mean?"

Holy fuck, bitch, I guess I have to make stupid conversation. "Are you travelling alone?"

"No," she answered.

"So, where's your guy?"

"Oh, no, I'm not travelling at all. I live here in town."

"And you just hang out at an airport hotel bar?"

"Well, I don't hang out. I just like to get out of the house, you know, and have a drink."

"I get it."

"You get what?" she asked.

I get that you're a bored housewife out looking for some action to break up the monotony of your life. "That you're just out having a drink."

"Yes, and I think I need another."

"Allow me." He raised his empty Jack glass and shook it. The waitress looked over and he pointed at the lady as well.

"So, are you travelling alone?" she asked.

"Me? Yes, I am."

"And where are you headed?"

Time to play. "Well, I'm kind of a bad boy," he said.

"Bad boy, really?" she said, smiling. "What's bad about you?"

Oh, you're gonna find out. "I'm headed back to New York. I just came here to take care of some business." He finished his food and put down his utensils.

"What type of business?"

The waitress placed their drinks in front of them. He thanked her and waited until she left. "I really can't talk about my business."

The lady's eyes got wide. "Really!" she said, excitedly. "Okay, of course, I understand. Are you from New York?"

"Yes, I live on the Upper East Side." He didn't know where or what the fuck that was, but he assumed she didn't, either. He slammed back his Jack Daniel's. "Have you ever been?" he asked.

"No," she said.

"Oh, you gotta go. It's like an adult playland."

"Wow, sounds fun," she giggled.

He moved his foot so it was touching hers. She didn't pull hers away.

"You lived here your whole life?"

"Yes, born and raised and still."

"I see. Well, you look like you're ready to fly now, and see what's out there—you're hanging out at an airport hotel, for God's sake. So, you know, you tell your husband and your kids that you need a break and just go somewhere. They'll be there when you get back. Just go experience things."

"Is it that obvious?" she said embarrassed.

"You'll love yourself for it."

"I should. I think I deserve it."

"Of course you do. Just remember one thing."

"What's that?" She looked at him intently.

"If you're ever in New York, you give me a call."

They both started laughing. He reached out, rubbed her hand, then picked up his glass and shook it at the waitress.

"I will, but I don't even know your name," she giggled.

"It's Clint, but if anyone is asking you, it's José."

She laughed and extended her hand. "I'm Sharon."

He shook it. "A pleasure," he said.

"Thank you." She was blushing

He got up. "If you'll excuse me, I have to go to the bad boy's room."

She laughed. When he was directly behind her, he placed his hand on her shoulder, leaned his head down, and spoke into her ear.

"I would like you to be here when I get back."

He stood back up and walked to the bathroom without looking at her. He pushed open the bathroom door and went to the urinal. *This is fuckin' fun. Out lookin' for some action, is she?* He started to laugh and shake his head. *Suburbia never seen anything like me, baby.* He finished up, washed his hands, and fixed his hair in the mirror. *You want some action? Showtime.* He pulled open the door and walked back to the table. She was still there. He sat down, picked up his glass, and slammed back another Jack.

"You good?" he asked her.

She looked at him and hesitated as if she was convincing herself. "Yeah," she said finally.

Good. Almost thought I was losing my touch. "Great," he said. He leaned over and gently touched her arm with one finger. "Listen, Sharon, I want you to go get us a room," he said to her.

She put her head down for a few seconds, then looked up and stared at him for another few. She looked in his eyes as if she was trying to look into his soul. *Don't go there, honey.*

"I'll be back," she said.

She may be a stupid bitch, but she's damn good for the ego. He looked at his two empty glasses, grabbed her drink, and threw it back.

***

Beth walked towards the ball field fence where Daniel stood waiting for her. She had butterflies in her stomach, and her legs felt weak. At that moment, she felt like just running away and avoiding the situation. The anticipation made her feel very uncomfortable. Daniel had his hands on his hips as if she were walking too slowly. *You're reading too much into it*, she told herself. *He's just standing there.*

"Hi," she said, barely squeezing the word out of her voice box.

"Hey," he said. "Gum?" He held a pack of gum toward her.

"No thanks." She was worried she would throw up all over him every time she opened her mouth.

Daniel coughed a bit then spoke. "Listen, I really think you're cool, and . . . and would you like to go to Kevin's party with me—I mean, as my date?"

And there it was. She was being asked on her first date. She had often wondered what it would be like. Where it would happen, who would ask her, what her answer would be. Those questions had just been answered, except for the last one. The wind blew the tuft of hair on the top of Daniel's head. She should say yes; he was not a bad-looking guy, and she surely didn't want to be dateless. She didn't know of any other prospects. Hayward wouldn't even be going to the party now, so there was no sense holding out on the chance that he might ask her. It was only one date for one date party, after all; it wasn't like she was marrying the guy. *Okay, here goes.*

Daniel looked away from her. She paused. When he looked back, his expression had changed from anticipation to agitation. It wasn't very appealing. *Well, what do you expect? The guy is probably nervous as hell, standing here with his ego in his hand waiting for you to say something.*

"Yes," she blurted out.

Daniel's smile was huge. "Great!" he said. "Gum?" He held the gum pack up again.

"No thanks, again."

"Oh, yeah, sorry. I'm kind of nervous."

Kind of! She was so nervous she was worried that her nerves had suffered some sort of irreparable damage.

"Me too . . . kind of."

They both laughed. *Maybe the nerves will be okay*, she thought. Laughing always made her feel better.

"They are still having the party, right? Even with this whole Davey Arcal accident?" Beth asked.

"Most of the people going to the party didn't even know the guy. It's still Kevin's birthday; he didn't die," Daniel replied.

Beth was surprised. Daniel's answer was really insensitive.

"I'll see ya later," Daniel said flatly. He turned and ran off, leaving her standing there.

A piece of paper blew by. She watched it as it kept blowing past the ball field fence until it was out of sight. She suddenly felt she had made a mistake; Daniel had never spoken like that before in all the time they had spent playing together. Maybe he wasn't himself; after all, it was his first time asking a girl out on a date. He had been, more than likely, under a lot of stress the past twenty-four hours. *Anyway, it's over*, she thought. *You have your first date. Now you have to pick out your first date outfit.* The wind blew her hair across her face as she walked away from the fence and back towards the school.

***

Hayward stood in the front window of his house, staring at the short path by the church. The path led through a couple of trees and joined his street to the schoolyard. He saw something move, and waited to see if anyone was coming down the path. A piece of paper came blowing out of the trees and disappeared behind the church. He stepped back from the window. He had a bad feeling, but what else was new?

***

He whistled the song "Afternoon Delight" as the elevator door opened and he walked out onto the eighth floor. She'd said room 814. He continued to whistle as he walked down the long corridor, looking at each number as he passed. People always checked each number just in case room 814 came after 802. He laughed to himself as he arrived at the door. He knocked and Sharon opened the door.

"Come in, I'm just going to finish freshening up."

"Yeah, yeah, you do what you gotta do."

Sharon went into the bathroom and started running the water. He made sure the door was closed, put the deadbolt on, and then pulled the chain over. He then walked over to the window and pulled the drapes closed. Sharon came out of the bathroom.

"Would you like me to order us some wine?" she asked.

He met her and put his hands on top of her hips.

"We don't need that right now." He leaned his head in and kissed her, then turned her around, pressed himself against her backside, and kissed her on the neck. She moved her head back and moaned with pleasure. He gently guided her over to the mirror where she could see them both. He stopped kissing her and rested his chin on her shoulder. They were looking at their reflection and both smiling. He took his hand off her hip and brought it up to the back of her neck, ran it under her hair, and caressed her there. He watched in the mirror as she closed her eyes and moaned again. He lifted his chin off her shoulder, grabbed a handful of hair on the back of her head, and drove her face into the mirror. She screamed as he pulled her head back. The top half of the mirror crashed to the floor. Most of the bottom portion remained in the frame, cracked and smeared with blood. He pulled her by the hair over to the bed and, pushing her head sideways on the mattress, leaned his head down and stuck his face in hers.

"You scream and I'll have to fucking kill you."

She whimpered as blood poured from various places on her face. He brought her head up and pushed it into the bed again.

"You fucking got that?" he asked, spittle flying into the side of her hair.

"Yes, yes," she cried.

He pulled her head up to what was left of the mirror, and her reflection showed the blood streaming down and flying off her lip as she sobbed.

"Now look. You see what happens when you leave your nice comfy house and try to be a fucking whore?" He held her there for a few more seconds then yanked her by the hair over to the desk. He bent her over the desk, smashing her head on the phone. She screamed. He brought his left hand up, made a fist, and punched her in the side of the face.

"Shut the fuck up, bitch. This is what you wanted." He pulled her dress up over her ass. She was still sobbing as he grabbed her panties by the side and pulled them. They made a ripping sound but didn't come right off. *Losing my touch.* He yanked again and this time the torn panties came right off in his hand. *Not a bad ass for a fucking soccer mom.* He reached over and picked up the phone receiver and cracked it over her head. She moaned loudly and continued to sob.

"Now don't you fucking move. This is what you wanted." He took his hands off her, undid his belt, and pulled down his khakis. *Fucking khakis.* He grabbed his dick in his hand and admired it.

"You lucky bitch." He put his dick in her and started to pump. She continued to sob, her head now in a dark pool of her own blood on the desk.

"This is what you wanted, wasn't it?"

She sobbed. He pulled back his arm and cranked her in the right side of her face.

"Say yes."

"Yes," she cried.

"This is what you fucking wanted." He started to pump her harder and could feel the train leaving the station. He pulled his dick out and pushed her onto the floor. He stood over her and jerked his cock.

"Oh yeah! Oh yeah! Oh yeah!" he said as cum flew out and fell on her as she lay there sobbing.

"This is what you wanted," he said again, as he squeezed the last bit out. He pulled his pants back up.

"I'm actually going to let you live. But if you go to the cops, I'll find you, torture you, kill you, and do what I just did to you to every living female in your family. Got it?"

"Yes," she sobbed.

He grabbed her purse and rifled through it. He took out her wallet, grabbed the cash, and tossed it aside. He pulled some makeup out of the purse, threw it at her, and laughed.

"You're probably gonna need some of this." He threw down the purse, walked over to the door, and undid the locks. "Well, now you know what a whore feels like."

He started to whistle "Afternoon Delight" as he opened the door to leave.

Chapter 11

Outside Looking In

"Is this the first visitation you've been to?" Hayward asked Joe.

"First and last," Joe replied.

"Last?"

"Yeah, these things creep me out."

"It's about respect, though," Hayward said.

"Yeah, and everyone should respect the fact that I'm creeped out. I mean, look at him up there, just lying there dead. It's hard for me to deal with. I just keep expecting him to open his eyes and sit up."

"I know what you mean."

Hayward plucked some white lint off the arm of his new black suit. He had tried on his old suit yesterday, but he had grown quite a bit since the last time he'd worn it, so his parents took him out to get a new one. It fit perfectly. He felt sophisticated in it.

Davey's family had asked Pete, Joe, and him to be pallbearers, along with three of Davey's cousins.

"Did they tell you about the casket, how we don't actually carry it?" Hayward asked Joe.

"Yeah, my mother explained it to me when I started to panic, thinking I would drop it or something."

"You thought you were gonna drop it? That's crazy," Hayward said.

"I did!" Joe said emphatically.

"So did I," Hayward admitted.

Hayward looked over at Pete. He was sitting beside them, but had been quiet all night. Up by the casket, a couple of old people stood over Davey. The man was rubbing the lady's shoulders and she was dabbing her eyes with a tissue. Hayward imagined Davey saying, "Take a picture, it will last longer." He smiled.

Hayward looked at the seats along the wall beside the casket, where Davey's family sat. His older sister, who Hayward had started to notice lately, looked pretty hot. "Sorry, buddy," he said to himself as he thought of Davey. Davey's mom hadn't stopped crying since he'd arrived. Davey's dad wore the same expression he always wore, whether he was yelling at Davey for something or talking to his wife about supper. Uncles, aunts, and cousins filled up the rest of the chairs along the wall. Hayward recognized a few, but not many. He saw Davey's Uncle John, who had come to his house and asked, on behalf of Davey's family, if he would be a pallbearer for the services.

Hayward looked at his watch. It was 8:00, halfway through his 7:00 to 9:00 shift. Davey's uncle had explained that the pallbearers should stay for the duration of the visitation to take people's coats, run errands, and be available in case the family needed help with anything.

Kevin's party was in full swing right about now. Hayward wondered what had happened at school—if people had made dates, who asked who, and who was dancing with whom. Did the class actually go along with his date party idea? Or did they scrap the whole thing . . . *You wouldn't be that lucky*, he thought.

He felt so far away from school and his school friends. It was like they were in a different world, a world he hoped to get back to soon. Hayward was going back to school on Monday, and he couldn't remember a time when he had wanted to go to school so badly. He needed to get back to normal in some parts of his life; that's what people meant when they talked about "moving on" or "moving past this." He was ready. He wondered what song was playing at the party right now, and if Beth was dancing or just standing, talking or looking around. *You're going to drive yourself nuts.*

"You back to school Monday?" Hayward asked Joe.

"Yeah, can't wait. You?"

"Yeah, me too," Hayward replied.

"I'm tired of crying," Joe said.

"I hear ya."

Hayward looked over at Pete. It was odd that he had said so little all night. Maybe he was really having a hard time.

"Hey, Pete," Hayward called.

Pete looked over and nodded his head in acknowledgment.

"You okay?"

Pete sighed. "As good as I can be."

Well, there you go, Hayward. Good work. You solved that case in record time, and we still have forty-seven minutes to fill on tonight's episode. He looked back at Davey's family. A lady was hugging Davey's sister, her arms on Davey's sister's hips. He thought of his arms on Beth's hips. He pictured himself and Beth slow dancing to Air Supply, looking into each other's eyes as the room spun around them. He then saw himself outside looking in a window, seeing Beth slow dancing with someone else that looked like Daniel Greensnot.

***

Pete watched as each person viewed Davey and then passed the family. People extended condolences to Davey's dad, mom, and sister. Davey's sister was wearing a short, tight black dress that looked really sexy. *Nice to look at, but not really appropriate for a visitation,* Pete thought. *Every guy coming through here was probably thinking the same thing.* Pete didn't understand why Davey's parents hadn't said something. *Their son is up there dead in a casket. I'm sure they aren't too worried about their daughter's clothes right now.* Pete had hugged

Davey's sister earlier, and she had squeezed him tight. The feel of her dress and her perfume had given him a semi-boner. *That's why it's not an appropriate dress. You're giving young men hard-ons at a visitation!*

He looked over at Hayward. He and Joe were yapping again. Normally, Pete would have leaned over and blasted them, saying that they shouldn't be chatting so much in here. It was disrespectful. If they wanted to yap, they should go outside. They'd been asked by the family to fill an important position, and they were making all three of them look bad. But that was before. Now, he would say nothing. He wasn't going to be hard on them because he thought he should. He was not going to try to control things. He would let others— especially those two—make their own decisions, and if they looked stupid or messed up, they'd learn from it. It had nothing to do with him. *Stay calm, and have confidence in yourself and what you're doing,* he told himself. He was in a good place, on his new path. *I'm going to make a difference.* He looked up at Davey. *I owe it to ya.*

***

Beth stood listening to the music. A small coloured light system made Kevin's basement look like a real dance hall. She stared at the wall, watching the different coloured lights swirl around. Daniel was standing beside her, but he wasn't saying much. *You're not sparking up any conversations either, there, honey,* she told herself.

Her thoughts were on her mother, who was still in rough shape. Her mom had come home yesterday evening with her face bandaged up and having trouble walking. She said she had been downtown and was shoved into an alley by a couple of homeless men who wanted some money to buy food. She had told them off and they had beaten her up. Her father had wanted to go find them but her mother had calmed him down. He insisted she go to the police, but she had talked him out of that, too. She said that they were just hungry and she shouldn't have told them off; she had made the situation worse.

Beth had noticed something very different about her mother. She had told her story with such passion, like she cared. Beth hadn't seen her care about anything in a long time. And she was talking to them differently—the way she used to, when things were good. Beth figured that was why her father didn't press the issue. He was happy that his wife was speaking to him normally. Beth had even heard them watching TV together and laughing. She wondered if her mother's story was entirely true. If it wasn't, did she really want to know the truth? Her mother, the good one, seemed to be coming back to them. She did not want to do anything to change or agitate her. Last night they had felt like a family.

Daniel leaned over and spoke in her ear. "Can I hold your hand?"

She felt a gush of warmth run through her body. Asking to hold her hand was so cute. "Sure," she said.

Daniel took her hand in his.

A boy is holding my hand! She hoped Daniel was a good guy, like her father. He was a good man. Her father had told her that they would be there for her mother as she went through her tough time, no matter what, because that's what families do. She was so proud of her father and happy for him. He loved her mother so much and it looked like she was coming around. Hopefully she would treat him like the great husband he was—like any good man should be treated.

She wondered how Hayward was holding up. She had heard that the visitation was tonight. She had tried to imagine what it would be like if one of her friends had died, trying to get a glimpse of what he was going through. She couldn't; the thought was too painful. Hayward would probably be back to school on Monday. She was looking forward to seeing him.

What are you doing, Beth? You are on your first date, and you're thinking about another guy. The lights, the music, and holding hands with a boy who likes you—it's about time you started enjoying the things right in front of you.

She'd had enough drama in her life lately. She looked at Daniel and smiled. He smiled back.

"Let's dance," she said, and without waiting for a response, led him to where the others were dancing.

***

The man was watching a cop show on TV, and the cops were friggin' geniuses. He laughed. In all these shows, the cops were so smart and the clues just popped up everywhere. He knew from being in his line of work that most cops weren't very smart. They were just on a power trip. If they were as smart as the cops on TV, they wouldn't be cops; they'd be the Fuckin' Dean of Admissions at Nosy Fucker University. He laughed. Maybe he should write a book. He seemed to come up with many good lines and little anecdotes about life. The story part would be a problem, because he couldn't write about his own life—no one would ever believe it. Case in point, here he was, sitting on the couch in a small, relatively clean apartment, drinkin' beer and watchin' TV all day. How did a man on the run find such accommodating accommodations? Charm. He laughed.

God must have fucked up with him. Really fucked up. Or he was a walking argument that there was no God, because he was someone who didn't give a fuck about anybody but himself, but he had charm enough to get what he wanted. And as a bonus, he had to live with the Push. He had kept the Push in check for a while now and was getting used to being in control. He liked being in control—a lot. *Pretty good at pattin' yourself on the back tonight, aren't ya?* He laughed. The door unlocked and Rita came into the apartment with some bags.

He had been out the night before at a local bar, just sittin' there having a few beers, keepin' a low profile, when Rita started up a conversation with him. He gave her some bullshit story about how he was in the army, but was discharged because he had punched his sergeant in the face when he saw him giving one of the female privates a hard time. Big fuckin' hero. Rita ate it right up, like everything else. She was overweight, single, and living alone. When he mentioned that he was just passin' through and didn't have a place to stay yet, she had practically dragged him to her place. She cooked for him and bought him beer and all he had to do was keep entertaining her with tall tales. He knew how to turn that bullshit tap on and let it flow. And he had to keep fucking her fat ass. *A man's got to do what a man's got to do.*

Rita had a fulltime job as a dispatcher with the transit buses, so fuck, he'd just hang here for a while. As long as she didn't see his face on the news, he could weasel his way into staying here till things cooled down. He knew it would eventually, because clues didn't just pop up for the real cops.

"Hey, how ya doin?" Rita asked.

"Great! Now that you're here."

Rita began opening the bags. "I got you some Budweiser, some Cheetos, and some beef jerky."

"Thanks."

"And I got us some ice cream for dessert. I'm gonna cook us up some pork chops, onions, and potatoes."

"You're too good to me."

"Oh stop," she said.

She must have been alone for a long time, 'cause she's just lovin' this company. Better keep it fresh, he reasoned, then reached over and smacked her big ass.

"Big Daddy wants some of that later tonight, too."

She turned around, bent down to his face, her fat cleavage hanging.

"Whatever Big Daddy wants," she kissed him and pulled back, "after dinner." She whipped around and headed for the kitchen.

No matter how much charm I got, I could never be this bitch's true love; it will always be food, he thought as she put the pans out on the stove. He turned back toward the TV. *Oh look, they found another clue, the fuckin' geniuses.*

***

Hayward turned around in his seat. He could not believe how many people were in the church. He thought it was full, but he was so close to the front that he couldn't see all the way to the back. He wondered if Beth had come. Maybe her family had some connection to Davey's family that he didn't know about.

Davey's casket was sitting at the front of the church. *Holy, all these people are here for you, buddy, and you're up there in that thing and can't see any of them. Well, maybe your soul is watching from up above.* He wondered if people could watch their own funerals, or if they were too busy having fun in heaven. You would have to be incredibly curious. *I know I would want to see mine, not that I want to die any time soon.* Was Davey up there watching people come into the church? If he saw people he didn't like, would he get mad? Do angels get angry? Hayward pictured Davey as an angry angel saying, "Oh man, what's he doing here?" and "How come so-and-so isn't here?" If he didn't like certain people coming up the church steps, could he make the wind blow and mess up their hair?

There was no flag draped over the coffin as Hayward had pictured a few days ago. Davey's school picture, blown up and in a frame, sat on an easel beside the casket. He thought of the many times he and Davey had sleepovers, and Davey had slept right beside him, and those cool nights they had slept in tents, sleeping close for warmth. Davey's casket was really fancy. He hadn't seen a real casket before yesterday and was surprised at how nice they were, considering they were just going to bury them in the ground.

Davey's uncle, the one who had asked him to be a pallbearer, was at the podium doing the eulogy. Hayward had only learned what a "eulogy" was yesterday. Davey's uncle talked about the clubs and things that Davey enjoyed, but he seemed to leave out a lot of things like chopping down trees, shooting birds with his air rifle, and burning things; the stuff his uncle was talking about made Davey sound like someone else. Hayward was old enough and observant enough to know that parents saw their kids the way they wanted to see them, not the way they really were. Or maybe they saw their kids as they really were, but would only talk about what they wanted to see in them. Davey was a good guy, so finding good things to say about him at his funeral shouldn't have been too hard. What about those miserable, old, cranky people who hadn't said or done a good thing in about thirty years? What do people say about them? They probably talk about their younger years, when they were cooks in the world wars and had lots of war buddies. There would be quite a few of those situations in this town.

He looked over at Davey's mother, who was still sobbing but had a smile on her face as she listened to Davey's uncle sum up her son's short life. Beside him, Joe was crying again. Hayward didn't think it was humanly possible for someone to cry so much. Pete was sitting next to Joe, his face expressionless, still not interested in conversation. Hayward understood. Davey had been Pete's best friend; but on the other hand, they were all close, and he and Joe were still alive and they should be there for each other. Pete just seemed to bottle it all up. Usually Pete was controlling the situation and giving Joe and himself advice. *I guess everybody deals with grief in their own way,* Hayward figured. *Joe cries it out, I wonder it out, and Pete buries it.*

The choir began to sing. It sounded good, but was a bit loud. Did Davey's parents select the songs? Or was it the priest? Or was it his uncle? Davey's uncle had a lot of jobs; did they give him that one, too? Hayward's parents hadn't taken him to church very much. He knew he was of the United faith, but could count on his hand how many times he had been to the United Church. Davey's funeral was being held in the Catholic Church. It was a lot bigger and fancier than the United Church. Hayward figured that was because a lot more people in town were Catholic, so when they passed around the collection plate, the Catholic Church got a lot more money. He looked up at the ceiling. It was made of wood that looked like bamboo, and it curved down to join the massive columns that came all the way down to the floor of the church. There were huge carved statues of Jesus and Mary, and every window was coloured glass that had pictures of crosses and shepherds. He had thought that the funeral would be horrible, having never experienced one before, but he found himself fascinated. This was a really beautiful place—a perfect place—to celebrate Davey's life.

***

Beth woke up and looked at the clock: 9:08 a.m. *Saturday morning. My favourite.* She took a deep breath and smelled something good coming from the kitchen. She smiled and slapped her hand on the bed. Her mother was cooking again.

"Awesome! Awesome! Awesome!" she cried out.

Beth sat up in bed and thought about the night before. When she finally decided to try and enjoy the evening, she had a great time. She and Daniel had literally danced all night. The shifting lights with the music were just fantastic; they had really made her want to move. A number of times Beth had to ask Daniel if he was okay because she could see the sides of his head were soaked with sweat. She had slow danced with Daniel, and it had felt good to be close to him; his hands on her hips made her head swoon. Daniel had gotten her a juice and a hot dog and been a perfect gentleman. He had thanked her for being his date. He told her she was pretty and how nice her outfit was. At the end of the night, he asked if he could kiss her on the cheek. She had shyly said "Okay" and had felt the warmth of his lips. She had to fight the urge to scream out with excitement. Beth hadn't felt it before, but now she was starting to get a crush on Daniel. She was already wondering when date number two would be. Her mind was racing. *I'm going to have to read a book today to keep myself from going insane thinking about last night*, she thought.

"Awesome!" she said, as she slapped her hand down on the bed again. She jumped up, put on her robe, and headed downstairs. Her father was seated at the kitchen table, eating pancakes. Her mother was at the stove. She had some more of the bandages off of her face now, and the scrapes looked like they were starting to heal.

"Would you like some pancakes, sweetheart?" her mother asked.

"I would love some pancakes."

Beth sat down and looked at her father. He gave her a big smile, and she smiled back at him with her eyes wide, showing him her excitement without exclaiming it.

"Good morning, Bunny."

"Good morning, Dad."

Her father went back to reading the paper. Beth looked toward her mother. She was a good-looking woman. She couldn't believe those men had cut up her beautiful face. How had it affected her? Was this the reason for the change of attitude toward her and her father? Had she thought she might not see her family again? Did she think she would die? Did she realize that their last memories of her would be the way she had treated them the last six months? Did she pledge to herself that, if she lived, she would appreciate what she had? Beth felt a horrible knot in her stomach at the thought of the men beating up her mother. Was that what it took? If that is what had to happen to get her mother back to acting like herself and back to her family, Beth was definitely sorry, but glad it happened. *Glad? How can you be glad? Look at her. Look at her bandages.* Beth was mad at herself for even thinking that. She looked away and decided she would never think about that again. Her mother placed the pancakes in front of her. Beth thanked her and reached for the syrup.

"How was your birthday party last night?" her mother asked.

Birthday party. That sounded so funny. With everything that happened leading up to the party, it kind of fell by the wayside—that "the party" was actually Kevin's birthday party.

"Great. It was . . . fun." Beth wished she could tell her mother that she'd had her first date—that she had been kissed by a boy. That it had been one of the greatest nights of her life. She knew she was too young to tell her mother any of these things. Besides, the last thing Beth wanted to do was make her mother unhappy. She had just gotten back.

"Whose party was it? Little Kevin McLeod?"

"Yes, but he's not that little anymore."

"No, I guess not. You're all growing up so fast."

You don't know the half of it.

"What did he get for his birthday? Anything good?" her mother asked.

Well, knowing Kevin's date, Jane Saunders, he probably got a bunch of kisses. She was an affectionate girl.

"Oh, you know, he got some cassette tapes, some clothes, a pocket knife," Beth replied. By the way Jane Saunders acted and talked about boys, Beth had a feeling she would be quite popular with them as they all got older.

"Do you have enough pancakes, Beth? Do you want some more?"

"No thanks, Mom. This is perfect."

"Do you have any plans for today?" Beth's father asked her.

"Well, I was planning on hanging around here, maybe start reading a book or just watch some TV."

"Big morning then," her father said, laughing.

I've had enough "big" for one week.

"I'm going to make some muffins this afternoon if you want to help me," her mother said.

Making muffins. Asking me to help. Her mother was back, and better than ever. Her mom walked over and stood behind her father and put her arm around him. It was a sight that made Beth want to cry. She was so happy for her family. She thought of Daniel with his arms around her last night and felt very lucky.

"Sure, Mom, I'd like that." A family filled with love, and a kind-of boyfriend who was a great guy: Beth was growing up, and she couldn't be more excited.

***

The wind was very cold and blowing hard. Hayward looked at the hole in the ground. *This is unbelievable,* he thought, *they're going to put Davey in there.* He knew funerals happened every day, all over the world, and figured everyone always remembered their first—the first time they realize that someone they know is dead in that casket and about to be put into the ground. The priest was giving the last rites. Hayward had seen it done on TV a lot, but on TV there was always some other drama going on with the people who were standing around at the burial. He didn't know of any drama that was going on with these people, and would bet any money that there wasn't. This was real life. It was emotional enough dealing with the guy in the casket, the fact that they were never going to see him again, and the way he had been ripped from their lives. There was only one star of this show.

Hayward looked around. Davey's mother was crying and his dad was hugging her. Davey's sister stood really close to them, and she too was crying. On his left, Joe was crying. He looked past Joe and saw a tear roll down Pete's cheek. Hayward looked at the casket. *How come I'm not crying?* he wondered. *It probably looks bad. Maybe I should try. I feel like crying, but don't know if I can.* He had cried a lot over the last four days. He listened as the priest talked about the Kingdom of Heaven. He closed his eyes really tight. He thought of Davey pillow fighting with him, how they would play the song Queen of Hearts by Juice Newton on the stereo and pass each other over and over like jousters, each time smacking each other with the pillows as they passed. Hayward's mouth started to tremble. He thought about he and Davey sitting on the woodpile in his backyard, using their air rifles to shoot cans they had placed up in the trees. The tears started to come. He thought about Davey trying different ways to shoot the cans, putting the gun in all kinds of crazy positions, making Hayward laugh so hard he almost lost his balance and fell off the woodpile. He felt a tear roll down his face but kept his eyes shut. *Oh God, I'm going to miss him.* The tears started to stream from both eyes. Hayward felt some movement beside him and opened his eyes. People were walking past him. He stood and watched as Joe and Pete turned and walked away with the others. He wanted to turn and walk too, but couldn't. He looked at the casket. *It's over? That's it?* He was confused. The cold wind sent a chill up his spine. He was the only one standing there. Even Davey's family was walking back to their cars. He forced his feet to move. He turned and started to walk away.

It's so cold out, he thought. He looked back at the casket. *We can't just leave him here. It's so cold.* The crowd had reached their cars and were getting in and starting them. He looked at the casket. *We have to leave him here. He's gone.*

Hayward put his head down and started to walk toward the cars. He looked over his shoulder at his childhood one last time while he continued to walk into the life of a young man.

Seventeen Years Later

Chapter 12

Maximum Amount of Pain

"Congratulations, Pete."

The training detective handed Pete a new badge that had his name and detective number on it. It gleamed in the light of the detective common area.

"Thank you," Pete replied.

The other detectives gave Pete a round of applause. It was a day he had worked toward for a long time. He had finally made detective, after working as a beat cop for six years and putting in half a year of detective training. Pete addressed the others.

"Well, I have dreamed of this day for a while now. Thank you all for your patience and your advice over the last six months. I am very lucky to work on such a great team. So thanks again, and well . . . let's put away some more bad guys!"

The other detectives began to hoot, holler, and clap wildly. The Chief motioned him into his office.

"Take a seat, Pete."

Pete sat down.

"I would like to personally express my congratulations, and from what I've seen during your training, having someone like yourself on board is very exciting."

"Thank you, Chief, I'm really glad to be here. Thank you for the opportunity."

"Okay, now we can be like Hollywood, pat each other on the back, and give out awards all day, or we can do some work."

Pete chuckled as the Chief continued, "Sometimes, as you know from being a beat cop, you have to go with your gut on things. I would like you to join the Max Killer Task Force."

Pete found it hard to believe what he was hearing. For the last seventeen years, the Max Killer was someone that the police believed was responsible for seven unsolved murders. He was called the Max Killer because psychologists believed that his victims had been killed in a specific way—the nerves relaying pain messages to the brain had been overloaded, and the victim subsequently went into shock. The killer had inflicted the maximum amount of pain a person could feel before they died.

"Already, sir?" Pete asked.

"Yes, the task force hasn't made enough progress towards catching this guy, so I'm making a change. I'm going to take Dubinsky off the case, and I'm putting you in. I think a fresh pair of eyes, and a new perspective on leads, will help this investigation."

"Well sir, I . . ." Pete stuttered, "I really don't know what to say."

The Chief stood up. "That is real easy," he replied. "You can tell me that you're gonna work your ass off and get that bastard off the street for good."

Pete stood up and extended his hand. "You can count on that, sir." The Chief shook Pete's hand.

"I know," said the Chief. Then he handed Pete a large file. "This is a synopsis of the investigation so far. Read this the rest of today and tonight, and then join up with the task force tomorrow."

"Okay," Pete said. He took the file and began walking towards the door. "Thank you again, Chief."

The Chief waved a dismissive hand. "You're welcome. Now get to work."

Pete walked into the main area where two detectives were talking. He recognized them as Dubinsky and Miller.

"Hey, Rook, what's your first case?" Detective Miller asked.

"Looks like I'm on the Max Killer Task Force."

"What!" Dubinsky exclaimed. "You've just finished your detective training and you're on my task force?"

Not yours for long, buddy. Pete pointed back at the office. "He's the boss."

The Chief's office door swung open.

"Dubinsky!" The Chief called out. Dubinsky gave Pete a quizzical look.

"Comin', Chief," Dubinsky said, still staring at Pete.

Pete didn't want to be around when Dubinsky found out. He left the station and walked across the parking lot to his car. He threw the Max Killer file onto the passenger seat, started the car and began the commute home. He was excited to tell his wife Alana that her husband was officially a detective now. He couldn't wait to tell his sons—Brett and Andrew—when they got home from school, either. Brett was in grade six and Andrew grade four.

"Detective," Pete said aloud as he rubbed his new badge. He was very proud of himself. He had wanted to be a cop since he was a kid. He had achieved that, and he had also taken hundreds of bad guys off the streets over the past six years. He thought of his childhood friend Davey, and the promise he had made. He was fulfilling it by making the world a better place.

Pete had an inner desire to succeed. He hadn't seen anyone in all of his years of policing, or in training at the Police Academy, who had his ambition and dedication. And now that he had made detective, he would use his brain and police skills to put away the baddest of the bad. And his first case would be the city's most notorious criminal for almost two decades. *This is heavy,* Pete thought.

It was believed that the Max Killer had started when Pete was only a boy. Pete thought about Davey, Hayward, and Joe and their childhood; it had truly had been a magical time up until Davey's death.

After Davey was gone, the boys had each followed their own paths, some of them not so good. Joe had become depressed in junior high and avoided any type of social, adolescent activity. He began to use drugs in high school, but still managed to graduate in five years. Joe's drug use became heavier after graduation. He began working as a shipper–receiver for the hardware store in town, but had lost his job because he couldn't stay clean. He eventually lost his apartment and lived with his parents for a while. He began stealing from them to support his habit. His parents had tried to help him until they could take no more. They threw him out and pretty much disowned him.

Pete had seen Joe on the streets while he was walking his beat. He tried to talk to him, get him some help. Joe said he didn't want any advice, or any programs—just money, so he could get his next fix. Pete never wanted to give him any money, but after exhausting all other options to get him help he would slip him some, trying to convince him to use it to buy food. Pete knew that Hayward sometimes brought Joe meals from home if he was heading downtown and could find him. Pete thought that was a great idea, because Joe couldn't buy drugs with the food; he also wanted to do it, but he never had. He also knew that Hayward had tried, many more times than he, to get Joe some help, but had gotten the same result. Hayward and Joe had been so close when they were kids, and Pete had hoped that Hayward, after moving back to town, would've been able to help Joe.

After high school, Hayward had moved to San Francisco to try to be an artist. Pete thought the real reason he moved out there was to get away from the pain. Ever since they were kids, Hayward had been in love with Beth Cooper. Throughout their school days, she had always had a boyfriend. Hayward never had (or had taken) the opportunity to tell her how he felt.

Hayward painted very well, but his work was dark and drab. He had tried to be part of the emerging artistic scene on the west coast, but had sold very little of his work. Hayward had worked as a waiter to make enough for food and clothes. He had either become tired of trying to make his art a career, or the scene had become tired of his art.

He'd moved back to Sifton and stayed with his parents, doing odd jobs such as painting houses. Pete ran into him at a bar. They'd shared a few drinks, talked about old times. Hayward had been impressed with how happy Pete was, and the great family life he had. Hayward had been at a point in his life where he wanted some stability. He wanted to start a career and a family. Pete had set Hayward up with an interview with the police force. He had been accepted, finished the Academy, and had been working as a beat cop for the past year. Pete and Hayward, working on the same force, had again become close. Once or twice a month they would go out for beers and talk shop.

Pete looked over in the passenger seat at the Max Killer file. Wow! *Gotta get up to speed on this tonight*, he figured. *Will have to cut the celebration with the family short.* He had work to do. Important work.

***

Hayward looked over at Jeff, who was driving their squad car. He had been partnered with Jeff for the better part of a year. Why did the police keep officers with the same partner for so long? He believed it must be some sort of mental test; if you can put up with being in the same car with a person for that many hours a day, that many days a year, and not go completely insane, then you could surely accomplish anything. Jeff wasn't a nice guy, and they really didn't have anything in common. Jeff was into heavy metal, NASCAR, and restoring an old pickup truck. They didn't have much to talk about, and they rode around in silence for much of the day.

Pete was training to be a detective, and Hayward had already decided that he wanted to follow that path. Hayward had worked the beat for almost a year, and he was fairly sick of it after three months. He liked being a cop—didn't *love* it, but if he wanted to become a detective he would have to work hard. He wasn't sure if he had the determination Pete had, and that's what they looked for.

The radio dispatcher broke the silence. "We have a shoplifter at Sunnyside Mall in custody, requiring presence."

Hayward picked up the radio mic. "Unit Twelve responding Sunnyside Mall."

"Ten-four," the radio blared back.

"Great," Jeff said, "a shoplifter. Booooooorrrriiinnnnggggg."

Boring yes, but these criminals usually weren't carrying any weapons. Hayward liked routine events. He wanted every shift to be a series of routine events so he could go home alive. He wasn't one of these cops on a power trip who ran around with a boner looking for trouble.

"Should've not even responded," Jeff muttered.

Hayward wanted to say something, but he knew better. Jeff loved to argue, and they had already gone through that stage a couple of months ago. They had argued about everything every hour of the day. Hayward had learned to say nothing so that he didn't give him ammunition. Often, Jeff would mutter things to try and goad Hayward into an argument. In the past, Jeff had argued with him so much and made such little sense that Hayward wanted to pack his bags and head back to San Francisco to paint and eat Kraft Dinner. *Muttering Jeff*, he said to himself.

They rolled into the parking lot of Sunnyside Mall and drove up to a door marked "Security." Hayward picked up the mic and told the dispatcher they were at the mall and responding. The officers got out of the car, opened the mall door, and walked in. Two mall security guards sat at a desk while a plainclothes floorwalker stood doing paperwork. In the corner of the room sat a young white boy, about twelve years old, wearing jeans, a red T-shirt with "Wicked" written on the front, and a ball cap twisted sideways. The security guards nodded their heads as a greeting. *A little overkill, eh boys?* Hayward grumbled internally. *Two guards, a floorwalker, and now two police officers for this twelve-year-old boy who stole what? A candy bar?*

"Hello, officers," the plainclothes floorwalker said.

"Hey," Hayward responded.

Jeff said nothing. Hayward was always fascinated by the respect that the police got from floorwalkers and security guards, because most of them wanted to be cops one day. They acted like they believed that if they kissed their asses enough times, the officers would just give them badges.

"This is Justin," the floorwalker said, pointing at the boy. Jeff walked over and bent down so his face was in front of Justin's. The floorwalker continued, "He stole an electric drill from the department store." Jeff grabbed Justin's hat off his head and threw it in his lap.

"Have some respect," Jeff snarled. "What did you need the drill for, son?" He continued before the boy could answer, "Gonna use it to break into houses? That it, boy?"

"No, it was a birthday gift for my father."

"Oh!" Jeff exclaimed as he stood up and threw his arms up in the air. "A birthday gift for your father."

Hayward hated how theatrical Jeff was. It was embarrassing.

"Well, you stole it, so you must have thought, 'Well, what If I get caught?'"

"No," Justin answered.

"So you just walked out with the drill in your hand?"

"He took it from the box and put it in the front of his pants," the floorwalker stated. Jeff held his hand up as if to say, *Quiet, I'm working here.*

"So, where was the drill when you walked out of the store?" Jeff asked.

"He told you," the boy answered.

"I asked you the question," Jeff pointed at Justin.

Hayward could see from the boy's face that he was scared. The security guards stared intently, studying Jeff's tactics so they could use them someday.

"In my pants," the boy answered, his voice cracking.

"So, why you would do that? Put it in your pants?" Jeff continued. "You were trying to not get caught, but you did, and now, let me guess, you didn't have enough money to buy him a gift?"

"That's why I took it," Justin said defensively.

Jeff raised his finger in the air. "But don't you see that you got caught? The risk you took has resulted in this." He then touched a different finger on his hand as he made each point. "You have no money, you have no gift, and we have to call your father, on his birthday, and tell him that his son is a thief."

The boy began to cry. Hayward felt empathy for Justin; his father would be devastated. Justin, crying, made him think of Joe crying when Davey died.

"Let's wrap this up," Hayward said to Jeff.

Jeff turned to the floorwalker. "Do you have his information?"

"Yes," the floorwalker responded.

"I want you call his parents, then. They can pick him up here. We are not going to charge him. I think Justin is going to think about things more carefully from now on."

Both officers' carry-on radios began to blare in unison. "We have a domestic dispute in progress at 15 Robin Lane. All available units in the fourth district requested to respond."

Hayward grabbed the mic on his shoulder and said, "Unit Twelve on its way to respond." He then uncued the mic. "Let's go, Jeff."

Jeff looked at the floorwalker. "You got this from here?"

"Sure, no problem," the floorwalker said.

Jeff turned back to Justin and pointed at his face. "I never want to have to deal with you again. You got that?"

The boy was still sobbing. "Yes," he replied. Jeff turned and walked out the door without saying a word.

"Goodbye, everyone," Hayward said and followed Jeff.

***

Beth grabbed her son by the arm and pulled him along.

"Mom!" the boy yelled.

She had pulled him a little harder than she had wanted to, but he would be fine. It sent a message to him, anyway. When Mommy says it's time to go, it's time to go. She walked out of the women's clothing store and started down the street. She hated taking Phillip with her when she was shopping for herself. It was almost impossible to entertain a six-year-old boy in women's clothing stores. Beth wished Daniel would spend more time with him and give her some "me time." She wanted to ask him again, but she already knew the answer. He was too busy, he was under a lot of stress with the company, and he had to keep an eye on his brother.

Daniel and his brother Rich had inherited a construction company from their father. For many years, the company had done well and kept the family somewhat wealthy. Lately it wasn't doing so well, and Daniel thought that Rich had made some bad business decisions. Daniel had worked hard and taken a lot of pride in the business that his father had built. Rich, on the other hand, had continued to use the company for his own personal expenses and to enhance his lifestyle. Rich had not put in the work that Daniel had and insisted that the company would remain small-time if he wasn't out there making connections. Rich planned to get the business big contracts through his connections to help the company expand to heights that their father had never dreamed of. Daniel thought his brother would run the company into the ground if he didn't work extra to keep the clients and staff happy. That came at a price, and Daniel was paying it with his family.

Beth sometimes believed that he loved the company more than Phillip and her. She had worked as a teacher until Phillip was born, and then, with Daniel's persistence, had decided to be a stay-at-home mom. They lived in a big house, had a summer cottage and a boat, and enjoyed an extravagant lifestyle, and none of it was necessary; she would rather have her husband. But anytime she brought up the business and its effect on their relationship, Daniel became aggressive and asked her if she wanted to move into a tiny house and live without the perks or let him do his job. When she protested that she didn't need the material things, Daniel said he'd worked too hard to get those things for his family, and that she should appreciate them and him. He argued that if he took his foot off the gas, or the reins off his brother, they would lose everything. Beth had suggested getting a nanny for Phillip so she could get things done on the weekends a little more easily, but Daniel said that would be an extra expense that they didn't need right now—although it could be an option when the company started doing better. Beth knew that Rich had a nanny for his two boys and was sure that he was paying her through the company. She wondered if the company going under would be such a bad thing. It would give Daniel more time to spend with his family.

She and Daniel had grown apart the last few years, and their marriage lacked the passion that it once had. Daniel used to treat her like she was the most important thing in his life; now she didn't think she was even in the top five. Over the past six months she had considered leaving him, but remembered her father and what he had told her: "Families stick together." Her father had stood by her mother during her rough patch, and her family had been great after that. Beth and her mother had become very close. What would her life have been like if her parents had gotten divorced? It would have been devastating. She did not want to do that to Phillip. She would stand by Daniel because this was her family, and families stick together.

Beth hurried along the sidewalk, glancing in a couple of store windows. She would have loved to have gone in and looked around, but Phillip was tired and wanted to go home. As she walked on, she saw two men standing outside a coffee shop. They looked homeless with their dirty clothes and dirty, unkempt beards. She shifted Phillip by the hand to the opposite side of her body that the men were on.

"Do you think you could spare some change, lady, for a guy who's down on his luck?"

She looked at the homeless man. "No, I'm sorry, I don't have anything right now." She glanced at the other man as she passed. He looked familiar. She took a mental picture and continued on. She tried to envision him without the beard, but found she couldn't. She knew she had seen the man before. Had it been lately? Or had it been long ago, when she was younger? That was it: it was Joe. She had gone to school with him. He was such a nice kid, but she remembered that as they got older, he had gotten into drugs. And now he was homeless. She wondered how someone from a good home and a good school—who had grown up in a middle-class neighbourhood—could become a homeless adult. She had heard that he had started doing a lot drugs in high school, and by the looks of it, he'd never stopped.

Joe had grown up on Campbell Street, the same street as Hayward, and they were once close friends. Hayward: what was he doing now? She had heard that he had moved out to San Francisco, but nothing after that. How was he doing? She thought about the crush she used to have on him in elementary school. As the years went on, they had hung out with very different crowds at school. Daniel had played hockey, so she had made friends with his teammates' girlfriends. Hayward's group of friends were more on the artistic side. Beth remembered that Hayward had won a contest for one of his paintings in high school. The school displayed the painting in the lobby for a week, although she couldn't imagine Hayward agreeing to that. The painting was of a lady wearing a crown sitting on a throne. In front of her sat a semicircle of shadowy figures with their hands on the sides of their heads and their mouths wide open as if they were screaming. The title of the painting was "The Tyranny of Democracy." Daniel had made fun of it, calling it the stupidest thing he'd ever seen. She'd thought the painting was dark, but appreciated his talent.

Hayward had a few girlfriends over the years, and Beth had found herself extremely critical of them. Sometimes she even expressed her judgements to her girlfriends, who'd then ask her, "Why do you care who Hayward Barry is dating, anyway?" She asked herself the same question a few times.

She wondered if she should go back and give Joe some money, but then thought better of it. She should get the Little Mister home.

Chapter 13

It's On Now

The man sat looking at her, sprawled out on the floor, blood still running from her nose and oozing from her ears and the part of her scalp that was torn from her skull. A bloody, broken picture frame lay beside her; it looked as though she had been beaten with it, although he didn't remember doing it. He had almost had her ready when she started to bite him. She bit him so hard that he lost his grip on her arm. She kept biting and used her free hand to claw at the side of his head. He had felt the first few bites, and then the rage in him continued to build until finally the Push started. And now he sat feeling cheated. How had he done this? He was dejected because he couldn't remember. Remembering was the main reason he did it. He loved the power, loved the control, and loved feeling the fear from his clients. He had started calling them "clients" years back; he found it very amusing. He loved feeling the fear in the room, felt like he could feel it, smell it, and wrap up in it. He usually closed the door if he was in a room with a client to keep the fear from escaping.

He reached up and wiped his forehead, noticing that he had her bloody panties in his hand. He quickly stuffed them into his pocket. He looked around her home; it was small, but cozy. Something was burning, so he got up and went into the kitchen, where she had been cooking and singing while he came in through the window. She was making so much noise that he was able to attack her with ease. He'd been able to control her fairly well until the biting. He reached over, turned the burner off, took the pan with the chicken in it off the hot burner and placed it on a cold one. What was she going to have with the chicken? He didn't see any other ingredients to make a meal. Was she just going to eat the chicken by itself? *Well, that's pretty fucking boring. Not exactly a chef. A good fuck though.* He laughed.

He didn't remember fucking her but knew he had because he felt vacated. He looked at the handle of the frying pan and thought of the old bag he'd hit with a pot a long time ago. He had smoked her good—one fucking shot. He used to be really good. He found himself having to work harder to control his clients these days. He had to get himself up for a game, whereas in his younger days, he was in the game before he knew it. He had to plan a lot more.

He had watched this girl for some time. She had worked at the Super Mart on Main Street. While observing her, he had found out where she lived, that she had broken up with a boyfriend, and that she lived alone. He noticed he was picking easier clients. She was a biter, though—not easy.

He looked at the chicken. Someone might be coming over for dinner, a nosy fucker; after all, he didn't know everything about her, didn't have a tap on her phone or anything. He walked back into the bedroom and went to the window. He had broken the latch on this window to get in with relative ease. He climbed out and walked across the backyard to the shed. He went behind it and picked up his knapsack. He unzipped it and took out a clean shirt, threw the soiled one in, and zipped it back up. He put the knapsack on his shoulder and walked out onto the street.

I've been walkin' the streets at night, he thought. He began to whistle the GNR song "Patience" as he walked. He felt a kink in his leg. *Gettin' old, can't keep this up. Should think about hanging them up*, he chuckled to himself. *Hanging them up.* He pictured his clients' bodies hanging in a meat locker. *Retire. From this.* Could he do it? Was it possible? What would happen when the urge came again? How would he ignore it? Could he go without that rush ever again? He thought not. This was his drug, and he was a full-fledged addict. And there was the collection. Would it just stop, and gather dust? Without new additions, wouldn't it get old? Lose its excitement? *If you keep going like this, you're gonna get hurt or caught.*

Caught. He had been doing shit so long it was like the police didn't even exist. Now they had a whole task force trying to catch him. *Holy, I'm pretty popular.* What were they doing in their daily meetings? He pictured a bunch of big-bellied cops sitting around a table with a bunch of files and pictures in front of them, saying things like, "Well, I think this and it looks like this, and he was doing this here and that there." He wondered if any one of those dumb cops just wanted to be honest and stand up and say, "I don't have a fucking clue who this guy is, where he's at, or when he'll strike again." He laughed.

He was still with Rita, and had been for seventeen years. He'd never gotten a job. She was the main provider. He took money from his clients, telling her that he was getting a pension from the military. For the most part, he had done nothing for the past seventeen years . . . *the collection.* He had avoided having any piece of identification, and apart from his old life, he didn't really exist. They had moved into a small house and lived comfortably. He did little things around the house—repairs, cooking, and keeping her happy. In the beginning, he'd only wanted to stay for a few days, but he'd grown fond of Rita. Unlike everybody else in his previous life, she didn't want anything from him, never complained to him. Basically, she just wanted his company. He came and went as he pleased, and she never asked questions. He had his hobbies, his collections, and sometimes he felt like he had the perfect life. She never angered him, nagged him, or pushed him.

There was another thing that had kept him with her all those years: she had never brought the Push out. He knew she would be dead if she had, and maybe she did too on some level. She was still heavy, but was game for anything, so it was never boring. He had his hobby, so if he had the urge to be with a smaller woman, he would. He smiled again.

He walked by a house and saw a woman in the window jumping up and down. He stopped just past the house and watched her. She was sweaty from her workout. He felt blood rushing to his penis. *Two in one night, do you think you're twenty or something?* he asked himself. *Do you really think you could pull this off?* This would be risky, even for someone with his level of experience. It wasn't planned out, he didn't know if there was anyone else home, there could be a man in the other room, and he could have a gun. He watched her bob up and down, the neck of her shirt covered in sweat. *A chance I'm gonna have to take. You're getting greedy. You're gonna get hurt. You're gonna get caught. They'll tie them all together. You'll get the chair.* As she bobbed, he wondered what colour panties she was wearing, if they were wet with sweat. *Gonna have to find out.* He ran down the driveway toward the side of the house. In the darkness, he unzipped the knapsack, took his shirt off, and put on the soiled one. It was still warm and comfortable. He looked at the blood all over the front.

This is a little much. Just go. Just turn around and go. You've already got something for the collection; you don't need this. Go home, think about this lady, and yank. Get Rita to give you a good blowjob, any-thing, just get the fuck outta here.

Fuck that. You fuckin' pussy.

He threw the knapsack down beside the house and walked into the backyard. All the windows were closed. *Sexy and a brain, what a waste.* She was working out to loud music. He figured she would never hear a window breaking; but if anyone else was home, they probably would. He kicked a basement window with just enough force to break it. A large piece of glass flew into the basement and the rest of the window hung in the frame in cracked pieces. He waited to hear a reaction from inside the house. Nothing. He bent down and pulled out the remaining pieces of glass, tossing them on the grass. He stuck his feet in the window and pushed himself down into the dark basement. He could see the shadow of the stairs that led up to the main floor in the centre of the basement.

You got to go back, dude. You're too old for this.

I thought I already told you to fuck off. It's on now.

He grabbed the hand railing and crept up the stairs. He'd have to close those drapes in the living room when the fun started. If he could see in easily, so could others. He reached the top of the stairs, the light coming from the crack under the door guiding his way. The music was still playing loudly, and he could hear her hopping up and down on the floor. He opened the door and walked into the bright light of the kitchen, crept across the kitchen, and peeked into the living room. There she was, still bobbing up and down. The rush came over him; it was exhilarating, and he took a deep breath, as if inhaling it like a drug. He exhaled and ran into the living room, grabbed her around the waist, picked her up, and threw her to the floor—almost like a wrestling body slam. She screamed. He grabbed the drapes from both sides and yanked them closed, turned around, and saw her hurriedly crawling towards the kitchen.

"Please don't hurt me," she repeated over and over again as she crawled.

He dove onto the floor, grabbing her by the sneaker. It was so white. Brand new Nikes, he figured, never worn outside. She screamed again. The music still blared, which helped dull her screams. He pulled her backwards and grabbed her upper thigh. She turned her body around and smacked him in the side of the head. He looked up at her face and the fear he saw there fuelled him. He pulled himself up onto his left arm, brought the right one back, and swung for the fences. His fist connected with her nose and blood shot out all over her sweaty workout top. She sat stunned, giving him just enough time to reload and connect with a barn-door swing that caught her right in the side of the head. She fell over on the floor, moaning and crying. This was his window of opportunity; he knew because he had done it many times before. He grabbed the waistband of her shorts and pulled them down, over her ankles and off her body. She was still moaning, holding her face. He flipped her over on her stomach, grabbed her by the back of the head, and undid his zipper with the other hand. He jammed his dick into her and started to pump.

"Please don't hurt me," she muttered again.

Hurt you? I'm fucking pleasuring you. You should be fucking enjoying this. He kept pumping, but something didn't feel right. He'd already done this tonight and realized his dick was desensitized and couldn't stay hard. He began to get angry; he had worked hard for this, had taken big risks, and this bitch sucked. He pulled his dick out and climbed onto her back. He reached around and grabbed her by the chin. He began to pull her head back while she screamed.

"You fuckin' tease! You fuckin' teased me in the window, but you ain't no good fuck. You're a fuckin' tease, aren't you?"

She screamed in pain as he pulled her head back farther.

"You fuckin' tease!" he screamed, yanking her head.

Her neck cracked loudly and she stopped screaming. He dropped her head. It hit the floor with a thud. The guy on the workout show was telling everyone to keep breathing.

"Kind of hard for her, buddy," he said aloud. He grabbed her workout shorts and pulled her panties out of them. He began to shove them into his front left pocket and realized there was already a pair in there. Busy night. He shoved them in his other front pocket and stood up. He looked down at her and smiled. *No pain, no gain.*

He walked back through the kitchen and opened the back door. He began to whistle "Patience" again as he walked out into the night.

***

"Thanks for helping me with my homework, Dad."

"No problem, Andrew," Pete replied as he rubbed his son's hair. "Now you go get ready for bed."

"Already? Don't I get some playtime after my homework?"

"It's late, bud. You've got to get to bed. As soon as your brother is out of the bathroom, it's time for him to go to bed too. I have to do some homework myself."

"You've got homework too?" Andrew asked, surprised.

"Yes. Yes, I do," Pete replied.

"Does it ever end?" Andrew cleverly asked.

"Bed," Pete pointed.

"Alright."

"Goodnight, bud," Pete said as he left the room and went downstairs.

Pete walked across the kitchen and took the Max Killer file off the top of the fridge and put it on the table. His wife came up from the basement.

"How does a family of four have enough laundry for a small army?" she asked. Pete smiled at her as she continued. "That's the last load for the evening. I'm gonna sit my ass in front of that TV and watch *Grey's*."

Pete walked over, put his hands on her waist, and kissed her. "Thanks for doing the laundry, making dinner, looking after the boys, and all the other amazing things you do around here," he said.

"You're welcome," she replied as she kissed him back. "Thank you for making detective."

"Yeah, I've got some work to do with this." Pete pointed at the file on the kitchen table.

"No worries. I'll make sure the boys are in bed."

"That would be great. Thanks. I don't want them to see anything in this file. They'd have nightmares for months."

His wife patted him gently on the chest and left the room. He sat down at the table and opened the file.

Well, Mr. Max Killer, look out, 'cause Peter Lyons is coming.

***

Jeff pulled the squad car up in front of a fair-sized split-level house. Hayward grabbed the two-way radio and keyed the mic.

"Officers on scene, 15 Robin Lane."

"Ten-four," the radio squawked back.

Jeff got out of the car with Hayward not far behind. The front door of the house swung open. Hayward grabbed the top of his gun, which he always did when he was startled on the job. An overweight white woman came running out.

"Throw him in jail, throw him in jail, I've had enough," the lady said, running up to Jeff. "I've had enough," she said again, trying to catch her breath.

"I get that. Please just calm down and tell me what the hell is going on. What have you had enough of?"

A man in a golf shirt came to the door and walked down the front stairs. "You called the cops! You really called the cops. I can't believe this," he said.

Jeff pointed at the man and barked, "Stay where you are, sir."

"What? I'll have you know . . ."

"Just stay where you are," Jeff barked again.

"Hayward," Jeff said sternly enough that Hayward didn't like it.

He motioned to Hayward to go and deal with the man.

"Every time he goes and plays golf, he gets drunk and then comes home and starts to bully me," the lady said.

"Bully you how?" Jeff asked.

"Delores. Let's go back in the house," the man said to the lady.

"Shut up, sir," Jeff shouted.

Hayward walked over to the man and gestured for him to come to the side, away from Jeff and the lady. Jeff had his notepad out and was taking down information as the lady spoke.

"Hello, sir, my name is Officer Barry," Hayward said. "Would you like to tell me what happened here today?"

"Well," the man started. Hayward could immediately tell the man had been drinking heavily. "I came home from a golf game with some good ol' boys and all I said was, 'What's for dinner?' and she flew off the handle."

"That seems odd, sir. She seems incensed, enough to call the police. Are you sure you didn't say anything else?"

The man wobbled a bit as he spoke. "I may have made a comment about her outfit."

"A derogatory remark, sir?" Hayward asked.

"What's derogatory is that outfit." The man spit a bit as he was getting the words out.

"Sir . . ."

"I used to take her to the club years ago, but look at her now, she's a friggin' embarrassment."

"Okay sir, I'm gonna take you down to the station where you can sleep this off, and then tomorrow you can go home with a clear head and you and your wife can sort this out."

"You're throwing me in the drunk tank?" the man slurred.

You guessed it, pal—hit the nail on the head, Hayward thought. "Yes. Will you get in the car, please?"

"I guess," he said as he walked to the car. "Do I have a choice?"

"I could charge you with domestic abuse."

"I never laid a hand on her," the man protested.

"Verbal abuse is abuse, sir." Hayward pushed the man in the car and shut the door. He walked back to the lady and Jeff.

"What are you doing with him?" the lady asked Hayward.

"I'm gonna let him sleep it off down at the station. He'll be home tomorrow."

"You're taking him to jail?" the lady said, shocked.

"Actually, that's what you told us to do when we arrived." The lady looked stunned as she realized the impact of her words.

"Well," she waved her arm, "whatever it takes to smarten' that man up."

"Just a little bit more information and we'll be on our way ma'am," Jeff said.

Hayward turned and walked back to the passenger side of the car, where he stopped. At the house across the street, he saw a woman and a little boy getting out of the car. The woman opened the trunk and grabbed some bags.

Beth. Was it her? He hadn't seen her since high school. Was that really her? He had to find out for sure.

"Beth!" Hayward shouted. The woman stopped and looked around. "Beth," he said again.

The woman turned and looked in his direction. He waved and started walking toward her. She didn't wave back, just watched him as he came closer. Hayward's heart felt like it was beating a hundred beats a second, and he was sweating. *If she doesn't recognize me soon, she's going to get spooked and run away.*

"It's Hayward!" he shouted.

"Hayward?" She sounded completely shocked. "Hayward Barry, holy shit, how long has it been?"

Hayward approached her. *Should I hug her? Better wait for her to make the first move.*

"Come here," she said, opening her arms.

Hayward walked into her embrace, his hands touching her back. *She feels amazing.* It was as though he was meant to be in this place. It was as if his body was designed to be in this position at this moment. He had never felt this comfortable in his life. They let go of each other. Just like that it was over, his body longing for more.

"How have you been?" Beth asked.

"Good," he replied. "And you?" Hayward gestured at the boy.

"Oh," she said, "this is Phillip."

"Hey there, Phillip."

Hayward bent down and held out his hand to the boy. The boy did not reciprocate. Hayward stood up.

"Phillip, Hayward was a friend of mine when I was a little girl. Wow, it's been a long time."

"It has been, yeah."

"Phillip, you can run along into the house and play. Mommy will be there in a few minutes."

"How old is he?" Hayward asked as the boy went into the house.

"He's six."

"Beautiful boy. Do you have any other kids?"

"No, just Phillip. He keeps me busy."

"I'm sure he does."

"Look at you, a policeman. I never would have pictured that, but I'm sure you're a great one. I just would never have guessed that would be your career path."

"Yeah, you and I both, but I was getting tired of eating mac and cheese and trying to sell paintings. I was getting older and figured I had better get a full-time job, maybe start a family."

"Oh, you don't have children?"

"No, no children, not married. I was in San Francisco for a bit."

"I heard you were out there. That must have been fun."

"The first few years were exciting, but you know, you get older and need more from life, so I came home to figure out what the next chapter would be. Then Pete—you know Pete Lyons?"

"Yes, yes, I remember him. I see him sometimes. He's a policeman here, right?"

"Yeah, he is, and well, we went out for a few beers, chatted, he put in a good word for me, and hey, here I am making a difference."

"Wow, that's pretty cool. Hayward, it was great seeing you, but I better get in there to Phillip. You know boys. I don't know what he'll get into.

"Yeah, of course. Yeah."

Beth bent to take the rest of the bags from the trunk of the car.

"Do you need some help with those?" Hayward asked.

"No, no, I've got these, thanks."

"Okay, well it was great seeing you."

"You too." As Beth walked toward the house, Hayward turned to leave—but then turned back around.

"Beth."

She stopped and turned. "Yes?"

Hayward jogged over and pulled a business card with his police officer information on it from his wallet.

"If you ever need a cop, you know, you can call me."

"Thanks." She tried to hold out her hand with the bags in it, causing them both to laugh. She put out her other hand and took the card.

"Okay, I'll see ya," Hayward said.

"Yeah, bye, Hayward."

Hayward crossed the street. *Wow. Beth. That was Beth.* He couldn't believe it. She was even more beautiful than he remembered. That was a nice house she lived in. He would've asked about Daniel, but knew she was still with him. The boy, Phillip, was his spitting image. Poor kid.

"Hey!" Jeff yelled, "Hey AWOL, I am working alone now. You turn in your badge?"

Hayward didn't answer—didn't really know what to say, anyway. He had just had his mind blown. He opened the door and got in the passenger side of the squad car. Jeff, standing at the driver side, shook his head and got in the car. The man in the back wasn't saying anything, but Jeff still turned and screamed at him to shut up before putting the car in gear, peeling the tires, and driving off.

***

Beth was putting away the contents of the bags with a smile; she'd been smiling since she closed the door behind her. *Hayward.*

Holy, it's been a long time. He looked good. Really good. And that police uniform, what a hottie.

She had always had a thing for a police uniform. She pulled his card from her pocket and turned it over in her hand. Officer Hayward Barry. She opened her purse, took out her wallet, and tucked it away in behind some other cards. She wanted to tell Hayward that she'd been thinking of him earlier that very day, when she had seen Joe downtown, but didn't want to mention Joe. She knew they'd been close.

A cop. She laughed. He'd always seemed so timid and shy, although she hadn't hung around with him much after elementary school. For all she knew, he could have been a monster. She laughed for even thinking that about Hayward. Being around him after all those years felt nice—it felt comfortable, a lot more comfortable than she'd been feeling lately. She opened the cupboard door and took out a pot and pan.

What will I make for King Daniel tonight? she wondered sourly. She slammed the door shut and put her head back. She thought about how long she'd been with Daniel: since fifth grade. What would it have been like to date other people, to have a different boyfriend? Had she made the right decision? She pictured Hayward and how he said he had been eating mac and cheese in San Francisco. Maybe if he'd painted something that wasn't so drab. Maybe he had, she didn't know. Maybe he painted clowns and carnivals and balloons and kids on rides and roller coasters having the time of their lives. He didn't though, she knew. That wasn't his style.

She hadn't even asked Hayward what he was doing in her neighbourhood, but she saw where the squad car was parked and figured that Delores had had enough. She should have called the cops on that pig about five years ago. Delores' husband, Al, came over when they had barbecues in the summer. He always got drunk and obnoxious, making racist and sexist jokes. The only person laughing at his jokes besides himself was Daniel's brother, Rich. Al and Rich were pig brothers. She laughed. A lot of the women at the barbecue would ask Delores to take him home, but the last thing she wanted to do was be home by herself with that drunk pig.

What time would Daniel be home this evening? He'd been getting home late these days, blaming his brother. They would always get into an argument when she asked about it. Beth pulled chicken out of the freezer, placed it in the sink, and started to run hot water over it.

She opened the newspaper and began to flip through it: more stories about the task force that had been assembled to catch the Max Killer, and a plea for the public's help. They had been after the guy for years. When the killings first began, the whole city was gripped by fear. People didn't want to leave their houses, everyone installed security systems, and everyone seemed like a suspect. Then the killing stopped for a while, and life in the city slowly returned to normal. Then there was another killing, and people got scared again, but life eventually got back to normal, more quickly than before. The community seemed to act differently after the next few killings; people lived normally as if they were defying the killer, making a statement that they were not going to live in fear. Even though the killer was still lurking, people went about their business. The police and their inability to catch him or come up with substantial leads or clues had given the story the status of a legend, as if the guy would never get caught—he'd just eventually retire or die. The government had increased the budget and resources for the task force.

We've heard all this before, she thought as she turned the page. Beth read the headline, "Seniors in old row houses forced out for new apartment complex." An old man was quoted as saying that they didn't have enough money to fight it in court, but their row houses on St. Margaret Street were all they had. The company that was responsible was Oak Tree Construction—Daniel's company. Why were they taking those seniors' homes? Probably another one of Rich's schemes. Surely Daniel didn't know about it, and he would

fix it. Once he found out about this, he would build somewhere else
. . . *He knows about it*, she concluded sadly. She looked over at the
sink. She had completely forgotten about the chicken. She jumped
up and turned the water off and looked at the soggy chicken. She
laughed. *Surf and Turf, I guess.*

She thought of Hayward again. Had he thrown the pig in his cell
yet? She pictured Hayward, in his uniform, throwing Al into the
jail cell and felt a rush of sensation to her genitals. She dropped the
soggy chicken in the sink and headed into the other room to check
on Phillip.

Chapter 14

Creatures of Habit

Pete flipped through the pictures. Each one seemed more gruesome than the last. They were of half-naked women who had been raped and killed in a variety of different ways. There were things they hadn't told the public that had linked every murder but two in the past seventeen years: each murdered girl's panties were missing from the crime scene. He looked at the rooms in the pictures, which were not disturbed much—no robbery fixation with this guy. Besides the rooms where the struggles had taken place, there wasn't much disorder in the houses. The killer didn't leave any messages. They had gotten lots of DNA, hair, and fingerprints from the crime scenes, but they could not connect any of them to any suspects or previous offenders in the police databank. They could not find any link to the killer; it was as if he didn't exist.

Didn't exist. Pete turned over another picture of a woman, her eyes wide and soulless. It reminded him of Davey's eyes when he had rolled him over all those years ago. He wondered what Davey would be doing now if he had lived. Looking around the kitchen, Pete saw toys on the floor and hand-drawn pictures from his sons on the fridge, and suddenly he felt an overwhelming guilt for what he had. He turned back to the file. *Got to get this son of a bitch who doesn't exist. This guy must do something. He must make a living somehow, unless he goes in and out of town, which is a possibility.*

Killers didn't usually do that, though; they were creatures of habit. The FBI had written an extensive profile. They had already checked the people in the system on social assistance or welfare, and none had brought up any red flags. The guy just didn't exist in Sifton. He started to write down the dates of the killings. Pete would check bus and plane records to see if there were any correlations with people arriving or leaving town around the days of the killings. He wasn't sure if anybody had checked these things out, but there was nothing in the file that indicated they had. He would check with the task force leader tomorrow.

Doesn't exist. These women don't exist now. He tapped the table. *Davey doesn't exist now. The person who did this?* He tapped the table again. *He exists, he lives, he breathes, and he leaves a trail, and someone knows who he is.*

The first murder had taken place seventeen years ago. What had the killer done before then? Had he always been in the city, and just decided to start killing? That didn't usually happen. He more than likely would have been a troubled teen, and they would have had his prints and such on file somewhere. If he came to town before the first killing, where had he come from? Pete would start with the surrounding cities and review unsolved murder cases that were over seventeen years old. He scratched some more things "to do" on a piece of paper for tomorrow. It would be a busy day. He loved doing detective work and felt good. He closed the file. *I'm coming for ya.*

Pete put the file on top of the fridge, went into the other room, sat on the couch, and took his wife's hand in his.

"Everything okay?" she asked.

"Perfect," he said. He kissed her on the cheek.

"Catch him yet?"

Pete chuckled. "Almost. Tomorrow probably."

She smiled, patted him on the hand, and leaned her head on his shoulder.

***

He got back to the little house where he and Rita lived and scanned the front. The lawn needed cutting, and the house needed a couple coats of paint. He would get to it; he had a list. He used to despise lists, thought they were for nosy fuckers, but over the years he had started making them. He had to, or else he would never remember to do fucking anything. His little handy jobs had kept Rita happy and him enjoying his way of life.

He headed for the detached garage in the backyard. He was feeling sore. He had done more tonight than he had in years, and he was feeling it. The television flickered in the living room. Rita would be there, plopped on the couch, watching the soaps she recorded during the day, probably with an empty pack of donuts or some ice cream. Even after all these years, he was still amazed at her appetite. He himself had gained about twenty pounds in the last ten years, probably because of her cooking.

He opened the side door of the garage, went in, and flicked on the light. This was his little sanctuary. It was a single car garage, but Rita did not keep her car in it, and she rarely disturbed him. She had her soap opera time, which worked out great for him and his hobbies. He went to the back of the garage and opened a cabinet, threw his knapsack in, closed the door. He opened a different cabinet and reached far into the back where there was a plain piece of plywood. He grabbed it, brought it out, and turned it around. It was covered with women's panties, nailed to the wood in neat rows. Some were covered with dried blood.

He scanned his eyes up and down the rows, smiling. He took a deep breath, smelling the fear, the excitement, the conquests. He reached into his pocket and pulled out the panties from the first client of the evening. Running his finger along the waist band, he thought about her ringing in purchases at the Super Mart, how her uniform pants had hugged her ass, how her hair was beautiful and curly and swayed back and forth as she moved about behind the register. He thought of her walk and the way she had had such a cute swagger. He brought the panties up, buried his face in them, and took a deep breath. Thinking about her fear, he breathed in again. The memory of the look on her face when she realized what was happening caused the blood to rush to his penis. Then came the biting. He would have to wear long sleeves the next few days to cover the bite marks.

He brought the panties away from his face. He couldn't remember anything after the biting until he was looking down at her dead body. He hated that; why did the Push have to be in him? Why didn't the Push go away? He had lived with the Push for too long. Might the Push retire? Would he ever be able to control the Push? He knew the answer. He was getting older and he would have to work harder at his hobbies to keep the Push at bay. He clenched the panties in a ball in his fist. It wasn't fair that the Push would cheat him of the moments that he worked for.

I do all the work, and the Push steals the glory. Fuckin' prick. He clenched the panties harder. *You fuckin' bastard. I did the planning, the scouting, the surveillance.* Then he laughed. *You sound like those dumb fuckin' cops. Surveillance: Let's sit in our cars, chat, eat junk food to fill our fat cop bellies, but we'll call it a word that makes it sound like we're doing such important work.* He squeezed his fist harder. *Fuckin' lazy fucks. Some of us have to work hard, and someone else takes the credit.* He squeezed his fist as hard as he could, welcoming the pain. *The Push took my moment. It was my moment.*

Then he had a horrifying thought that he'd only had a few times in his life. He had to calm down. If he got angry enough at the Push, would the Push turn on him? Would it try to destroy him? What would he do? He wouldn't even know it was happening. How would he be able to save himself?

He shook his head. *Got to stop thinking about this right fuckin' now.* He could feel sweat starting to develop on various points of his body. He unclenched his fist. *What the fuck is wrong with you?* He imagined sitting in a psychiatrist's office and trying to explain himself; she wouldn't be able to call 9-1-1 fast enough.

He opened a drawer on the counter and took out a hammer. He opened another drawer, this one filled with different-sized nails neatly arranged in appropriately sized boxes. He fished out some finishing nails, which were the ones he always used for the collection. He carefully spread the panties out and placed them against the wood at the end of the bottom of the last row. He tacked the panties in place, sat back, and examined the board.

Wow! Everybody's good at something. He smiled as he reached into his pocket, pulled out the other pair of panties, and held them up. *And some people are the motherfuckin' MVP.*

***

Hayward entered his apartment. His head swirling from the day, he tossed his keys on the counter, went into his bedroom, and took his uniform off. Did people realize what it's like to be a cop? Until he had become a cop, he had no idea what they did on a daily basis. Fixing disagreements, chasing people with guns. What kind of crazy-ass job was that? He'd come to believe that cops should be paid a million bucks.

He pulled on gym shorts and a T-shirt and headed for the kitchen. Maybe in a few years he could be a detective like Pete, and then he wouldn't have to answer the beat cop calls. He didn't know if he had the passion to get to that level. Maybe he would just do this job for a while, and then figure out what he wanted to do. When would that happen? Would anything that he did make him happy? He opened the freezer door and took out a Chinese food frozen dinner, peeled the top back on the corner, popped it in the microwave, and hit four minutes. He didn't have to read the instructions anymore; he'd been living alone and eating frozen dinners for a long time; it was just repetition.

What did the guidance counsellors say when he was in high school? "You had to think of something that you liked in life, and then think of a job that related to that thing." He had told them he liked to draw and paint, but they hadn't told him to be an artist, which would have been the logical choice. They told him to be an art teacher. Hayward thought, at the time, that that was such a narrow-minded view of the world. All they wanted to promote was educa-tion. Well, he showed them; he tried to be an artist, he went to San Francisco, he was going make it. Hayward had always thought he could make art a career, but it turned out the counsellors might have been right. He had tried hard in San Fran, but when he looked back at it now, it seemed like a waste of time. Although, how could it have been a waste of time when he was following a dream?

And look what that got you? he asked himself. *Look at your life. If you had listened to them, you would be an art teacher, with a secure, non-dangerous job, probably settled down with a couple kids.*

The microwave beeped. He popped open the door, pulled the food out, sat on the couch, and put his dinner on the coffee table. He took a deep breath and looked around the room. He would have been an art teacher who always wondered "What if?"

He started to eat his food and picked up the television remote from the table. He thought about turning it on, but then decided he liked the silence better. His head was full, and it would take some time for his brain to sort everything out. It wasn't too late to be an art teacher; he could paint when he wanted and pass along his art knowledge to a younger generation of ambitious minds. And teachers had a great work schedule. But becoming a teacher would take a lot of time and money. He was also thinking it was time to settle down. How many women were attracted to a thirty-year-old student? He could see her bragging now: "Well, he was a starving artist, then a cop, but he couldn't hack that, so now he's going be a teacher, and who knows how long he'll be doing that?"

Man, you're in some funk tonight.

The Chinese food was good. He wondered why frozen dinners kept tasting better and better but he couldn't get his life on track. It was as if frozen dinners were progressing faster than him. Such an odd thought. But it was true.

Hayward thought of hugging Beth. It had been amazing. If he were coming home to Beth every night, would he think about his job the way he did? He would clean horse stalls all day and love it if he could home to the feeling of that hug every night. That was the answer. He needed to find a wife and stop bitching about his career. His job was a good one in the eyes of others. A lot of women loved the excitement of dating a police officer.

You just have to get out there and play the game, son, he reminded himel. *You also need to stop comparing every woman you meet to Beth, she's happily—well, you don't know that—married, has a beautiful boy, and is never going to be with you. You should have realized that long ago, but you haven't, you've been hanging on to this crush. That's all it is, a boyhood crush that didn't get to take its course. You need to get over it. It wasn't Davey's death that kept you and Beth apart; it was life, and here you are watching it pass you by. Seeing her today was a sign. You now know she's doing great, she's not alone sitting around waiting for you, and she has a great life and a great family. That's what you want, that's what you need, so go get it. Use what you have, you're on the right track. You've got a career, now use it to get the rest of the things you want. Then see if you want to be an art teacher.*

Hayward finished his last bite of food, got up, and tossed the empty carton in the garbage. *That's it. Gonna go look for that special lady, tomorrow.*

Why not start tonight? His brain was exhausted, and he didn't want to look for a wife at a bar. He'd start looking during everyday tasks; that would be the best way to find her. He grabbed the remote from the table and flopped down on the couch. *Let's just relax tonight. Tomorrow is going to be a busy day.*

***

"Cy," Craig yelled. "Cy."

Cy turned around. "What?" He was standing in the parking lot of their high school.

"Where ya going, man?"

"I told you where I was goin', Craig."

"I thought you were jokin', Cy."

"Well, I ain't. You in or what?"

"Cy, if you get caught skippin', you can't go to the prom."

"Holy fuck, Craig, you really believe that shit?" Craig lowered his head as Cy continued. "You really think that this late in the year, teachers give a fuck if you skip? Their fuckin' minds have checked out already. And not let you go to the prom—the prom is such a huge part of a young person's life, do ya think they are gonna take that away 'cause I skipped a fuckin' English class?"

"I guess not," Craig said sheepishly.

"No, of course they're not. So what you gotta do is stop acting like a fucking pussy, get in the truck, go up on Bill Hill with me. We'll get fucked up and go with the way the wind blows the rest of the day."

"Yeah, man. Fuck it, let's go."

They both turned and walked towards Cy's truck.

"You know," Craig said, "my mom paid a lot of money for the tux and shit and you know Tamara probably spent a lot of money on her dress." They opened the doors of the rusty Ford and got in. "And you know—"

Cy cut him off. "Listen, get it all the fuck out now, 'cause when we get fucked up I don't want to hear any of this shit."

"Holy fuck, Cy, calm down."

"I'm as calm as the cucumber sticking up your mother's ass." Cy cackled as he started the truck.

"You fucker," Craig said, holding up his fist. "I should fuckin' pop you for that."

Cy kept laughing, pointing at the side of his cheek to give Craig a target. Then he reached across to open the glove box and pulled out a big bag of weed. "Well, if you're not gonna hit me then roll one up, fucker," he cackled again.

Craig took the bag, smiled, and shook his head.

Cy saw someone come out of the school and walk toward the edge of the sidewalk. "What the fuck?" he said.

Craig looked up.

"Hey, isn't that Neil Delgrande?"

"Yes it is," Cy answered.

"He still owe you money?"

"He sure does, for that ounce about a month ago. Haven't seen him around though, till now. You stay here and finish that." Cy jumped out of the truck and jogged toward Neil. Neil saw him coming and shifted his feet as if he wanted to run, but the rest of his body had decided against it.

"Hey, Cy," Neil said, his voice cracking. Cy came right up to his face.

"Dude, where's my money?" Cy was practically talking in his ear.

"Oh yeah, I owe you some money," Neil said nervously.

"You're fucking right you do." Cy spoke calmly. Neil shifted his feet.

"Yeah, well, I don't have any right now, but I'll get it to ya next couple of weeks."

"Tomorrow," Cy said.

Neil shook his head.

"I can't get it by tomorrow."

Cy grabbed his arm and squeezed it hard. A car pulled up beside the sidewalk, but Cy didn't let go.

"Hey, please man, that's my mother. She's here to pick me up to go to the orthodontist."

"I don't care if it's Santa fuckin' Claus, you better have my money tomorrow."

"Okay, yeah, I'll get it tomorrow."

Cy loosened his grip. Neil quickly pulled his arm away and jumped into the car. Cy leaned down so he could see Neil's mother and waved. She didn't wave back, just drove off. Cy laughed and walked back to his truck.

Fucker better have that thing rolled. Even if it was, Cy had already decided he would give Craig a hard time about the way it was rolled. He stopped smiling, pulled the truck door open, and hopped in. He put the truck in gear, looked at Craig and the joint he'd rolled, took it from him, and held it up.

"What the fuck is this?"

Craig looked at him, confused.

"What the fuck is this?" Cy repeated, but couldn't contain himself and began to laugh. He tossed the joint into Craig's lap and peeled out of the parking spot.

***

The morning sun shone in Beth's eyes as she poured milk in a bowl of cereal for Phillip, who sat at the table banging his spoon.

"Please stop banging that," she said. She brought the bowl over and placed it in front of him. He continued to bang his spoon.

"Please stop that!" she said, more sternly this time.

He paused for a minute then began to eat his cereal.

"Any prize yet, Mom?"

Beth looked at the box of cereal. A toy rooster was somewhere inside the box. "I don't see it yet, Phillip."

When she was a child, her father used to say, "Bunny, when the prize falls into your bowl, then it's a surprise, that's what makes it fun." She loved her father, but she had hated that shit. She was a parent herself now, and still didn't understand it. She plunged her hand into the box and fished out the rooster, walked over, and placed it on the table.

"Now we can all get on with our lives."

Phillip looked at her strangely. She would apologize but that would just confuse him more. He took the rooster and made it jump around the table with one hand while he shovelled spoonfuls of cereal into his mouth with the other.

She looked out at the sun and felt its warmth penetrating through the closed window. It would be a nice day outside, but there was a storm brewing in the house this morning. Beth was already cranky when she heard Daniel come down the steps. She wondered what the next level up from cranky was. Daniel walked into the kitchen.

"Good morning," he said.

Beth said nothing.

"Hi, Dad," Phillip said, still bouncing the rooster up and down. Daniel walked over, bent down, and kissed Phillip on the top of the head.

"Hey, hey, what you got there, a chicken?"

"Yeah," Phillip answered.

"It's a rooster," said Beth.

"Whatever." Daniel walked over to the fridge and opened the door.

"Not whatever. You have to teach him the proper names of things. He's at an important age."

Daniel closed the fridge door and looked at her, then looked back at Phillip.

"That's a rooster, son."

"Okay," Phillip said, still bouncing it.

Daniel turned back to Beth. "There. Happy?"

"Far from it," she huffed, storming out of the kitchen. She went into the living room and plopped herself in a chair. Daniel followed her.

"What the hell is wrong with you?" he asked.

"Where were you so late last night?"

"At work—where do you think I was?"

"I don't know anymore."

"What the hell, are you out of your mind?"

"I made dinner," Beth said, and then started to cry.

"I know; I ate it when I got home."

"I made it for dinner, for our family, to be eaten at dinner time, to sit as a family." Beth usually kept quiet because of how mad Daniel could get and the magnitude of the fight that would happen, but today she was ready. She wasn't happy with him, and he would hear about it; she had kept it bottled up for too long.

"I had to work—you know, that thing I do so we can keep this house and buy food and pay bills."

"You work too much, too damn much, you're never here. Phillip needs his father."

Daniel began to yell. "He needs to have a roof over his head and a mother that's not a fucking psycho."

Beth could feel the blood rushing to her cheeks. "Psycho, for wanting my family to spend time together, that's psycho? You bastard!"

"Look, where is this coming from?" Daniel asked.

"From you! What's going on? Are you having an affair or something?"

"An affair!" Daniel yelled. "What the fuck are you talking about? I am at work, trying to do two people's jobs with my brother trying to run us into the ground, and you can't understand that. You can't understand that I'm doing this for us, for our family."

"I'm tired of that excuse, Daniel."

"It's not an excuse, Beth. You act like I'm avoiding our family, like I want to be at work that much."

"Do you?"

Daniel took a deep breath. "Look, I will try to make some changes at work so I am home more."

"Just let the damn company go under if you have to."

"You know I can't do that, Beth."

"Why not? You can get another job. You're skilled; you won't have any trouble."

"Beth, that company means a lot to me."

"More than us?" She jumped up and went back into the kitchen. Phillip was still sitting at the table; his cereal was done but he was wrapped up in playing with the rooster. Daniel followed her.

"Please," Beth said. "I don't want to fight in front of Phillip."

"Listen," Daniel said calmly, "I'll stay home from work today. I'll spend the day with you and Phillip. We'll have lunch together, dinner together, and you can do whatever you want this afternoon."

"Really?" She was shocked.

"Really. I'll start making changes right now."

"I would like to get some yard work done this afternoon, if you could watch Phillip."

"Sure, whatever you want."

Beth nodded her head in appreciation.

"Okay, how's that?" Daniel asked.

"That's a start," she said.

"Now, can you give me a hug?"

Beth gave him a hug.

***

Pete sat at his desk, scrolling through the police database. He had asked the task force leader if anyone had gone through the specific dates of bus, plane, and train schedules to see if anybody was coming in and out of town right around the dates that the murders had taken place. They had, but he was told that revisiting them with a fresh pair of eyes wouldn't hurt. He sent out requests for those travel records, and while he was waiting for them to come back he would check out some other things. He had a gut feeling that he should look into unsolved murders that had occurred over seventeen years ago in towns or cities in a five-hundred-mile radius of Sifton. He pulled up a map of the geographic region, printed it off, and tacked it on his wall. It was a long shot, but it was a new angle, according to the file. He would work backwards by town. He had always been taught that your gut was your gut for a reason, and it usually came up with the best answers.

He would start with the town closest to Sifton. He typed the town of "Brocton" into the database and started to look for any murders from seventeen to twenty years ago. There were two: one was a murder–suicide, and the other was done by a neighbour of the victim. No unsolved murders. Pete reached up with his pen and put an "X" through Brocton. He had to change the search parameters. He was only interested in the unsolved murders. He felt good—this was a good angle.

He adjusted himself in his chair and decided it would be a long morning. He would be staring at his screen for a while today. He grabbed his mug and headed to the coffee machine. Dubinsky was standing in the hallway, the detective he had replaced on the Max Killer Task Force.

"Hey," Dubinsky said.

"Hello," Pete replied. "I was just going to get a coffee."

"What are you workin' on?" Dubinsky asked.

Who the hell is this guy? Pete wondered. *Who the fuck does he think he is asking what I'm workin' on?*

"Well," Pete said, "I'm just getting into the file, but basically I'm looking at what the task force has already done and building on that."

"Oh yeah, that's cool. You know, I was on this task force for the past three years, and I know this case inside and out."

Well, it doesn't matter how fucking well you know it, because you didn't catch him did you?

"Thanks, I'll remember that," Pete said.

"Okay, yeah." Dubinsky turned and walked away.

Pete hoped that nutbar wouldn't be looking over his shoulder every day. He really needed that coffee now. He continued on toward the machine.

Chapter 15

Missing Person

Ready for another great day with Jeff, Hayward thought as he closed the passenger door of the squad car.

"You ready, dickless?" Jeff said as he started up the car.

Hayward usually never said anything to Jeff, but today was different. Jeff started to pull out of the parking lot.

"Dickless? What the hell was I sticking in your mom last night, then?"

Jeff slammed on the brakes. Hayward jerked forward, his seatbelt stopping his body from being thrown up against the dash. Jeff turned and stared at Hayward.

Uh oh, guess I struck a chord here. Hayward wasn't afraid of physical confrontation with Jeff; he just didn't want to get into a situation of violence with his partner. It wouldn't look good for either of them.

He stared back at Jeff, ready for Jeff if he tried to hit him. Hayward's hands were ready to do some serious blocking.

"That was funny, Barry, that was fucking funny," Jeff said, and started laughing.

Hayward smiled back.

"This is gonna be a good day," Jeff said as he put the car in gear and peeled the tires.

It's never a good day with you, Jeff.

Hayward remembered his revelation the previous night: to look for a woman he could see spending his life with. Heavy stuff. He didn't want to be with another cop, because he was worried enough for his own safety, and doubling that worry didn't seem like an attractive option. He made a pact with himself that he would be constantly aware of women in his surroundings and ask at least one out in the next few days. The places that he and Jeff usually went for lunches had some good-looking waitresses. Next time he would pay more attention to the women, and maybe even ask about their situations if he thought they had strong potential.

Jeff began to sing "Welcome to the Jungle" as they passed through the projects. Hayward hated Jeff's singing; it sucked. Even if Jeff had been a good singer, Hayward figured he would hate it because he hated him.

"Where are we going?" Hayward asked.

"To hell," Jeff replied in a devilish voice and a shrill, mock laugh.

What the fuck was wrong with this guy? He was such a dick. No wonder Jeff lived alone. Then he made a connection.

Holy shit, I live alone. Am I as bad as this fucking guy? Do people look at me the way they look at him? Hayward was beginning to scare himself. *Get it together, Hay. You got to get it together, man. Look at this guy; there is no way you can compare yourself to him. Holy fuck, I think I'm starting to go crazy. It makes sense, all of those years in love with someone who will never be mine. Now this guy? He's my final straw. This is going to push me over the edge. I was going to change things in my life, but it may be too late.* Hayward began to take deep breaths. *Stay the course. It's going to be okay, Hay buddy. You know it is. Just calm down.*

The two-way radio cackled. "Unit to respond to 72 Meech Street. Possible missing person, female lives alone."

"Possible missing person, my ass," Jeff snarled.

Hayward picked up the mic. "Unit Twelve responding, 72 Meech Street," he said.

"Ten-four," the radio babbled back.

"Ahh! What did you do that for?" Jeff said, frustrated.

"Responding to a call, man. That's what we do."

"There are probably other units closer, and those calls are so fuckin' boring. It's just some stupid bitch who forgot to set her wake-up alarm, and all the other soap-opera-watching hens who talk to each other make a kafuffle for nothing."

Hayward felt butterflies in his stomach. He had a bad feeling. This would be far from nothing.

"Let's check it out," he said. "If it's nothing, we'll be at Delicious Donuts in twenty minutes having a coffee break."

"Now you're starting to make sense. Funny today, and making sense today. You're gonna have to mark this day on the calendar."

Hayward's butterflies had evolved into a nauseous feeling. *I don't think that we'll have to mark this day. I think we are going to remember it.* He hoped he was wrong, and that Jeff was right. He was actually praying that was the case.

The squad car turned the corner onto Meech Street. Hayward watched the house numbers as they went by. They pulled up in front of 72. Showtime. He opened the passenger door.

"Let's go wake this bitch up!" Jeff yelled as he got out of the car.

They approached the front door and Hayward noticed that the front window drapes were drawn. Jeff arrived at the door first and rapped on it hard.

"Time to wake up Miss Bitch!" he said loudly.

Hayward stood at the bottom of the steps and hung his head in shame after Jeff's comment. He knew the neighbours had probably heard that one. Jeff, always the professional.

Jeff rapped on the door again. The house stood silent.

"I'll check around back," Hayward said. As he walked away, he could hear Jeff rapping on the door again.

"Hello!" Jeff yelled.

As Hayward walked around the side of the house, his chest started to tighten. It was the feeling he had when he was rushing down the hill to Davey's body. He had never forgotten that feeling. It was the most scared he had ever been in his life, and here, at this house, he was feeling it again. He came around the back of the house and saw the broken basement window and his heart sank. He placed his hand on top of his revolver and walked up to the window.

"Jeff!" Hayward yelled.

He saw the broken glass inside the frame, meaning the glass had been pushed in and someone had used the window to gain access. Hayward had a flash of Davey's face when Pete rolled him over. Jeff came jogging into the backyard.

"What is it?"

Hayward pointed at the window.

"Forced entry!" Jeff said. His face lit up.

Although Jeff lacked professionalism and human compassion, he loved his job and lived for moments like this. Unlike Hayward, he fed on the nervous rush. Jeff cued the microphone on his shoulder.

"Unit Twelve, requesting back up 72 Meech Street, signs of forced entry, officers entering."

Hayward could feel the sweat building on the back of his neck. Jeff ran over to the back door and stepped back a few feet. Hayward hesitated. *This is your job; this is what you do*, he told himself. It didn't matter how many calls he responded to; he would never get used to this. Hayward walked back a couple of steps and started to feel dizzy.

Man, get it together. Your partner needs you, and there could be someone in there who needs help . . . It's too late for her. He got his legs moving and positioned himself behind Jeff.

"You ready?" Jeff asked.

"Yes," Hayward said, nodding.

Hayward began to breathe rapidly. Jeff pulled his gun from its holster. Hayward did the same.

"Let's see what's up," Jeff said.

Hayward realized he wasn't the crazy one; Jeff was. Jeff charged at the door. Hayward wasn't worried at all that the door wouldn't give, because Jeff was hurling every molecule of his body at it. Jeff's body hit the door with such incredible force that the door flew in. It happened so fast that Hayward didn't even hear a crack. Jeff stumbled in the doorway and then headed into the house. Hayward ran in behind him. Jeff raised his weapon and walked across the kitchen. Hayward did the same. Jeff stopped at the entrance into the living room and raised his left hand to tell Hayward to stay where he was. He looked back at Hayward and put his left hand to his throat and made a slicing motion, then pointed into the living room. He then pointed down the hall.

"Secure the house," he whispered to Hayward.

Hayward made his way down the hall. There were three rooms. He jumped in each doorway with his revolver pointed, knowing anything could be waiting for him each time. Becoming an art teacher suddenly seemed like a great idea. Hayward checked the last room. Empty.

"Clear!" Hayward yelled as he ran back to living the room.

Jeff was kneeling over a woman's body. She was lying face down in a pool of dried blood. Jeff had her hand in his as he checked for a pulse. Her pants were down around her ankles.

"She's gone, and has been for a while," Jeff said as he placed her hand back down.

Hayward looked at the body. It was something he knew he would never get used to. *What a waste*, he thought. *Sick bastard. This sick, sick fucker has to be stopped.*

Jeff stood up and said, "I'll call in the details here. You better go put up some police tape, secure the crime scene. The neighbours will be gathering out there as we speak."

Hayward was relieved. He didn't want to be in the room with this body anymore. He also didn't want to be around to see her face. He had a vision of the crime scene investigator rolling her over—only he didn't see the face of a woman, he saw Davey's face. He got to the squad car, opened the trunk, and grabbed the famous yellow police tape. He hadn't seen anyone when he opened the trunk, but when he closed it there were three people standing there, a man and two women.

"What's going on, officer?" one of the ladies asked.

"Can't really discuss that right now, ma'am," Hayward said.

"Well, we live in these houses. Are we in any danger?"

"No, ma'am. Just go home, and there will be an officer around shortly to fill you in on the situation."

"Has Janet been hurt?"

Hayward was looking for a fence post or tree to begin unravelling the tape when he stopped. Janet. Her name was Janet. *I'll bet that sick fucker didn't even know her name. Her name was Janet.* He snapped out of it.

"I can't discuss that right now, ma'am."

The lady began to cry into the man's shoulder. "He got her," she said. "He got Janet." She sobbed loudly. "You need to catch this guy!"

Hayward kept unravelling the tape. He'd never felt more like a cop than in that moment.

***

He was lying on the couch with a tub of ice cream sitting on his chest. He was sore this morning and had stayed in bed until Rita had left for work. Better to have no questions than any. He could feel the condensation forming on his chest as the bottom of the ice cream container started to warm. He wondered if the nosy fuckers had come across his latest work yet; at least one of them must have found one of those bitches by now. He often thought that the nosy fuckers would do a better job than the cops sometimes.

He lifted the remote control and flipped through the channels, stopping on the local morning news. They were talking about some traffic tie-ups and a baseball tournament scheduled for the upcoming weekend, but he knew what they'd be talking about later. Once the nosy fuckers made their rounds, it would be a very interesting day, because for the first time there were two—two separate ones. Double your pleasure.

My pleasure. He smirked. His work would be the top story everywhere. He hoped they came up with a better name. The Max Killer: that sucked so bad. It sounded like an episode of *Saved by the Bell*. He wanted to send them a communication, come up with his own name and tell them it, but he knew they always tested, analyzed, and traced that shit. It increased the odds of getting caught. Maybe that's why they gave him that stupid name; maybe they weren't that fuckin' dumb—but yes, they were. *I'm laying here eating ice cream after all these years. Yeah, they're fucking geniuses.*

They would probably think that it was the work of more than one person. The thought of this made him swell with pride. His work, at his age, considered to be done by two or more persons. Fantastic. Maybe he wasn't as close to retirement as he thought. He would have to check out CNN later in the day; this would be bigger than just the local news. His work would probably be nationwide news. He put the ice cream container on the floor. In doing so, he moved his legs and pain shot through his hip. Better just to stay here on the couch and lay low—*recuperate*—for a few days. With all of the upcoming exposure, the cops would be feverishly hunting. They'd have to call in the FBI. The local cops were dumb, but the FBI had a couple smart fuckers. They would be able to get answers quicker than the local Andy and Barney Fifes.

But he didn't care how smart they were; they weren't as smart as him. He was smart with "God fucked up" talent. Fuck them all. *Come fuckin' get me if you can.*

He had already decided that he would not do more of his work for a long time. He would let his latest masterpiece play out, let fear grip the community, let those donut fucks chase their tails. Watch them try to find some answers. Let's see them tell the public, with jelly donut filling hanging from their stupid mouths, that they are following up on many leads. He would wait. Wait until things got back to normal. Wait until people began to think he had left town or died. He would wait until that Mickey Fuckin' Mouse Club Task Force was disbanded for budget reasons and more pressing cases. He would satisfy his urges in the garage, with his collection. He could go out to the garage and see his "girls" whenever he wanted. He would wait until it was all just a bad memory to the city, a story of legend. Then and only then would he return with a wrath never seen before, his grand finale, his greatest show. He would plan it for years. He would give the cops, the public, and the world the one that would put him in the history books, alongside Bundy, Manson, Gacy—only he would be top billing, he would make sure of it.

Only the best for the motherfuckin' MVP.

***

Pete got out of the car and walked over to Hayward, who was guarding the perimeter of the house. Pete surveyed the taped-off area and the front of the house, took a deep breath, and put his hands on his hips. He looked at Hayward.

"How bad is it?"

"Looks like he raped her, then broke her neck."

"Fuck," Pete said and looked at the ground.

"Pete." Pete looked back at Hayward, who continued, "We got to get this sick fucker, man, we got to get—"

Pete interrupted. "Look, I know. This is my first day on the task force, and I can't think of a worse scenario to start it off."

"I'm sorry, Pete, I just . . . she . . ." He nodded at the house. Pete put his hand on Hayward's shoulder.

"I know, buddy, it doesn't get any easier. Never does."

"Pete, I know you've got the task force; but if you need any help following up leads, I'll do it when I'm off duty— anything I can do to help."

"Thanks, Hayward, I know I can count on you. Alright, I better get in there." Hayward nodded in acknowledgement, and Pete walked up the front walk and into the house.

In the living room, the medical examiner knelt over the body.

"Hey, George," Pete said.

George zipped cotton sample swabs into some bags. "Hello, Peter."

"What have we got here, George?"

"Female, thirty-five, killed by what looks like a broken neck rather than strangulation. Partially nude." George stopped there. Pete cocked his head, waiting for something else. Nothing came.

"Rape?" Pete asked.

"As far as I can tell without doing tests at the lab, no, I don't believe so. No signs of vaginal penetration, aggravated or otherwise."

Pete walked closer to the body.

"That's odd. Is this the same guy?"

"Don't know. I believe that's your job to find out."

Pete was more than a little annoyed with his response, but thought it better to keep his reaction subdued.

"Any panties?" he asked.

"Not that I can see," George replied, then zipped up his bag and stood up. "Well, Peter, she's all yours." George promptly walked out the front door without saying more.

"Thanks," Pete said to a closing door.

Kirk, the crime photographer, was taking pictures of the body. Pete walked into the kitchen and looked out into the backyard. Jeff was out there, watching the back perimeter. Pete had known Jeff from his days as a beat cop, and like everyone else, didn't care for him or his tactics. But he knew he was a good cop; he probably would have made detective if he wasn't such an asshole. Pete walked out the back door and turned toward the house.

"Jeff," Pete said, acknowledging the officer.

"Hey, Detective Lyons."

Pete looked at the broken window.

"Entry point?"

"Yeah, looks like it."

"George said our victim wasn't raped." Pete waited for Jeff's reaction. Jeff looked confused.

"Then why the fuck did he take her clothes off . . . to peek?" he said angrily.

"That we don't know."

Jeff looked at Pete then looked away a couple of times. Pete noticed, and figured Jeff would eventually tell him something. Pete knelt down and looked at the broken glass of the basement window and the remaining shards that were still in place.

"Maybe he was spent," Jeff said. Pete stood up and looked at him.

"What?"

"You know, spent, like he had already emptied the tank." Pete stared at him. "Do you know what I mean?" Jeff asked.

"I know what you mean," Pete replied, his mind racing. He was going over everything that he had seen or read to discount Jeff's theory.

"Makes sense," Pete said in a low voice.

"What's that?" Jeff asked.

"I hope you're wrong, but that fits. This could be the second victim of the evening. Panties were taken but no rape, no beating. Just a snapped neck, snapped in frustration." Pete pulled out his cell phone to call the task force leader.

***

Beth had just finished putting away a load of laundry when she heard a loud revving engine. She looked out her bedroom window and saw a Maserati sports car pull into her driveway. She could tell Daniel's brother Rich was driving.

Not today, she thought. She headed downstairs and opened the front door. Rich was walking up the front step.

"Hi, Beth," Rich said, his eyes shaded by dark sunglasses.

"Daniel's not feeling well. He'll talk to you tomorrow," Beth said, knowing that wouldn't make him go away.

"Come on now, Beth, I need to speak with my brother."

Beth could feel Daniel standing behind her, but she said it anyway. "Yeah, he said he didn't want to speak to you." Daniel moved forward and Beth retreated into the house.

"Don't be like that, Beth," Rich said in a mock begging voice. "Come on now, we're family."

"Knock it off," Daniel said as he went outside and closed the door.

Beth went into the living room and stood by the opened window where she could eavesdrop on their conversation.

"What's up, Rich?"

"Hey, just wondering what's up with you, taking today off. What's up with that?

"I've got some family things to deal with today."

"Hey," Rich said, taking off his sunglasses, "I'm family. Can I help?"

Beth squeezed the drapes so hard she thought she would leave a bloodstain. Daniel became agitated.

"What did you come here for? Just come out with it."

"Look, the deal with the row houses, it's running into some problems. The mayor is starting to get some political backlash. We knew that would happen, but now there's a small group of tree huggers protesting and they're starting to gain momentum. The mayor's not happy—the money's not as important to him as it is to us. His main concern is protecting his public image."

"He's backing out?" Daniel sounded surprised.

"No, no, not yet."

"We need this deal, Rich. Without it the company is going under."

"Hold up for a minute now. He is asking us to ensure that, if this thing turns into a 'seniors out on the street' thing, none of it sticks to him."

"So, if that happens he wants our company to take the blame?"

"Look at it this way," said Rich, "we get the deal, the money, and a little bit of negative press."

"The mayor also gets his money, though," Daniel said.

"Yes, but he then owes us," Rich said, pointing a finger in the air.

"Owes us what?"

"The mayor said, and I quote, 'If we can swing it this way, he'll look after us.' That means favours, Daniel. We'll be able to swing a lot bigger money deals with the mayor's help. Where we don't have to deal with a political circus surrounding them. I'm talkin' us getting government bids—what do ya say? Do I tell him we've got a deal?"

"I really don't think I have a choice. We need this deal to survive," Daniel said apprehensively.

"Great!" Rich said, putting his sunglasses back on. "I'll inform the mayor of the good news."

Beth hurried toward the kitchen. She opened a cupboard, took out some spices, and looked at them. She heard Daniel come in and close the door and waited for him to enter the kitchen.

"What was that all about?" she asked.

"Just business. It looks like one of the deals I was working on is going through."

"What kind of deal?"

"Hey, it's my day off, I don't want to talk about work," Daniel said, smiling.

"Fine. I'm going to do some yard work, okay?"

"Yeah, sweetheart, you do whatever you want. I'll watch the boy."

Beth headed for the door.

"Wait," Daniel said.

Beth turned.

"Where's Phillip?"

"In the den watching cartoons," Beth said with disdain before going out the back door.

***

Hayward stood at his post and watched as each detective from the task force arrived and went into the house. The forensic team had finished in the house and was now combing the yard for evidence. Pete had explained Jeff's theory to Hayward. The task force also thought it was plausible and had put out a press release asking the public to report anyone who hadn't shown up for work and hadn't called in sick. Detectives had begun to canvass the neighbourhood.

Hayward watched as a security company car drove up to the house. The car had an emblem on the side that read "Knightright Security." Two men in uniforms got out, one tall and lanky and the other short and stalky.

After greeting the guards, Pete approached Hayward.

"Hey, Hayward," he said. "You and Jeff can get on with your beat now. The security company will take over the perimeter." The security company would be there in shifts for the next twenty-four hours until the police released the house back to the next of kin.

"Thanks for your help," Pete said.

"Yeah, sure, no problem. And Pete—remember what I said if you need help with anything." They shook hands and gave each other a half hug.

"Always buddy, always. I'll be in touch."

"Okay, Pete."

Jeff was walking toward the squad car. He had seen the half hug.

"Holy shit, Hayward, have you gone gay on me? Shit, I could see it comin' but thought it would take a little longer."

Hayward began walking over to the car. He wanted to say something back, but this was a crime scene and there was a murdered woman inside, so he just quietly got into the passenger seat. Jeff jumped in the driver's seat.

"You trying to blow your way to detective?"

"Yeah, something like that," Hayward responded, not wanting to play Jeff's game. Jeff pulled the squad car away from the house.

"So you really think that he already got someone else?" Hayward asked.

"I have no idea. Just seems odd that this one wasn't raped but her panties were gone. Doesn't make sense for him to go out and prowl and go after her with an empty tank, you know. He's only heading out that night for one reason. He was probably finished and on his way home, sees her doing a workout in the window and boom, he can't resist, he literally can't help himself." Jeff turned the car onto the expressway.

"That makes total sense," Hayward said.

"Pete thought so too," Jeff said confidently.

"Man, how come you never went for detective?"

"Not for me man, got to kiss too much ass, you know, like your buddy Pete there." Hayward was about to defend Pete, but he realized he didn't know much about becoming a detective and what went on behind the scenes.

"If that theory is true, he was more than likely walking by the house," Hayward said.

"And . . ."

Hayward continued, "Probably lives close to the area."

"Holy shit!" Jeff said sarcastically. "You're the goddam detective."

"Shut the fuck up. I just can't stop thinking about this sick fuck. We need to get him off the streets."

"Well, young grasshopper, that's not your job, that's the Johnny Lick Hole Detective's job. Your job is beat cop, which is simply to make sure, on a daily basis, that these useless pieces of shit in our fair city don't get to the point where they kill each other."

Jeff took the squad car off the expressway and into a suburb. Hayward knew this was Jeff's way of throwing his line in the water: trying to get Hayward to bite so they could argue. This prime argument territory was Jeff's magical fucking fun land. Hayward said nothing, so Jeff continued.

"And that's what we are going to do now, our beat cop job. We are going to follow up on the domestic disturbance from yesterday, and you can go to the door and play detective and see how our old-ass couple is doing."

"The couple from yesterday?" Hayward asked, surprised.

"Yeah, remember that memo we got, how we need to follow up on domestic cases? That our attention to the seriousness of these acts can serve as a deterrent for future incidents? In other words, show these wife-beaters that the cops have an eye on them."

Hayward realized they would be travelling right past Beth's house. He remembered reading the memo, but they hadn't experienced a situation yet that had required a follow-up, so he'd forgotten about it. He began to feel dizzy as they drove up Beth's street and his heart started to flutter. *Just go do your job*, he told himself.

Jeff brought the car to a stop just in front of the couples' home. Hayward looked at Beth's house and there she was, in the front yard clipping a shrub with some large shears.

"Well," Jeff said, "go check it out, Detective . . ." he rolled his tongue, "Lick Hole."

"Look, could you just take care of this one? I need to speak to that woman over there."

Jeff looked over at Beth and asked, "The MILF from yesterday? What you got goin' on there, homey?"

"Nothing, absolutely nothing. I just want her to take extra precautions because of this sicko running around."

"Alright." Jeff snickered. "But you're fuckin' buyin' me lunch."

"Sure, whatever."

"And don't do something stupid like tell her about the crime scene."

Hayward was getting out of the car before Jeff could change his mind or come up with anymore demands.

"Wouldn't think of it," he said, closing the door. *Glutton for punishment, aren't you? Just serving and protecting.*

Beth watched as Hayward crossed the street. He waved.

"Hey there, Beth."

"Hello, Hayward," she said, looking up at him from beneath a wide-brimmed gardener's hat. "You had better not keep showing up here, or you're going to bring the property values down." Then she quickly added, "Just kidding." Hayward laughed.

"That is true, but we're just following up on the couple over there."

"Delores and Al. Yeah, this neighbourhood has been real quiet the whole time I've been out in the yard."

"That's not why I'm here. Well, it is why we're here, but there is something else."

Beth was smiling at him.

"What's that, Hayward?"

"You know how we've had a few unsolved rapes and murders over the past few years?"

"Yes, of course, how could I not know that?"

"Well, there was a murder last night, about five miles from here, and we think it's the same guy."

"Oh no," Beth said with a note of compassion but more notes of worry in her voice.

"I just thought I would let you know—you know, since we were just here, in the neighbourhood, and you were just here." Hayward was in full-babble mode. "And you know, I've known you for a while."

"Thank you. Thanks for letting me know. I'll make sure I'm extra careful."

"Okay, great. Well, that's about it, I better get back, to . . ." Losing his words, he pointed at the car.

"Okay," Beth said, giggling. Hayward began to shuffle backward.

"Hayward," Beth said. Hayward, who was already turning around, turned back awkwardly. "Would you like to go for coffee some time? Maybe catch up a bit?"

"Sure, yeah sure, that'd be great. You've got my card, right?"

"Yes, yes I do."

"Okay, yeah, great." Hayward turned back around.

"Hayward," Beth said again.

He turned to face her again.

"Thanks," Beth said, still smiling.

"Yeah sure, no problem." Hayward smiled back.

Hayward headed back toward the car. Jeff was leaning on the roof of the driver's side with his head leaning in his hands.

"Ahh, my hero, you saved the MILF."

Hayward knew he had said it loud enough that Beth could hear.

"Would you just get in the car and shut the fuck up?" he said to Jeff.

Hayward opened the door and got in. Jeff jumped in, put the car in gear, and pulled away.

"What's the deal with her, anyway?" Jeff asked.

"I knew her when I was a kid."

"Oh, now I get it."

"Get what?"

"The one that got away."

Hayward stared ahead. *Can't get away if you've never had it,* he thought.

***

Beth, finished with her gardening, came in the front door. Daniel was standing in the kitchen doorway, arms folded, leaning on the door casing.

"Daniel, you scared me."

"What was that police officer doing here?"

"Saying hi," Beth responded as she took off her gloves.

"Police don't just drop by to say hi. What did he want? What was he asking you?" Daniel persisted.

"Calm down, Daniel." She took her boots off and walked past him into the kitchen.

"I'll calm down when you start answering some of my goddamn questions!" he yelled. Beth wheeled around.

"It was Hayward!" she yelled back. "Hayward, saying hi."

"Hayward," Daniel said. He looked stunned. "Hayward Barry?"

"Yes, he's a policeman, here in Sifton."

"I thought he was an artist somewhere."

"Well, he's not."

"So he just comes here after all these years to say hi?"

"No, he and his partner were responding to a call from Delores across the street. Remember yesterday? I told you she finally called the cops on the pig. Anyway, Hayward saw Phillip and I in the driveway, when I was unpacking groceries. He came over and said hi."

"So he comes back again today to say hi?"

"No," Beth said calmly. "They were doing a follow-up on yesterday's incident, and I was out in the yard, so he let me know that they had found another woman murdered about five miles from here."

"And he told you because you're working on the case?" Daniel said sarcastically.

"He just saw me in the yard and mentioned it so I would take extra caution for my own safety. You can appreciate that, can't you? My safety?"

"Of course, I care about your safety. You're my wife. I just don't know why he cares so much."

"What are you saying, Daniel?"

"I'm saying, the artsy-fartsy-turned-cop probably still has the hots for you."

"Are you serious? Are we really having this conversation? After all these years?" Beth asked. The conversation was exasperating.

"Well, after all these years, he is in our front yard," Daniel fired back.

"I told you why he was here. It was a coincidence."

"Was it?" Daniel said accusingly.

"What do you think? We've been secretly corresponding since fifth grade, and only now, after you and I are married and have a child, we decide to do something about it?"

"No."

"Well then, would you just drop it?"

"Fine, alright, whatever." Daniel threw up his hands and left the kitchen.

Beth put the kettle on to make herself some tea. Coincidence. She flipped the word over in her head like a burger. Was it coincidence, or something else? Like fate. Maybe going for a coffee with Hayward wasn't such a good idea. If she did, she couldn't tell Daniel about it. She would have to think about it, and there were so many things to consider. It was probably best if she didn't have coffee with him; that would be the safest route.

Keep everyone happy . . . except you.

She thought again how cute he looked in his police uniform. What would a coffee hurt?

Chapter 16

A Crime of Hatred

Pete was in his office going over the latest murder and comparing it to others. If the theory—or even a portion of it—was true, the killer lived in the city. He didn't travel in and out, but lived here and didn't have any record of a fingerprint or a blood sample on file. The killer hadn't been picked up for anything illegal in the past seventeen-plus years, or as long as the city had been keeping a database. Pete began to look back at the work he was doing before he had gotten the murder call. He looked at the map he had been working on, at Sifton and the surrounding towns. He typed in the name "Arcana" to search for possible unsolved murders from seventeen to twenty years ago. Nothing. He looked at the map, and typed in the name "Brighton." Nothing. He typed in the names "Innisville," "Tomson," "Long Branch," "Broad Cove," and "Spaniard's Pass." Nothing.

"Uniontown" was a hit, though, with one unsolved murder, eighteen years previous. An elderly woman had been beaten to death, and her valuables were stolen. The prime suspect, Clayton Graves, disappeared after the incident and was never seen again. Pete brought up his picture and printed it off. A start. He kept typing towns until he had compiled a list with pictures of seven men wanted for unsolved murders in towns within a five-hundred-mile radius. One more would give him eight possibilities.

He typed in the town of "Chapelton" and a hit came up: a man named Tommy Kelch, wanted in connection with the death of a woman and her elderly neighbours. Pete's eyes widened when he saw the date: October 8th, 1987. The day Davey died.

Pete brought up Kelch's picture. He thought of Davey falling. An image he'd been able to put out of his head for the past ten years seemed to have been resurrected at the sight of the man in the photo. Pete printed the picture and added it to the rest. He would distribute them around town and post them on bulletin boards. He spaced the pictures so they all fit on one page, then added a caption that read, "If you know any of these men, please call 555-7272 immediately."

He got up from his desk and headed for the task force leader's office, looking at the men on the paper. He tried to remember if he had seen any of them living in Sifton. As he looked at each one without any recognition, he got an uneasy feeling that he was on the wrong track. He pushed it away. He was new, he was the fresh pair of eyes, he had to do things that nobody had done yet. He knocked on the door of the task force leader.

"Come in."

Pete entered the office .

"Hello, Captain," he said.

"Hey, Pete, I just got back from our crime scene. What did you think over there?" the Captain asked.

"Well, sir, I think the theory of a previous victim is the one that the evidence leads me to believe. We have to investigate it thoroughly."

"We won't know much until we find a previous victim," the Captain said.

"Sir, I have something to show you." Pete placed the sheet in front of Captain Thomas. "These men are all wanted for murder in towns within a five-hundred-mile radius of Sifton. These murders occurred between seventeen and twenty years ago. I have a hunch that the killer moved here somewhere in that time frame, before the first homicides were reported. This would assume that one of these men killed in one of these towns, then fled and landed in ours, and has been able to elude capture. The killer has stayed and killed because he hasn't had a reason to run."

"That's a pretty far-fetched, astronomical-odds hunch you have there, Pete, but good work. It's an angle we haven't explored. Get those signs up around the city. If somebody recognizes one of these dirt bags, well, even if we don't have our city's killer, hey, we'll have somebody else's."

"Yes, sir, I'll start on that right now."

The Captain's phone rang. He held up one finger to get Pete to wait as he answered it.

"Hello. Okay. Where? I'll be there in twenty minutes." He hung up the phone.

"Looks like we have a previous victim. Young lady lived alone, didn't show up for her late-afternoon shift at the department store, a couple of officers went over to her apartment and found her. We've got to get down there."

Pete felt nauseous. Being right had never felt so shitty.

***

He was lying on the couch, watching *Oprah*, as he did every day when Rita came through the door. How could Oprah have so many shows dedicated to moms and wives when she was neither? And he found it odd that her audience was mostly white women. Yet her show kept on truckin', and her audiences kept cheering, and cheering loudly.

"How's burgers for supper?" Rita asked.

"Great," he said as he sat up. "Oprah's like a chameleon." Rita didn't respond to that.

"Did you hear that they found a murdered woman just, like, a mile from here?" she asked. He had been watching the coverage throughout the day since the story broke.

"I heard something about a murdered woman, but I didn't realize that it was close to here."

"Yeah, too close for me, really gives me the creeps. I think maybe we should get stronger deadbolts."

Don't lose fifty pounds and work out in the window, and you'll be fine, he mused, then said, "I wouldn't worry about it."

She took the frying pan out from underneath the oven and placed it on the stove.

"Don't worry about a murderer?" she questioned.

"What I mean is," he cocked his head back and smiled at her, "I'll protect you."

"That's great, but you aren't here all the time. This lady was murdered last night, and you were out, so I think we should consider the deadbolts."

"Consider them? You want them, we'll get them."

"Well," she said, "I guess that settles that. I'll talk to the other girls at work tomorrow and see if there's a good affordable locksmith they could recommend."

"Locksmith. You don't have to worry about a locksmith. I'll get some deadbolts tomorrow at the hardware store, and I'll install them."

"You know how to install locks?" she asked.

He had been smashing them his whole life. It would be fun to try to install one.

"Of course I know how. In the military we were trained to infiltrate enemy buildings, and part of that was dismantling deadbolts."

"That's not installing."

"No," he said, laughing. "I'll just do it backwards."

Rita chuckled and placed the burger patties in the frying pan.

"You sure you don't want me to call a locksmith?"

He persisted. "Let me try to do it first. If I have trouble, then you can call a locksmith to install the locks I buy."

"Fair enough. They haven't released the name of the murder victim, but the girls at work were saying it was Janet Rigby."

"Really. How was she killed?"

"Oh, the girls didn't know that, just that it was Janet's house that was taped off as a crime scene."

"That's so sad. Was she married?"

"No, she was divorced, and never had any kids."

No wonder she was divorced; she wouldn't put out.

"I just wish they would catch this guy," she sighed. "He scares the bejesus out of me, out of everyone."

"Yeah, I can see that. I'm sure the police are doing everything they can."

Those stupid, jelly-lipped, coffee-stained, stupid fucks. I know I said "stupid" twice.

"It has been happening so long, that the girls at work are saying the police have kind of accepted it," she continued.

"Accepted it?"

"Yes, just have realized they can't catch him, so they are just waiting until he makes a mistake."

"I really don't think that's the case," he replied.

"Well, how else you explain not being able to catch someone for seventeen years?" She turned back towards the burgers. Seventeen years was how long he had been with Rita. Seventeen years ago he arrived in town. Seventeen years ago the killings began. Rita had never given him any indication that she suspected him, but she knew the timeline. It was time to put out any kind of flame. He walked over and put his arms around her as she stood in front of the stove.

"I'll protect you from murderers and monsters and vampires and any other fucking thing that tries to take you away from me."

He kissed her neck. She tilted her head back. He began to undo the front of her belt.

"The burgers," she said.

He reached over, turned off the burner, and took her in the kitchen.

***

Jeff sat waiting as Hayward walked across the food court with two baskets of tacos.

"Hurry up, hurry up, I'm fuckin' starving. Just 'cause you're sore about buying me lunch, doesn't mean you have to fuckin' starve me."

"That's the most unusual thank-you I've ever heard."

"You want a fuckin' thank-you? You're lucky I didn't shoot you."

"You're welcome," Hayward said sarcastically.

"Did you hear that radio call?" Jeff asked.

"Which one?"

"The 11-98D call."

"I think so, but what does it have to do with us?"

"11-98D is a detective's meeting at the station. Why would they be called for a meeting when they were already all together once today?" Jeff asked. Hayward thought for a few seconds.

"The first victim!" he said.

"You might as well submit your application for detective right now, 'cause it's only a matter of time, my friend," Jeff said before beginning to shovel a taco into his mouth.

Another victim. Before it had just been a theory. It hit him as hard as the last one. Such a senseless waste. How could a human do that to another?

"We need to get this guy," Hayward said as he pushed his basket of tacos away. He'd lost his appetite.

"You might as well head over to that meeting, then," Jeff said.

He was getting tired of Jeff. It had been a horrible day, two innocent women found murdered. Hayward didn't know if he would be able to handle this job for a few years—maybe not even the rest of the week. He was losing his faith in the human spirit, which he had enjoyed seeing during his days in San Francisco. Here in Sifton, he was on a collision course with evil every time he went to work.

He had to focus on the positives. Keep his head in the game. He had to think good thoughts. Beth. She had said she would call him for coffee. What about the pact? He was supposed to try and find someone else. Ask someone out on a date today. Take the initial step that leads to settling down and raising a family. He looked around the food court and saw a Spanish women yelling at her two children, a couple of young girls laughing, and a few other ladies in business suits eating Subway sandwiches. It didn't matter. He wasn't going to ask anybody here out on a date. Might as well stop looking.

Jeff had finished his taco basket and was eyeing Hayward's.

Why did Beth want to have coffee with him after all these years?

"Are you gonna eat that?" Jeff asked. Hayward pushed the basket at him without saying a word. "Pussy," Jeff said and began to throw Hayward's tacos into his gob.

"To catch up": that's what she had said, wasn't it? Shouldn't read any more into it. Beth was a married woman with a child. *She is just going for coffee and to chat, talk about old times, that's all. You need to move on, find someone who's looking for a lot more than coffee. That's where you need to focus.*

Hayward glanced over at the women in the business suits again. One of them was pretty, and she wasn't wearing a wedding ring. *Just go over there and ask her to go for a coffee; it's that simple. Simple.* He almost laughed out loud.

"What are you staring at?" Jeff asked, looking over in the direction of the women.

"Nothing, just looking."

"Well, aren't you hornier than a dog with two peckers today?"

Hayward ignored the comment. He couldn't ask anyone out with this asshole around. There was no telling what Jeff might do. *That's an excuse*, he told himself. *Just go over there and ask her out, never mind him. Are you going to live alone the rest of your life 'cause your partner's an asshole? Come on.*

Their radios babbled, "Possible 966 in progress, Regans Plaza, 874 Fuller Street." 966, a drug deal.

Hayward grabbed his mic and said, "Unit Twelve, responding." Jeff looked at him.

"What the fuck did you do that for? We're having lunch."

Hayward got up. "Let's go," he said. Jeff pushed back his basket of tacos.

"You owe me another lunch. This one doesn't count," he proclaimed.

"Listen," Hayward said, "behind Regans Plaza is the back of this mall. We can get out the receiving doors to the back. Come on, I know the way."

Hayward began to jog and Jeff followed. Hayward had worked part-time at the department store in the mall during high school, collecting shopping carts and stocking shelves at Christmas. He jogged past the washrooms and down the long corridor. It was the same as he remembered it. He had dated a girl who had also worked at the mall. She had loved his artwork but had such a negative view of the world, like the government was conducting experiments and there were conspiracies behind everything. He came to the end of the hall and busted through the door. The sun was blinding. He looked to the right and saw a group of three men and started running toward them. One of them looked up and pointed at him.

"Freeze, police!" Hayward shouted. The men jostled with another and then they all took off running. One went east and two started running away from Hayward to the north. Hayward pointed to the guy going east.

"Take him, Jeff." Hayward glanced that way as he passed. The man who had headed east had fallen. He continued chasing the other two. *Let's see if I can get one of these bad boys.*

The men up ahead came to a fence. They both climbed up and hurled themselves over. Hayward was starting to get winded but he jumped at the fence, got halfway up, and hauled himself up the rest of the way. The two men ran along the back of a building, and it looked like one was using a cell phone. Hayward jumped off the other side of the fence and landed on the ground. His ankle wobbled but didn't go over. He saw the men reach the end of the building, and a car came screeching out from the side. Hayward drew his weapon and ran along the back of the building. The men jumped in the car, a '90s Camaro. The car reversed and disappeared toward the front of the building with the sound of squealing tires. He didn't get the licence plate because he'd only seen the car from the side. Hayward reached the end of the building. The car and the two men were gone. Gasping for breath, he grabbed his shoulder mic and called in the description of the car. He took a couple more deep breaths and then started back to find his partner.

***

"Goodnight, Phillip," Beth said as she kissed him on the forehead then walked to the door.

"Mommy."

Beth turned in the doorway.

"Do you think Daddy had fun today?"

"I'm sure he did, Phillip. Why do you ask, sweetie?"

"If Daddy had fun with me today, then maybe he might spend more days with me."

"Oh, sweetie," Beth said as she fought back tears. "Daddy has a lot of work to do with his business, but I'm sure it's only temporary. He'll have more time home soon."

"I hope so," Phillip said.

"Go to sleep now, son," she said, closing the door behind her.

Beth stood on the other side of the door for a few minutes as tears spilled down her face. She sniffled, wiped her nose with her sleeve, glanced back at the door, and composed herself before heading down the stairs. She found Daniel in the den on the computer.

"He's all set?" Daniel asked.

"Yes," she said as she sat on the couch. Daniel turned to her.

"I tucked him in, but he said he wouldn't be able to sleep unless Mommy tucked him in too."

Beth let out a laugh, but the tears started flowing again.

"What is it, Beth?" Daniel, still seated in the computer chair, asked.

"He was just asking if you had fun with him today."

"Why would he ask that?" Daniel asked, surprised.

"Because—" Beth said, sobbing, "because, he thinks that if you had fun with him today, that you'll spend more time with him."

"Ahhh. Well, like I said, Beth, I'm going do what I can at work to free up more time. We just have to get a couple of deals to go through and the company will be on solid footing."

Beth grabbed a tissue from the end table. "Well, you know how I feel, and now you know how your son feels," she said.

"And I told you how I feel—we need this company." Daniel got up from the chair. "Now listen, I'm heading down to work for a few hours." Beth looked at him in disbelief. "I spent the day with Phillip, and you got to do what you wanted," he continued.

"Whatever," she said.

"Do you think I want to go down there?"

"Whatever," she said again as she picked up the remote control and turned on the TV.

"I meant what I said, Beth."

She ignored him and stared at the television. Daniel didn't say anything else, just got his jacket from the front door closet and left the house. Beth listened as his car pulled out of the driveway. She went to the computer and typed in a search for row house opposition.

A citizens' group lobbying to keep the row houses—or build the seniors new and affordable housing—came up. There was a memo detailing why the group was started. The city had approved a project for a new high-rise condo building, built by Oak Tree Construction, at the location where the row houses stood. The houses had been built by war veterans, who erected them after WWII. When the soldiers returned home, the city was in a real estate crunch with all the new and growing families. They sold the lots to the soldiers in half portions. Now the city had given them next to nothing for the appraised value of the old conjoined homes, and the veterans couldn't afford to move anywhere else based on their pensions. The group was lobbying the mayor to do something about it.

Daniel's company, throwing vets out into the street. His father, the founder of the company, would be rolling over in his grave right now. How could he do this? It was morally wrong. The company couldn't be that important, but it seemed like it was. She would have a talk with him about this. Daniel had told Beth not to inquire about the business, and now she knew why. It was because of the type of businessman he was; he didn't want her to see that side of him, the side that threw veterans out into the street. What drove him? He had said it was his father, but his father would never approve of this. The money? They weren't rich, they were well off, and she was sure with his experience and skills that he could probably get the same money and work a lot less if he worked for somebody else. What was it, then? Was it the power? Was it the power of owning a company that could push people around? Was that why he was so scared of his brother ruining the company—because he *was* the company? The power and control were a part of his personality. Beth had always felt that she didn't agree with Daniel's opinion on aspects of her life. He was like a dog with a bone until he got his way. He was a good man, protector, provider, father. Was he, though? She was starting to doubt all of those things.

***

Hayward arrived back at the parking lot. His leg muscles were still on fire, and he figured he wouldn't be able to walk tomorrow morning. He had regained his breath on the way back, but the collar and underarms of his uniform were completely covered in sweat. *Man, I gotta pick up some beer on the way home, 'cause I'm really gonna need a cold one tonight*, he thought.

He had heard on the radio that Jeff had made the apprehension. When he arrived at the car, Jeff was in the driver seat and the perp was in the back on Jeff's side. He opened the passenger door and got in.

"Hay . . . Hay . . . Hayward," a stuttering voice called from the back of the squad car.

Hayward turned around. "Joe?"

The man in the back was very thin, with red scabs on his face and clothes that looked like they used to fit him last year, but now just hung there. He had a scraggly beard and his hair was a mass of long tangles, like a Rasta hairdo after a hurricane. Joe leaned forward.

"Oh," Jeff said, "I see you already know Mr. Crackhead."

"What the hell, Joe? What were you doing with those guys?"

Hayward hadn't seen Joe in the last couple of months, and it looked like his old friend had aged another five years—five hard years. Joe had developed speech problems from a mini stroke caused by an overdose years ago.

"I . . . I . . . was just . . . I just needed a little hit, you know. I've been cuttin' back though, I've been cuttin' back though, Hay," Joe explained.

"Cutting back?" Jeff exclaimed as he pulled up the evidence bag from below his seat. It was a large bag filled with crack cocaine.

"Holy fuck, Joe, you had this?" Hayward practically yelled at him.

"It's . . . It's . . . It's not mine. That . . . that . . . that guy, he . . . he . . . he jammed it in my jacket when they saw you coming."

"That's what you all say, ya fuckin' scumbag," yelled Jeff.

"Hey," Hayward said, "just let me talk to him, okay?"

Jeff raised his hands as if to say, *Fine, go right a-fuckin'-head.*

"Why did you keep it when he gave it to you, Joe?"

"C . . . c . . . 'cause I never had that much before. I could sell it, maybe."

"Oh fuck, Joe," Hayward said, his head in his hands.

"Of course you would sell it," Jeff said. "You fuckin' try to smoke a hundredth of that bag, you'd be dead in hours." Hayward grabbed Jeff by the arm.

"I need to talk to you outside," he said.

"Alright." Jeff yanked his arm away and got out of the car. Hayward got out of the car and walked over to Jeff's side.

"Look, I know this guy. He's not a dealer."

"He just told us he was gonna sell that shit," Jeff fired back.

"Yes, he did, but he's not a regular dealer, just a homeless addict who saw an opportunity to better his situation."

Jeff looked confused. "You sound like one of those fuckin' intervention doctors on TV."

"You gotta understand, I grew up with this guy. One of our friends died in front of us, he never got over it."

"Are you fuckin' serious? You better not be shitting me."

"No, I swear," Hayward said. "That's the truth. Do you think I would be this upset if the guy didn't mean a lot to me?"

"That's fucked, dude. How old were you when this happened?" Jeff asked.

"We were eleven."

"And he started using drugs then?"

"No, no," Hayward explained. "He was just a lot more sensitive than us, and had a harder time getting over it. In junior high he began experimenting, and by the time he finished high school he was a full addict. He had a stroke a couple of years back, and part of his brain never recovered. That's why he seems a bit touched and talks like that."

"That's fucked," Jeff said again.

"Do you think we could cut this guy a break?"

"What?" Jeff said. "What are you talking about?"

Hayward knew what he was doing was wrong—jeopardizing his job, and asking Jeff to jeopardize his—but he had to try. Joe was facing the possibility of life in prison based on the amount of drugs he had in his possession. It automatically carried the charge of intent to distribute. That would put him with all the worst criminals. Given his condition, and the length of the sentence, Joe would die in jail. He would never get the chance to be rehabilitated. Jeff stared at him in silence.

"Just look the other way, man. I'll take the blame," Hayward begged. Jeff stared straight into Hayward's eyes.

"Officer Barry, the suspect in the back seat was arrested with the street value of about $500,000 worth of crack cocaine, which means intent to distribute, which he already admitted he would do. And by the look of him, he probably would have sold it to any pregnant woman, school kid, any-fuckin'-body who gave him some money. He would have enabled them to leave their lives and start down the road that he took to become this useless maggot of society." Hayward grabbed Jeff by the front of his uniform, and Jeff grabbed Hayward's.

"Think about what you're fucking doing here, Hayward," Jeff continued. "Don't throw your shit away because he cares nothing for his own life."

Hayward let go of Jeff, and Jeff let go of him. Hayward looked up at the sky. "Fuck, fuck, fuck," he yelled. What he had asked Jeff to do was insane, and they would probably both go down for it. The arrest had been made, the suspect was in custody, Joe's name had been called in, and charges against him were pending. "You're right, Jeff, I'm sorry. I just—"

Jeff cut him off. "Fuckin' right you're sorry, and the next time you put your fuckin' hands on me like that you better plan to do something, 'cause I'm gonna beat the fuck outta you. Now get in the fuckin' car so I can lock this guy up and go the fuck home."

Hayward looked up at the sky again. "Fuck!" he yelled.

Jeff opened the car door. "No, fuck *you*, now get in."

Jeff and Hayward climbed in the car, both slamming their doors.

***

Pete looked at the lady lying facedown on the floor, naked below the waist. Her head was lying in a giant pool of her own blood. The pool was about three feet in diameter, and a portion ran in a stream toward the kitchen. Pete had to keep swallowing to maintain his stomach contents. *Can't let your emotions get in the way of your focus,* he reminded himself.

He examined the stream of blood that snaked toward the kitchen like a boney outstretched arm. He bet she hadn't even known there was a slight tilt in her living room floor that sloped to the kitchen. She would never know. A shudder went up his back. Maybe she knew. Maybe she spilled something once, and it had made that exact path. He had to focus.

"This one is really violent, Captain. Looks like he knew her, a crime of hatred," Pete said. The Captain stared at the body, his fingers under his chin, as the forensics team buzzed around, gathering their evidence and taking pictures. Pete waited for a response from the Captain, but none came. Pete studied the body. He had to evaluate all angles, all possible theories, and eliminate them based on the evidence. There was blood splatter on the legs of the coffee table, which was on the opposite side of the blood stream flow. Due to the missing panties, they were likely looking for the same guy. The coroner called for the Captain to come over to look at her face—she had some skin clenched in her teeth. Pete followed the Captain and they both looked as the coroner shone his small flashlight into her mouth. She had bitten him, and that changed things. The Captain squinted, his fingers still underneath his chin.

"She enraged him with the biting," Pete said. "That's why he became so violent. She fought back hard enough to hurt him. This is the same as the Heather Wells case from back in '91. She had been violently beaten with a broom handle, and the evidence showed she had first tried to use it for protection."

"That's right, Detective. We know from his profile that our perp has a short fuse when it comes to anger, and when the fuse is lit, it turns to blind rage," said the Captain.

Captain Thomas walked into the kitchen, Pete trailing him. They looked at the chicken on the stove.

"Not cooked yet," the Captain said.

"He shut off the burner, Captain," Pete responded.

"Probably when he was done. He wants us to find the bodies. He doesn't want the house to burn down and ruin his artwork before it can be examined. He enjoys it, thinks we're all so stupid. Pete, I am going to finish up here with the forensic team. Why don't you head back to the office and continue working that angle you showed me this morning?"

"Okay, Captain. You sure you don't want me to follow up anything with this case?"

"No, I'll have the other detectives continue with this one. Do you have a hunch about the poster? Do you think it could get us some leads?"

The poster. The date of one of the murders was the same day as Davey's death.

"I do, Captain."

"Well, go with it. I want you to call the TV station and make sure those pictures are on the next broadcast of the local news."

"Will do, Captain."

Pete walked toward the door, nodding at a few members of the forensic team; although they were so busy that only one noticed him. He left the house relieved he didn't have to look at that poor lady anymore.

The Captain had given him some positive feedback on his work. He hoped his gut feeling led the investigation somewhere. Pete climbed into his car and pulled away from the house. Follow your gut, they said. The date of Davey's death had never left his gut.

Chapter 17

Here We Go

Rita picked up the empty supper dishes from the table and walked over to the kitchen. "Do you want anything else?" she asked.

"No, that was great," the man said as he got up from the table, walked over, and plopped down on the couch.

"Could you put on the news? I want to see if they've released anymore details."

"Sure," he said, excited to see how the Keystone Fucks were gonna explain themselves again, because all they were doing was chasing their own tails.

He switched to the local news channel and watched a talking dog sell dog food. Rita filled the sink with soapy water. He laughed at the talking dog asking for the particular food. He called to Rita.

"If he could talk, I bet when those cameras stop rolling, he says, 'Hey, would one of you fuckers get me a goddamn steak?'"

Rita smiled but didn't laugh.

Wow, what's wrong with her? he wondered. *That was funny as hell.*

The local news came back on.

"If you are just joining us, we regret to report that a second woman has been found murdered in the city's north end."

Rita let out a sigh. He turned up the volume.

Quiet, bitch. I'm the star of the show.

"We know the victim lived on Douglas Street, but her name has not been released. The community is on high alert tonight with a possible serial killer walking our streets. Police have said that they haven't determined yet if the killings are related.

"The police have said that the latest victim put up a fight and the person responsible should have some visible injuries on his hands or arms."

Holy shit! They really have figured out something. He looked at his hands. She had only gotten him on the right arm, but he checked anyway.

"Oh, my God," Rita said, on the verge of tears.

He pulled down his right sleeve. "Relax, relax," he cooed.

"How am I supposed to relax when there is a killer running around?"

"Because," he got up from the couch and walked over to her, "like I said, I'm gonna protect you."

"Are you gonna protect my friends, the girls from work? What if it's more than one person? Are you going to protect me then?"

He began to get angry. *If you made it this long, bitch, you're pretty much home free. Don't fuck that up. Time to reel this bitch back in.*

"We'll get some locks tomorrow, and an alarm system if you want," he suggested. "I'll bring my gun in from the garage."

"You have a gun in the garage?" she asked.

"Well, yeah, I was in the military."

"That was a long time ago. Why do you have one now?"

"Because they train us to always be prepared. If I need a gun I have one, and I'm trained to use it."

"How come you never told me about it before?"

"Because I thought you might freak out, like you are now. Won't you feel safer tonight, if I have a gun in the night table drawer?"

She looked at him confused. *What the fuck, bitch?* He was beginning to get impatient.

"Let's just watch a movie tonight and take your mind off this. You are safe, okay?" She looked at him without responding. "Okay?" he asked again, giving her shoulders a bit of shake.

"Okay, okay," she said.

"Alright, that's better. Let's keep it together."

"I'm still a little overwhelmed. I need to sit down." Rita sat down at the kitchen table, fanning her face with her hand. "Would you mind just finishing up those dishes?"

"Sure," he said. "Just sit down, relax. I'll finish these dishes."

"Thank you."

He walked over to the sink, grabbed his sleeve, and caught himself just before he pulled it up. He looked over at her; she was staring at him. He stepped back from the sink.

"I just have to go to the bathroom."

He went into the bathroom and closed the door. He could feel her eyes follow him and try to see right through the door. He flushed the toilet.

Well, this isn't good. Got to get myself out of this one. She can't really suspect me after all these years, can she? After all I've done for her. Okay, need to get out of these dishes. Have to leave, get out of the house for a while. She'll probably freak out. Holy fuck, do I have to kill her? She's my fuckin' meal ticket. Talk about smashing in the skull of the hand that feeds you.

He laughed. *I have to. I'm too damn funny. Alright, just got to leave. She'll do the dishes by the time I get back. Okay, I'll go rent a movie. If she hasn't done them by the time I get back, I'll do them after the movie when she goes to bed.*

Holy fuck, big tough guy, what happened to you?

I've been looking after you, keeping you outta the fuckin' joint for the past twenty years.

If the plan didn't work, he'd have to kick it old school and kill her, get his things together, and move on. That had been a lot easier when he was younger, and hitting the road, going on the run again, was the last thing he wanted to do. He had gotten . . . *soft*, used to his lifestyle. Didn't want to get off this gravy train yet. *Time to put your skills to work.*

He opened the bathroom door. She was still seated at the table.

"Listen," he began. "I'm kind of freaked out by this stuff, too. I'm gonna go get some deadbolts right now and rent us a movie so we can get ourselves sealed in here, take our minds off this, and enjoy the evening. I'll do the dishes later."

"Can I come with you?" she asked.

This bitch can't take a hint. I may have to kill her.

"I'll be back in a minute. Just take some aspirin, sit back, and watch some TV. Don't watch any of the local channels; they may upset you. I'll be back before you know it."

"Alright," she said.

He led her from the kitchen table over to the sofa. "I'll grab some chips and ice cream, too," he said.

"Okay."

Wow, he had his work cut out for him tonight. She was so subdued. Her fat ass would usually light up like a fuckin' Christmas tree for chips and ice cream.

"I'll be back soon," he said as he hurried out the door without waiting for her response.

***

Beth was on the computer checking the top news stories. As she browsed, one caught her eye: "Two deaths in Sifton ruled homicides. City on high alert." She clicked on the headline and read the article. They hadn't released any of the victims' names, but police did believe it might be the work of the same man. They recommended that people travel in groups and make sure all doors and windows were locked. Holy shit—this was the type of thing you would see in the movies. She felt a shiver of fear go through her body.

Beth jumped up from the couch and headed for the front door. She remembered that Hayward had told her there was a killer at large. She had almost forgotten about it until now. She looked at the lock on the front door; the deadbolt was in the locked position. She placed her hand on it anyway and tried to turn it to a more locked position. It didn't move. Satisfied, she headed for the back door.

Had Daniel heard about this and gone to work anyway? Had he not told her because she would have wanted him to stay home? Could he have done that? She began to get angry. Well, he had better get his ass home right now. She arrived at the back sliding door in the kitchen that led to the backyard, checked the lock latch, then grabbed the phone from the kitchen counter and called Daniel's office. The machine answered with the company's motto, "Building dreams with our clients." Beth scowled thinking about the row houses and the war vets. She pictured the vets being herded out as if they were cattle. The machine stated the hours of operation. She hung up and dialled Daniel's cell phone number. Daniel's voicemail picked up. She hung up without leaving a message. Beth was infuriated, but she knew it would be a mistake to leave a message while angry. She redialled the number again and listened again as the message indicator began to play.

She hung up, put the phone down, and walked over to the counter where she picked up her purse, dug in it, and pulled out a card. Officer Hayward Barry. She flipped it over and looked at the cell phone number written on the back. She flipped it back over and read the front again.

***

"Ha-Ha-Hay, how long am I going t-t-t-to stay in jail?" Joe asked from the back of the squad car.

"A long time," Jeff responded.

"Listen, Jeff, can you just . . ." Hayward didn't know what to say next, so he turned and began talking to Joe.

"Hard to say, Joe. It doesn't look good, you carrying all those drugs. You're gonna do some time, but I promise ya, buddy, I'm gonna do all I can."

"What ab-b-b-b-bout P-P-Pete, do you think he can get me out, Hay?"

"You won't be going home anytime soon," Hayward said, although he knew Joe was homeless.

"Home," Jeff laughed. "You got a new home now."

Hayward ignored Jeff, tired of talking to him. "Joe, I'll get ahold of Pete as soon as we get to the precinct and let him know the situation."

"I'm c-c-c-cold," Joe said.

"You're gonna have a big black dick to keep you warm soon," Jeff said, snickering.

"That's enough. Shut the fuck up. This is my friend, no matter what you think, and I swear to God, don't push me."

Jeff looked at him. Hayward was mad, but a little frightened of what Jeff would do. Jeff began to laugh. Hayward put his head in his hands.

"Fuck, fuck, fuck," Hayward muttered. *Why does life have to be so fucking difficult sometimes?*

"H-H-H-Hay?"

"What?" Hayward pulled his head back up.

"Remember Davey, Hay? Ya remember Davey?"

Hayward sighed. As if this couldn't get any worse. He surely didn't want to go down that road.

"Of course I do."

"H-H-H-He was a good guy, eh, Hay?"

The squad car pulled up to the precinct.

"He sure was. Listen, Joe, I want you to do everything they ask during processing, Okay? I'll meet up with you later after I talk to Pete and we get you a lawyer."

"H-H-He was a good guy," Joe repeated, as if he didn't hear anything Hayward had just told him.

The car came to a stop and Jeff put it in park.

"Let's go, bosom buddies," Jeff said as he chuckled and got out of the car.

***

Pete tapped his pen on his desk. He had given stacks of posters to the beat cops that had just started shift and had emailed the pictures to the local news stations, who indicated they would start airing them immediately. He looked at his phone and waited.

They have been trying to catch this guy for seventeen years, and you, who have only been on the task force for a couple of days, think you are gonna get the lead to break the case, he mused. *Really, Pete. Maybe you need to get out there and start doing some old-fashioned police work. Sitting by the phone waiting is not a good use of your detective skills. That's probably what Dubinsky did, and that's why he was removed.*

Pete hadn't talked to his wife and boys all day; he'd been wrapped up in the case, and his family understood, but he missed them. He felt a chill go up his back. He picked up the phone and dialled his house. His wife answered.

"Hello."

"Hey, sweetheart."

"Hey, there," she said. "How's it going?"

"Wow, it's intense."

"I can imagine. Are you gonna get home soon?"

"Not sure, but I have a feeling with the way things are going it will be late."

"I put some supper, wrapped in foil, in the fridge for you. It's potatoes and roast beef."

"Thanks," Pete said, remembering that he hadn't eaten all day. "How are the boys?"

"Great. Brett is asleep and Andrew is working on his project for school."

"Are the doors locked?" he asked.

"Of course."

"You're sure?"

"Pete," she said angrily.

"Sorry. You know."

"I understand," she said. "They're showing pictures of some men on the news. Are any of these guys involved?"

"Not sure. It's a hunch we're trying. They're suspects in unsolved murders from a long time ago, in towns as far as five hundred miles away. It was kind of my idea."

"Really! Well, I hope it works out and somebody recognizes one of them. Good work, honey."

"Thanks, I better get back to work."

"Okay, I'll keep the bed warm for you."

"Thanks, honey. Tell the boys I love them, and I'll talk to ya later. Bye."

Pete hung up the phone, put his hands behind his head, and stretched backwards. He looked around his office. Detective. He was still busting with pride.

Well, Detective, let's stop sitting here and get in the game. He got up from his chair and put on his jacket. His phone rang and he picked it up.

"Detective Lyons, can I help you?"

"Hi," a cracking voice said.

"Hi there, what can I do for you?" Pete said.

"My name is Rita . . ."

***

After dropping Joe off at processing, Hayward plopped down on a bench in the hallway. He put his head back and sighed. Life had seemed so much simpler when he was a kid: no drug use, no bills, and no job stress. How did boys with such a great childhood go so wrong in life? Joe was the extreme, but Hayward had also disappointed his parents by not going to college and moving out to San Francisco. They had tried to talk him out of it. They told him he was nuts and throwing his life away. That only fuelled him to get out of town, get away from everything that reminded him of Beth.

He missed his art. Painting was his drug, an escape from real life. Maybe he'd break out the easel tonight, give his mind a rest. He knew he wouldn't, though. No, when he got home he would have a frozen dinner and a beer, sit down on the couch, and watch TV until he was too tired to stay awake—just like every other working schlub. He was goal-oriented now, and that's what you did—you didn't waste your life painting. He had to stay focused. Joe was first on the list. He and Pete had to try and come up with something to help their old friend.

Hayward's cell phone rang. He fished out of his pocket and answered it.

"Hello," he said.

"Hi, Hayward?" a lady's voice asked.

"Yes."

"It's Beth."

A flood of emotion came over him—seventeen years worth of longing, of dreaming that he would answer his phone and hear her voice.

"Hello, Beth. What can I do for you?"

"How are you doing? You must be busy with all the stuff I've been seeing on the news lately."

"Yes, it's been busy, but I can handle it. What do you need?"

"I was wondering if you were available for a quick cup of coffee tomorrow afternoon?"

"Sure, what time?"

"I have to pick Phillip up from school at three, so how about around two at the coffee shop at Maple and Walnut? It's close to Phillip's school.

"Okay, yeah. I'll save your number here on my phone, and if things are chaotic tomorrow, I'll give you a call before then."

Hayward knew that a catastrophic sequence of events signalling the end of mankind was the only thing that maybe, just maybe, could keep him from meeting her.

"Okay, great. I'll see you tomorrow."

"Okay, bye," he said and hung up the phone.

Hayward sat in amazement. Did that just happen? Was he dreaming? He punched his leg and felt it.

This is real. Wow. Calm down, ol' boy, it's just coffee. It's not like you will ride off into the sunset together. Just coffee. Probably going to take another seventeen years to get over this one.

He laughed and stood up. The he stopped laughing. He had never gotten over the first time.

***

He got back to Rita's and noticed that her car was gone. That was odd. He walked in the door, put the ice cream in the freezer. He looked around. The lights were on and the TV was still blaring. She never left the house without shutting them off.

"Rita?" he said aloud to the empty house.

"Rita?" he said again, louder.

Nothing. He tossed the movie he had rented on the table and hung his jacket on the back of the chair. He looked in the bedrooms. Maybe she had been beaten, raped, or killed. What would be the chances of that happening? Those were some pretty astounding odds, that there was somebody like him and he was that close, on his turf. He began to get angry, as if there actually was somebody trying to move into his neighbourhood, into his house. Or had this newcomer taken her out to wine and dine her, take his spot, and steal his meal ticket?

Not the motherfuckin' MVP, not on my watch.

He sat down in front of the television. He'd wait a little while and then call her cell phone. He quickly got up and went over to the sink. The dishes were still there, and this was his opportunity to get them done. He mentally patted himself on the back for remembering. He rolled his sleeves up a bit.

Get ready, dishes, this is the fastest that you'll ever get washed.

"We have shown these men a number of times tonight, and we will continue to show their pictures. These men are all wanted fugitives," said the news anchor on the TV.

He whipped around and glared at the TV, his pulse quickening. He watched as face after face went by. How many fuckin' guys were there? The dish he was holding crashed to the floor. There on the television was his picture, taken about twenty years ago, but it was him. Tommy Kelch: his old name.

"Fuck!" he yelled at the screen.

The TV anchor continued, "If you recognize any of these men, contact authorities immediately." A phone number flashed up.

"Fuck!" he yelled again.

Here we go.

In the first few years he had been here, he'd thought this day would come; but as time went on he had gotten used to thinking that he would live out his days doing what he was doing. As the years went by, he began to feel invincible. Surely Rita had seen the picture, and surely she had recognized him. He had to go. He shuddered at the thought, wishing he were younger, wishing he still had that fire, that he hadn't gotten soft.

He went into the bedroom and grabbed a duffle bag and threw some clothes in it. Time to dust off the old skills. Everyone was good at something. He chuckled as he carried the duffle bag into the living room and looked around. He could feel a small fire beginning to start in the bottom of his belly. He welcomed it.

"I need anything I can get," he said aloud as he walked over to the kitchen and grabbed some big knives from the drawer.

He wrapped the knives in a tea towel and threw them into the duffle bag.

Have to get my gun and my collection, he reminded himself. *My life's work.* He opened the back door and walked out in the back-yard towards the detached garage. He heard something on his left and turned.

"Get on the ground!"

Two figures dressed in black emerged from the driveway with guns pointed. He lunged for the side garage door and swung it open. He had just gotten through the door casing when he was grabbed from the right. Another man in black had come from around the back of the garage. He could hear a chorus of "Get on the ground" as the man on the right tried to force him down. He looked over at the cabinet where his gun was. The man from the right, the other two, and maybe a fourth, he thought, shoved him down onto the garage floor. His chin cracked off the concrete, his arms were pinned from both sides. He was bleeding from his mouth.

"Don't fuckin' move!" one of the men yelled.

If I could, I'd kill all of you motherfuckers. Rita the Rat. The cuffs were put on and he was lifted to his feet. A man appeared in front of him.

"Thomas Kelch," the man said.

He thought about denying it, but he might as well start working on a new game plan now. They had too much physical evidence, and once they got his DNA he was toast. He said nothing.

"I'm Detective Peter Lyons, and you are under arrest."

The rest of his rights were read as he felt the Push beginning. He began to thrash. He looked at the cabinet that contained his collection, wanting to see it one last time, and these fuckers wouldn't . . . He thrashed wildly. As the Push was about to totally take over, he felt electricity ripping through his body like getting a million shocks at once. He looked at the cabinet with his collection as he fell.

Chapter 18

It's Only Coffee

Joe stood with his hands holding the bars.

"S-S-S-So I gotta stay here t-t-t—tonight?"

Hayward stood in a hallway lined with jail cells on both sides.

"Yeah, buddy, they need to hold you. Pete is out working on a big case. I'll go and see him in the morning. You gonna be okay?"

Hayward felt dumb for asking. Who wanted to be in jail? Even homeless people don't want to be in jail.

"I-I-I-It's not home, b-b-b-but it'll do, Hay," Joe said and then stared at the floor. The prison jumpsuit they had given him hung loosely from his skeletal frame.

Hayward felt helpless, knowing he had to go home and leave Joe here. He thought of the Joe from their younger days. He had been such a large figure, one of the biggest in his class every year. No one picked on him because of his size. No one wanted to see someone that big lose his temper.

"Listen, buddy," Hayward said, his voice cracking a little. He didn't want to say what he was about to say, but they were both grown men who had made choices in life that had brought them to this point.

"I gotta go home and get some rest for work tomorrow."

To Hayward's surprise, Joe lifted his head.

"Y-Y-Y-Yeah, Hay, I'll see ya tomorrow," Joe said as he took another disheartened look around his cell. Hayward wished there was something he could do to change the situation, but no more could be done tonight.

"I'll see you tomorrow," Hayward said as he turned and walked away. He bit down on his lip to try to keep from crying.

***

Beth walked into the closet in the large master bedroom she shared with Daniel. She perused her clothes. She felt like wearing something nice tomorrow when she went to pick up Phillip. She began to feel guilty. She was a married woman; she shouldn't be picking out outfits to see another man. It was wrong. *It's only coffee,* she tried to convince herself, then failed. *If it's only coffee, why don't you tell Daniel?*

"Are you out of your mind?" she said out loud. *There are enough things that man isn't telling me. He doesn't respect me enough to tell me.*

She scowled, let out a grunt, and suddenly had a strange feeling. She looked at her clothes, but they weren't her clothes; they were her clothes from when she was eleven years old. She would pick out her outfit for the next school day—the day Daniel asked her to the date party at the ball field fence. What if she had said no? Where would she be now? She thought of Hayward standing in her front yard in his police uniform. She thought of Phillip and how she loved that boy more than anything in the world. If she had said no, she wouldn't have Phillip. She shuddered at the thought.

Downstairs, the front door opened. She quickly shut off the lights and climbed into bed. She didn't want to talk to him right now; there was too much swirling around in her head. She wasn't a great actor and was never good at lying, so she figured he would be able to read something on her face. Over the years he had been fairly good at reading her guilt. She closed her eyes as tightly as she could to try to force the thoughts away, listening to him rustling about in the kitchen.

Gone was her rage from earlier. Daniel had probably seen that she had called. He figured she was mad. He wouldn't come up to bed for a long time; he didn't want to talk to her any more than she wanted to talk to him. Great marriage. She thought of her mother when she went through her rough time. Her family stuck together. *They stuck together,* she repeated again, *but I'm going for coffee.*

***

A team of cops were going through Rita's house and garage. Pete looked up into the night sky and took a deep breath; the last few hours had been intense. Was it him? Did they really have their guy? Did they have the Max Killer in custody?

The Captain of the task force walked up to Pete. "That happened fast. This could be our guy," he said.

"Well, he is wanted for murder, so hopefully we help solve that case," Pete replied.

"Yes, we'll see. Pete, I don't want you to get the wrong idea, but I am not going to have you lead the interrogation. I'm gonna go with Magnerson. He's got a lot of experience in this area, and this is going to be a high-profile case."

"Of course," Pete said. He felt a little slighted, but he understood. This was, after all, his first case as detective, and he didn't want to mess anything up . . . *They wouldn't even have the guy if it wasn't for you,* he told himself.

"That was some great work though, Pete. Hopefully we find some evidence that this is our guy. If we do, we'll bring you in, okay?" Pete nodded in acknowledgement, and the Captain continued. "While we are working on this case, I want you to keep looking, as if this isn't the Max Killer. If this isn't our guy, I don't want this thing blowing up in our face."

Holy crap! Is he serious? I probably just made the biggest arrest in the history of this police force, and he wants me to pretend that it didn't happen.

Pete wanted to say something, but he didn't want his first case to be his last. He decided he had better keep quiet and go along with what the captain wanted.

"Sure thing, Captain," Pete said.

A member of the search team was standing in the door of the garage.

"Could I see you, Detectives?"

"Yes, of course," the Captain said.

The search team member led them to the back of the garage where he and two others had been working.

"We found this."

Pete's heart began to beat loudly as he looked at the board with all the panties nailed on it, in neat rows.

"Jesus!" the Captain exclaimed.

***

Two cops led him down a hallway of cells. He had to shuffle his feet as he was shackled with cuffs around his ankles as well as his wrists. He was tired. They had questioned him for eight hours. He had told them he didn't know what they were talking about for eight hours. Only once did he worry about cracking, when they'd first mentioned that they had the collection. But he regained his composure and again acted like he didn't know what they were talking about.

He looked at a tall, extremely skinny guy in a cell with his hands on the bars. They opened the cell next to his and pushed him in. A corrections officer removed his cuffs as he looked at the small bed, eager to get some rest before his next interrogation, if there was one. He laughed. They were busy mulling over their pages of the crazy answers he'd given to their dumb questions.

Stupid fucks, ruin my fuckin' life. I'd like to ruin their fuckin' lives. They closed the cell door behind him. He sat on the bed. *This sucks. Better relax—gonna be in jail for a while.*

He knew he would never be free again in his life. He accepted it. Better retire. Fuck that! Retire from what? Being a tough guy? That was never going to happen. Tough guys needed rest too, though. He lay on the bed and closed his eyes. He had spent so much time with those detectives he could see their faces when he closed his eyes. He had looked them in the eyes each time they had asked the question and wanted them to look at him. He wanted them to see evil. He noticed that they looked away sometimes when they were asking the questions.

You fuckin' gutless pukes, take these shackles off. I'll kill all of you with one arm, you fucking pussies. Get some rest before those fucks come back. He took a deep breath to try and reset his brain.

"H-H-H-Hey there."

He heard it coming from the next cell and ignored it.

"H-H-H-Hey, buddy."

Great, what does the freaky-looking fag want?

"Fuck off!" he shouted from his new bed. He figured that would shut him up. He took another deep breath and tried to sleep. Another minute went by before the guy spoke again.

"H-H-H-Hey, you wanna get outta here?"

He lifted his head from the pillow. There were only a few things that fag could have said that would make him interested enough to listen, and that was one.

"What the fuck are you talking about?"

"I kn-n-n-now some people," Joe said from the next cell.

He got up off the bed, moved closer to the fag.

"Who do you know?"

"H-H-H-Hayward, he's my friend."

"Who the fuck is Hayward?"

"H-H-H-He's a cop."

"So how's he gonna help you?"

Why are you talking to this fucking junkie, anyway?

What have you got to lose?

You're gonna rot in here.

You can. I'm not.

"H-H-H-He's gonna get Pete to help me."

"Who's Pete?"

"P-P-P-Pete Lyons, he's my friend from w-w-w-w-hen we were kids."

Lyons. That was the name of that stupid fuckin' detective fuck that had arrested him and asked him the same stupid fucking questions for the past eight hours.

"H-H-H-He was Davey's best friend."

"Who's Davey?"

He was beginning to think this wasn't going anywhere and that he should go back to bed. But something kept telling him to talk to this crackhead fuck and find out about the people he claimed to know. He had a feeling in his gut.

"He had a feeling in his gut": that was a pig expression. Did the other side of the law have gut feelings, too? He began to argue with himself again. Everyone has gut feelings: butchers, garbage men, janitors, Super Mart girls.

He thought about the collection and the Super Mart girl's place on it. He noticed the crackhead was still talking. He didn't know what he was talking about and had missed the answer of who Davey was. Probably the judge. Wouldn't that be funny? He had to get back on track and get this crackhead on track with him.

"So, you and Detective Lyons are close?"

"O-o-o-o-yeah, we were. O-o-o-o-yeah, we were."

Funny how some things just fall into your lap. He laughed. *MVPs make it look easy.* He walked around his cell, puffed out his chest, his confidence brimming. He thought of his grand finale. Maybe it was gonna start right here.

***

Hayward arrived at the precinct early because he needed to talk to Pete. He knew Pete would be there already, because Pete was the most driven guy he had ever known. He knocked on Pete's door and a muffled voice told him to come in. Hayward pushed open the door. It was immediately obvious that Pete had just woken up as he raised his head from the desk.

"Hey, Hayward," Pete said, seeming relieved that it was Hayward and not someone who needed a professional Pete.

"Hey, Pete, I just need a few minutes of your time. I know you're busy with the big case."

"Ya think?" Pete chuckled. "Never even made it home last night."

"It's Joe," Hayward said. Pete began to tidy up some papers on his desk as Hayward took a seat.

"What about Joe?"

"He was busted yesterday, and he's being held downstairs."

"Busted! For what?" Pete asked, sounding annoyed. Hayward figured Pete's annoyance was aimed at Joe rather than him.

"He was carrying two kilos."

"What? Wait, I know, I know. He was trying to get a hit, the deal went south, and he was stuck with the product."

"Yes."

"That's a trafficking charge," Pete said in a disbelieving tone.

"Yeah, I know. Do you think we could do anything to lessen the charge? He's going to federal prison if we can't."

"Shit," Pete said, slowly running his hand through his hair. "With that amount, Hay, that's . . . that's . . . holy shit."

Hayward didn't say anything. He could tell from Pete's expression that there was little he could do.

"Does he have a lawyer?" Pete asked.

"Not yet. I guess they are gonna give him a public defender."

"Fuck that." Pete grabbed a piece of paper and a pen, scribbled a name down, and handed the paper to Hayward.

"Get this guy for him, and I'll cover the cost."

"I'd like to cover some of it too."

"Sounds good. Just get him this morning. I've got a lot of work to do today."

"Yeah, I heard you got him. Congratulations. When is it hitting the press?"

"Already out there. The Captain wanted our citizens to feel safe and to try and repair the image of the department. We just have to get the DNA tests done, and that should be the final nail in this sick fuck's coffin."

"Hell of a way to start off your detective career."

"Yeah. So Joe's still here, downstairs?"

"For this morning, but they're going to send him up to the penitentiary this afternoon. He doesn't know it yet. He thinks we're going to get him out."

"I wish I could. Take care of contacting that guy for me," Pete pointed at the piece of paper he had given to Hayward, "and I'll stop by and try and explain some things to him before he's sent up."

"Thanks, he'd like that. The visit, I mean."

Pete's phone rang and he picked it up. "Hello. Yeah. He's right here. Okay, sure, bye." He hung up. "The Sergeant wants to see you."

"Really?" Hayward was surprised. "Okay," he said as he got up.

"I'll give you a call later," Pete said.

"Right on," Hayward said as he left the office.

***

Beth awoke as the alarm sounded. Daniel's side of the bed was untouched. She remembered him coming home, but he hadn't come to bed. Not a surprise. It used to make her mad, but now she didn't care. She felt better when she was alone. She had been so mad at him lately that she didn't want to see his face. He had probably gone to work already.

She wondered what life would be like without him. What about Phillip? He loved his father; she had to keep the family together. She remembered what her mother had put her father through, knowing she couldn't do that—not to her family. She pulled herself up from the bed and put on her robe. She remembered her coffee date with Hayward and got a wave of nervous butterflies. She walked down the hall and opened the door to Phillip's room.

"Time to get up, sweetie. Mommy's going to make your breakfast."

What would she and Hayward talk about? Old times? What they've been up to? She was curious about his time in San Francisco. As she walked downstairs, she had a horrible thought. *What if I'm not interesting? I really haven't done anything that isn't obvious. Married, child, teacher, no real stories.* She thought about Hayward's shy demeanour and figured he didn't have too many tales of wild adventure himself. She smiled as she walked into the kitchen. The smile faded quickly. Daniel was standing with his backside against the counter. He looked serious, which wasn't unusual, but there was something different in his expression.

"Oh, Daniel! You scared me."

"What's going on here?" he said as he lifted his hand. He was holding her cell phone.

"What?" Beth acted surprised. She knew what he was talking about.

He had looked through her cell phone and had seen Hayward's number and that she had called him. She was disgusted with Daniel.

"What are you doing calling him?"

233

She paused as she formulated her answer. She was nervous about where the conversation would go.

"Well, there is a serial rapist and killer running around the city, and you left your wife and child home alone."

Daniel slammed the phone on the counter so hard it made Beth jump. She had never seen him express anger physically.

"So you call that loser?" he said loudly.

"Give me my phone before you break it." Beth walked toward Daniel with her arm extended.

Daniel left the phone on the counter, grabbed her arm, and gave her a shake. A wave of fear came over her. Never before in his anger had he physically put his hands on her, and she wasn't sure what he would do next.

"Just remember what I do for this family," he said sternly.

"Let go of me!" She could feel her fear begin to transform into anger. "Let go of me now!"

"Mommy," Phillip said from the entrance to the kitchen.

Beth felt horrible. She didn't want Phillip to see this. *Fuck, I don't want to see this.*

"Stay away from him," Daniel said in her ear with more meanness than she had ever heard before. He gave her a hard squeeze, and pain shot through her arm.

"Ouch!"

He let go and walked past her. She grabbed her arm, trying to rub the pain away.

"What's wrong?" Phillip asked as Daniel walked by him.

"Nothing, buddy," he replied as he grabbed his coat and keys. He slammed the door behind him.

Beth tried to fight the urge to cry.

"Mommy, Mommy, what's wrong?"

She couldn't contain her grief. She burst into tears as she knelt down on the floor. She felt Phillip place his hand on her back. It made her cry even more.

***

Cy pulled the rusty truck up in front of the convenience store.

"Are we going to class today?" Craig asked.

"Na. I got to go in here and get some smokes." They hopped out of the truck.

"So, why did we get up so early?"

Cy pushed open the door and walked in with Craig following.

"What the fuck are you talking about?" Cy asked as he approached the counter.

"I mean, why didn't we sleep in? 'Cause we got up for school, and we're not even going to go."

"Won't your old lady tear you a new asshole if she thought you weren't going to school?"

"I guess," Craig responded.

"Camels," Cy said to the overweight clerk behind the counter.

"Do you have some proof of age identification?" the clerk asked snidely. Cy held up his fist.

"Identification," Cy laughed. "How about some, I-dent-your-face-in?"

The clerk looked stunned for a second then quickly threw the cigarettes on the counter. Cy turned around.

"You got any rolling papers?" he asked Craig.

"No."

"Well, get some now, you stupid fuck," Cy said and walked over by the door.

Craig asked the clerk for some rolling papers. Cy knew that the fat-fuck clerk wasn't going to ask him shit about an ID. He laughed and looked down at the rack holding the newspapers.

"Holy motherfucker!" Cy said loudly.

Craig, having bought the rolling papers, went over to see what Cy was so excited about.

"What is it?"

Cy pointed at the newspaper headline: "Suspect in seventeen-year-old murder caught." And there was a mug shot of Tommy Kelch on the front page.

"That's my fucking father."

Chapter 19

Elvis Black Hair

Hayward knocked on the door of the Sergeant's office. It swung open, revealing a stern-faced, short, stocky Sergeant Reynolds.

"You wanted to see me," Hayward said, already knowing this didn't look good.

"Yes. Please, come in."

"Sure, Serge."

Jeff was seated in the office when Hayward entered.

"Thank you, Officer Martell," the Sergeant said.

"I look forward to hearing from you," Jeff said as he got up.

The Sergeant said nothing; he just gave Jeff a disgruntled look and motioned toward the door with his arm. Jeff gave Hayward a small grin and closed the door.

What's going on here? Hayward wondered.

"Have a seat."

"What's this about, Serge?" Hayward asked as he sat.

"Well, Hayward, I think you're a good cop, and until now you've had a perfect record of service. I got a complaint today about your conduct and integrity yesterday involving the arrest."

"A complaint?"

"Yes. It seems a felony charge suspect was in your custody, and it's been reported that you wanted to release the suspect. Is this true?"

"Well, kind of. You see, I have known the suspect since I was a boy, and—"

The Sergeant cut him off. "Is this true?"

"Sir, the circumstances of the arrest were—"

"Look," the Sergeant said, "we have been put in a situation, and we've been asked to investigate your conduct."

"What?" Hayward couldn't believe what he was hearing.

"I'll need you to answer the question. Did you ask your fellow officer to release a suspect?"

Hayward looked at the floor. He didn't know what to say. He didn't know if Jeff had worn a wire, or if there were cameras in the car. He decided that denying it could only make it worse. He probably wouldn't get fired, but he would be suspended and all of his actions involving cases and suspects since he had become a police officer would be scrutinized. He would also be embarrassed. The precinct, like any other workplace, was a cauldron of steamy gossip, and he would be front-page news for the next few days. He started to feel his blood temperature rise. How could that fuck Jeff rat him out?

Ironically, Jeff was always using the word "rat" in that context about perps, people on the street, and even fellow cops. Jeff had always warned him to stay away from this person and that person because they were a fuckin' rat. This whole thing seemed so unlike him.

"I need an answer," the Sergeant said again.

Hayward thought about Joe and how he had ruined his life with drugs. What the fuck? For the first time in his life he was mad at Joe. His problems had started when Davey died. He had always felt sorry for Joe, until now. Maybe he had gotten what he deserved. Maybe he should be thrown in jail with the other leeches of society because that's what he was. It was time to admit it.

Pete and I had to live with Davey's death, he thought. *Had to move on, had to make a life for ourselves. Why the fuck couldn't you, Joe? Why the fuck couldn't you just face it instead of hiding behind the drugs, you fucking coward?*

"Hayward," the Sergeant said.

And now, Joe, you're dragging other people down with you.

"Officer Barry," the Sergeant said sternly.

That's the problem, Joe, that's the fucking problem. Not only do you fucking selfish drug addicts ruin your own lives, you take everyone close to you on your stupid selfish ride.

"Officer—"

Hayward cut him off. "Yes, I knew that he wasn't the dealer, just a buyer, so I wanted to let him go."

"Well, Officer, that's for the courts to decide."

Hayward wanted to respond, but thought better of it.

"I have no choice but to place you on a suspension from your police services until a detailed investigation is conducted into your conduct as a police officer."

Hayward kept his head down. "How long will that take?" he asked. How could Jeff have ratted him out?

"Not sure. As I stated, there is going to be an investigation."

"And if they don't find anything else, what happens?"

"Hayward, I'm going to level with you. We got this request from above. A preliminary investigation was requested to determine if there had to be a full one. The first person I question is your partner, and right off the hop, I get some shit on my shoe and I have to follow the trail."

"Requested from above?" Hayward asked.

He had always tried to fly below the radar. How could he be under investigation if Jeff hadn't started this?

"This is serious, Hayward, and it doesn`t look good. I have to be very careful and cover my ass here. This is from the Commissioner of Police, through the Mayor's Office."

Hayward sat in bewilderment, his mind racing a thousand miles a minute.

"I'll need you to place your gun and badge on the desk."

The Mayor's Office. What the hell?

***

The man awoke to a banging sound on the bars of his cell.

"Let's go! Let's go!" a voice yelled.

He opened his eyes, exhausted after only a couple hours of sleep. He had listened to the life story of the crackhead and his two cop buddies. *We'll see how much his pig friends care if I get my hands on him*, he thought.

"Let's go!" the voice yelled again.

He hated being told what to do. Better get used to that quick, but he knew that he wouldn't. Without a good living situation in prison, he would die relatively quickly. His only option right now was to try and better it. If this crackhead was really close to the two cops, maybe he could use that angle, get into these cops' heads, and create fear. He might be able to get that to work.

Wow, look at you, adjusting your strategy for the situation, changing the plays. Well, everyone's good at something. Just another game on the schedule.

The cop banging on the bars was a fat black guy, and it looked like he had eaten junk food every day since he was five years old; he probably had. The man hated black people, and he figured this cop probably got some sort of rush bossing him around.

"Turn around and face the wall," the officer said.

He glared at the cop. *Sure thing, nigger.* He turned around.

The cop grabbed his arm. "Hands behind your back."

He placed his hands behind his back, and the officer put a pair of cuffs around his wrists and yanked him. He figured this guy liked yanking him around. The cop pushed him outside the cell and then led him over to the crackhead's cell. Another cop was just down the hall. A white guy. The black cop had probably volunteered to get them so he could yank around some white boys.

"Stand there," the cop instructed him, and then unlocked the other cell.

"W-W-W-Where's Pete?" the crackhead said.

"Don't know who you're talking about, and don't care. You boys are going up to Lakehead."

He was surprised, because Lakehead was the penitentiary, and he figured they would be questioning him again here today. *I guess they realize the only thing they are getting from me is a big, heartfelt, "Fuck you."*

"W-W-W-Where's Pete?" the crackhead said again.

The man looked at the officer down the hall. He was talking to someone that was in a different hallway, out of his sight.

"Face the wall," the cop told the crackhead. The crackhead turned around, and the cop put the cuffs on him and led him out into the hall. "You guys got to get ready for your bus ride." The cop was half facing them while locking the cell door.

I'll show you who's the boss, fucking nigger.

He kicked the cop in the nuts. The cop fell to his knees. He glanced down the hall, and the officer was still talking to someone. He rammed his body against the cop's head and smashed it against the bars. The cop fell unconscious to the concrete floor. He could hear the crackhead trying to say something and stuttering like a son of a bitch. He raised his leg and stomped the side of the crackhead's knee. The crackhead yelped with pain and fell to his knees. Now the officer at the end of the hall was coming over. He quickly positioned himself with his back to the crackhead's head. He got his cuffed hands underneath the crackhead's chin and pulled the chain on his throat. He pulled the crackhead's head against his ass as hard as he could. He could hear the officer from down the hall running now. He squeezed. The crackhead made some sounds that made him think of his collection, about his work to acquire the collection. Some of the women who had made donations had made similar sounds.

The cop was yelling something, but he couldn't hear what it was; he was lost in the symphony of the choking sounds. The officer cranked his arm with his baton. His arm exploded in pain, but he kept choking. He could feel the life escaping the crackhead. Even from behind, he knew the feeling. The officer cranked his arm again, lower this time. Didn't hurt as much as the first one. The officer was screaming something, but he only heard the gargled sound of the crackhead's last breath. He felt the crackhead's head fall limp, but he continued to squeeze. The officer brought the baton back, and this time he knew where it was going. The baton caught him square in the side of the head. His knees buckled, and he fell to the floor. He felt the officer pulling on his arms, trying to free the crackhead. He was semiconscious from the baton blow, but he was happy.

I got him. Right in your fucking house, you keystone fucks. I got him.

He could see more cops running down the hall toward them. They would do everything they could to try and save the crackhead, try and resuscitate him. But they wouldn't.

I got him.

***

Hayward stood at his locker, not knowing what to think. What the hell was happening? How could he have gotten suspended? It didn't make sense. He felt someone standing at the end of the row of lockers. He looked over and saw it was Jeff. Hayward hadn't heard footsteps; he was just standing there.

"Look, I know you're mad."

"Fuck you," Hayward said, and put his head down.

"Listen for a minute. I don't know what the fuck happened today, alright. I got here today and was hauled into the office. I was asked a bunch of questions about you and your conduct. They said they were investigating you. I didn't know why. I didn't know for how long they had been. I didn't know if I was being set up, or being investigated myself. I didn't know if you had been wearing a wire. I only knew that to protect my ass, I needed to say exactly what happened. If I tried to cover for you and they found out, it would be my ass, my fucking career, and that wasn't going to happen. I'm a cop that loves this shit."

Hayward wanted to say a thousand things. On the other hand, he didn't want to say anything. Suddenly he heard shouting.

"Hayward! Hayward!" An officer appeared behind Jeff at the end of the row of lockers. "Hayward! Pete told me to get you. He needs you down at the holding cells right away."

"Joe," Hayward said and slammed his locker and started to run to the exit. He gave Jeff a push as he ran past. Hayward understood Jeff had done what he thought he should in the situation, but he wanted to shove him anyway.

***

Pete turned the corner of the holding cells and ran towards the group of officers and paramedics. As he approached, he could see that they were pumping on someone's chest, trying to resuscitate him. He knew who it was. He arrived at the group and looked down into Joe's lifeless face. The paramedics continued to pump and count, but he knew. Joe's face then turned into Davey's face. Davey's wide, dead eyes.

"Fuck!" Pete screamed.

Hayward came running down the hall. He grabbed Pete by the arm and looked down at Joe. Hayward had seen a childhood friend dead before; he knew Joe was gone. His eyes locked with Pete's. He had never been more sure of what someone else was thinking. How could this be happening again? They embraced. Hayward closed his eyes and began to cry.

"What the fuck, Pete?"

Hayward suddenly felt like that scared little boy that day at the brook. He could feel the wet leaves around his feet.

Pete broke the embrace and looked over at the officers standing by the cell.

"Who?" Pete asked.

The officers said nothing, unsure of the question. The paramedic that was pumping on Joe's chest stopped and felt the wrist for a pulse for the last time.

"Who did this?" Pete barked at the officers.

One of them pointed at the cell, and Pete walked over and looked in. He was seated on the cot and did not look up. Pete placed his hands on the bars.

Hayward opened his sobbing eyes. He didn't want to look at Joe again. He knew it would take years to get the image out of his head. *Davey's image never left.*

"Open this door," Pete said calmly.

"I can't do that, detective," the officer responded.

Hayward was relieved. He was afraid of what Pete would do; he'd seen enough death.

"Why?" Pete said to the man seated on the cot.

The man didn't respond.

"Why, Tommy?" Pete yelled.

Tommy spoke. "He was your friend, wasn't he?"

Hayward played the question over in his head a few times. What was this guy talking about?

"He was our friend," Pete said, "and you fucking killed him. Why?"

"I need you to see that I have power," Tommy said calmly.

"What the fuck?" Pete said.

"I want you to make sure that I'm taken care of in the penitentiary," Tommy said.

"I'm gonna kill this fucking scumbag," Pete yelled and shook the bars wildly.

Tommy continued calmly, "Your dead crackhead friend told me a lot about you. I don't think you want anything to happen to your family or the love of your life, do you?"

"Fuck you," Pete said so viciously that spit flew from his mouth onto the bars.

"You need to realize my power," Tommy said, standing and looking directly at Pete. He walked toward him, stopping just out of arm's reach. "You puke cop fuck!" he then screamed.

Hayward looked into Tommy's eyes. He'd never seen anything more evil in his life. Pete's hands shot into the cell and he tried to grab him.

"You fuck! I'm gonna fucking kill you!"

The officers grabbed Pete and pulled him off the bars. Hayward stood stunned as the officers pulled Pete away from the cell and ushered him down the hall. Pete shrugged a few times but went with the officers. Hayward looked at Tommy, who was staring back at him. Hayward felt like he would vomit. Another officer walked over to him and gestured for him to go down the hall where Pete had gone. Hayward did so. He just wanted to be away from Tommy. From evil.

"The bus is ready. Let's get him up to the penitentiary," someone yelled.

As Hayward walked down the hall, a paramedic passed, pushing a gurney the other way. He remembered wondering if Davey was watching the people walking into his funeral. He wondered if Joe was watching the man wheeling in the gurney for his body.

***

Cy looked at the gas gauge of the truck. It was just above "E."

"You got any money?" he asked Craig.

"No."

"Holy fuck, I wonder if I could have a more useless friend."

"Fuck, man," Craig replied.

"Roll us up one. I'm gonna have to get us some money, and I wanna be fucked up when I do it. I don't want to be all fuckin' nervous and shit. When people think you're nervous, they get brave."

"What are we gonna do when we get there?" Craig asked.

"Don't know."

"Then why are we going?"

"Just fuckin' roll, would ya, or I'll drop your fucking ass out here in the middle of nowhere."

"Alright, fuck, man. You want a big one or snack size?"

"Have I ever said snack size?"

"No, but you might now."

Cy shook his head and looked out the window as they passed a sign that read "Sifton: 250 miles."

***

Beth was sitting at the kitchen table looking out into the backyard. She had taken Phillip to school and had decided to have a cup of tea when she got home. She couldn't stop staring out at the trees and the birds. The knowledge that she had to leave Daniel had been accepted, but how would she do it? Her mind went over a number of possibilities. She couldn't kick him out, not after his outburst; she was afraid of how he would take it. She had to take Phillip and go somewhere herself. Her parents had moved to Florida after she had finished high school. She didn't really have any friends; Daniel had pushed everyone away from her. She worried she might have to stay with him, that she had no place else to go, and realized why many women stay in abusive relationships. She had always judged and chastised these women, and here she was, considering it herself. *No, not me.*

She got to her feet and headed to her bedroom. *I'll pack some things, and we'll go to a hotel until I can figure the rest out. We'll go to a hotel after I pick him up from school.*

She pulled a suitcase out from the closet and perused her clothes, and then remembered she had a coffee date with Hayward. *Should I call and cancel? No, I should meet him. After all, he is the police. I may need them when Daniel finds out I have left with Phillip.* And there was the fact that she really wanted to see him.

She began to put some clothes in the suitcase. She put aside a pair of pants that made her ass look good, and a sweater she thought made her boobs look bigger. *What are you doing? Your marriage is falling apart, and you're dressing up for another man.* She began to feel guilty. But Daniel had gotten physical. The marriage was over. She pushed the guilt out, folded more clothes, and put them in the suitcase.

"That's the last time you'll grab me, you bastard."

***

Hayward pushed open the door and walked out of the precinct, his head spinning. He should have found Pete and talked with him, but he needed to be out of there. It was too much. He walked across the employee parking lot. Joe was gone. Actually, Joe was gone a long time ago. He had always hoped that Joe could pull it together and one day get his life back on track. Hayward was devastated. There was no chance now. Davey's death had dictated the rest of Joe's life. It was as if Joe had died that day, too. Joe's funeral would be like reliving Davey's all over again.

He opened his car door and got in. Could he have done more? Could he have done anything to change this? He couldn't have. Everyone Joe was close to had tried to help him over the years, but to no avail. Hayward figured the only person that Joe would have listened to would have been Davey; only he, back from the dead, would have been able to stop Joe's path of self-destruction.

"Life is so fucked up," Hayward informed his car. He turned the ignition and the car roared to life.

Suspended too, what the fuck? What am I gonna do at home besides feel lonely and miserable? He paused. *You could paint.*

He put the car in gear and pulled out of the parking lot. He thought again that he should go back and see how Pete was, but he didn't want to. He wanted to do his own thing. Do whatever it took to get his mind off all this misery. He had a coffee date with Beth this afternoon. Could he go now? After all that had happened? He had to. Now more than ever, he wanted to see Beth. Just sit in her presence for a while, and maybe life might make some sense. Davey's death had made him miss his chance way back in the fifth grade. He couldn't let Joe's death do the same. He'd never gotten a chance to express his feelings for her, had never gotten closure from that time. Maybe he could get some today. The death of another one of his boyhood friends was not going to stop him from seeing Beth. It was his destiny—unless she called and cancelled. That destiny seemed more fitting for his life and this fucking day.

***

Pete sat in his office holding the picture of his wife and kids in his hand. Joe was gone. Happened right in his precinct, in his barn. He had devoted his life to saving lives after Davey had died, and his childhood friend died in his own precinct. He had been told in the morning that Joe was there, in the holding cells, and he hadn't done anything. He hadn't made any phone calls. He hadn't tried to help him at all. Why?

Because you were too busy basking in your own glow from your big arrest. You, Mr. Big Shot, put your friend on hold, and now he's gone.

Pete grabbed his hair and pulled on it slightly, then shook his head in frustration. *You could have helped him. You have some pull. You left him there. Down where that animal was. Some detective. You're supposed to always be one step ahead. You were looking in the mirror with your chest pushed out, and you fell way fucking behind. You could have helped him.*

He began to hear a faint humming noise in his ears. What could he have done? *You could have tried,* he snapped back at himself. The humming was still there. He looked at the picture of his wife and kids. Where were Joe's wife and kids? Where were Davey's wife and kids? He dropped the picture on the desk, put his head in his hands, and moaned. He grabbed his phone, opened it, and scrolled to Hayward's number. He put his thumb on the call button but didn't press down. He took a deep breath and exhaled. He closed the phone and threw it on the desk. The humming had gotten a little louder.

You could have helped him.

Shut up, he told his mind. It didn't listen.

***

Tommy looked around at his new room. It was small. A little bigger than the six-by-eight, like they always say on the TV shows. He could hear the howls of the other inmates. He would have to establish his power. He wished he had gotten sent here when he was younger, when he had more fire in his belly. But he had one advantage—he had decided that his life had ended and he had nothing to lose. So they were gonna get a show when they fucked with him, and he knew they would. They would surely bring the Push out, and if he survived after that, he figured he would end up going completely insane in solitary confinement.

He was sure he had scared those pig-fuck cops. Were they ready to come through for him yet? He needed someone on the outside that could do him favours. He needed a second wave of Operation

Scare Those Pig-Fuck Cops to show his power. Force them to make his life easier in here. He had already planted the seed; he just needed someone to water it while he was stuck in here.

A guard walked up to the bars of his cell with two other guards behind him.

"Kelch."

"Yeah," he replied, unenthusiastically.

"You got a visitor."

The guard unlocked his cell. A visitor. Who? Rita the Rat? Couldn't be. Maybe his court-appointed attorney? The court wouldn't have had time to even appoint one yet. Why would they let him see anyone that wasn't family? Whoever it was, he knew what he had to do. Get them to help him. Get something done on the outside any way they could.

The guard led him through a series of doors and into a room with glass barriers and phones. He motioned to a booth, and Tommy walked over and sat down. He picked up the phone, and as he did, a scrawny teenage boy appeared on the other side of the window. He looked at Tommy for a few seconds, and then picked up the phone. Tommy didn't say anything—he had no idea who this was, and was ready to tell him he had the wrong person, when the boy spoke.

"You, uhhh," the boy said nervously, "you, uhhh, Tommy Kelch?"

"Maybe. Who the fuck are you?"

The boy looked around the room nervously, making very little eye contact with Tommy.

"Did you, uhhh," the boy paused again. "Did you, uhhhh, leave a baby in a trailer home seventeen years ago?"

Tommy said nothing, just stared at the boy who continued to look at him and then away.

"I'm, uhhh . . . I'm, uhhhh, I'm that baby," Cy said.

***

Hayward pulled into the coffee shop parking lot, his heart thudding in his chest about a thousand beats per second. He parked and got out. As he walked to the door and pulled it open, he wondered if he should have worn the brown pants. He scanned the patrons and then he saw Beth waving, down at the end. He walked towards her table. *Just calm down, buddy. Should have worn the brown pants.* Beth got up, gave him a small hug, and then they sat down.

"Thanks for coming, Hayward. I just, well, just seeing you the other day, well, I just wanted to see you, see how you've been, what you've been up to. Catch up, you know."

Wow! She's as nervous as I am. That made him feel better, and he began to relax a little. As he looked her over, he thought, *She's more beautiful today than ever.*

***

Tommy was lying on his cot with his hands clasped behind his head. He was grinning from ear to ear. *The legend continues.* He laughed.

"The legend continues," he said aloud, and laughed again.

"Shut the fuck up," someone called out from a nearby cell.

He laughed even louder.

***

"I don't think this is a good idea," Craig said, as he fiddled with the map.

"Good fucking thing I didn't ask ya what ya think, then," Cy replied.

"So, what do we gotta do again?" Craig asked.

"Tommy said he's gonna rot in there because there's a couple of bitches going to testify against him, and so I'm gonna do him a favour and take care of them."

"Take care—what do ya mean, 'take care?'"

"Like, I'm gonna take care of you if you keep on pissin' me off."

"Maybe he deserves to be there, Cy."

"Listen, if you found out your old man was alive, wouldn't you do just about anything to spend time with him?"

"I guess."

"Well, there you fuckin' go. Is this the street?"

Craig looked at the map quickly. "Yeah, pretty sure, number twelve is the house. Probably this one up ahead with all the police tape in the front yard and driveway."

Cy slowed down, pulled alongside the curb, and looked at the front of the house.

"Twelve. That's the place. So what now?"

"Well," Cy said, "Tommy said that she was a fat pig with Elvis-black hair."

"What's 'Elvis-black?'" Craig asked.

"Don't know really, that's just what he said. I think it's just a fat bitch with black hair."

A truck rolled by and parked along the curb on the opposite side of the house cordoned off with police tape. A large woman with dark black hair got out of the driver side. She went around to the back of the truck, opened the tailgate, and took out some bags.

"Showtime," Cy said as he put the truck into gear and eased away from the curb and into the road.

The lady closed the tailgate and began to walk across the street with her grocery bags. Cy dropped his foot to the floor and the truck sped towards her. She heard the sound, looked toward the truck, and started to waddle fast. Cy angled the steering wheel toward her. *Wham*! The truck smashed into her and drove her to the pavement. The truck continued its forward progression, jumping about two feet in the air as it rebounded from running over her carcass. Cy and Craig were jostled around in the cab. Cy continued to press the accelerator to the floor, and the truck got back to all four wheels and started to speed up again.

"Yeeehaw!" Cy yelled.

"That was fuckin' sick," Craig said as he looked through the truck's back window, trying to see the carnage.

***

"You said something about the Mayor's Office," Hayward said. Some things were starting to make sense.

"Yes, Daniel's company is tearing down the row houses that the veterans live in, and he and his brother are working with the Mayor's Office."

"I'm on suspension after being investigated due to an order by the Mayor's Office."

"No! Oh my God! He's crazy. Hayward, that's horrible. He's just doing that because he's jealous. I'll make some calls later and try to straighten that out."

As she said it, Hayward was taking a drink of coffee and started to choke. *Daniel's been with the girl of my dreams for the past seventeen years, and he is jealous of me? You cannot be serious.*

"So, I'm telling him tonight that I'm leaving him."

"Oh! Wow, that's crazy."

"I know. I was just going to go to a hotel, but I've been thinking that we've been together so long I really need to tell him this in person. I owe it to him."

"Well, you should be happy. You deserve to be happy. And if you ever need anything, even a place to stay, you know, rather than a hotel, you call my number."

"Thanks, Hayward, that's really sweet. I don't know how Daniel is going to react. I may need the police," Beth said jokingly. He could tell it wasn't completely a joke to her.

She looked at her watch. "I have to pick Phillip up from school now, but it was so great catching up. We should do it again sometime."

"Yeah, for sure, you have my number."

"Yes, I'll call you in the next few days and let you know where we're staying."

"That would be great. Call me anytime."

Beth gave him a small hug and left the coffee shop. Hayward sat back down.

What a fucking day! She's leaving Daniel! She just said she was actually leaving him. You gotta play this cool, man. Real cool and stay outta that friend zone. Leaving him! She should have never gone out with that Daniel Greensnot in the first place.

Hayward's phone rang. Pete. He felt shitty about running out of the precinct earlier, but he had to. He would just explain his mindset at the time to Pete if he asked.

"Hello," Hayward said.

"Hayward, I need to talk to you."

"Okay, Pete. When?"

"Right now. Can you come to Pier 28? I'm just parked on the dock here."

"Sure, buddy. I'm on my way."

"Thanks," Pete said, his voice cracking a little as he hung up.

He was relieved. The opportunity to talk to Pete meant he could stop feeling guilty about not talking to him earlier.

Was this day for real? Joe was dead. He felt a wave of sadness. And here he was, out on a coffee date. The wave of sadness crashed, and a wave of guilt rose right behind it. It didn't matter. It was all worth it. Just sitting with her for those forty-five minutes was magical. Hayward got up and walked to the door. *Catch up*, he laughed. All she had talked about was herself.

***

Cy brought his truck to a stop in front of Beth's house.

"This looks like the place," he said.

"What's this one look like?" Craig asked.

"Don't know, but she ain't fat with Elvis black hair. Probably with a young boy, Tommy had said. No cars in the driveway, so we'll wait and see what happens. Roll one up."

"Are you sure?"

"Roll one up," Cy said loudly.

***

"Why are we going here?" Phillip asked.

Beth guided the car into a parking spot at McDonald's.

"You like McDonald's, don't you?"

"Yes, Mommy."

"Well, we are gonna have a treat night."

She sighed. *This is it. This is what it's going to be like with no home for a while.* She fought back tears. She had to face him, but she was starting to doubt if she was ready to do it tonight.

***

Hayward pulled onto Pier 28 and saw Pete's car. He pulled up alongside and Pete got out. Hayward parked and got out. They walked to the front of the cars and embraced.

"Listen," Hayward said, "I'm sorry about running out of there today. I just . . ."

Pete waved a dismissive hand as his phone rang. He looked at the caller ID.

"It's the station," he said to Hayward as he answered. "Detective Lyons here. What? Okay. Yeah. Okay. I'll call you. Send somebody over there now."

He hung up and turned to Hayward.

"Rita, the one who gave up Kelch, just got run over in front of her house. Turns out, that crazy fucker has accomplices running around out here. I gotta call Alana, just be a second."

Accomplices. The sick fuck that killed Joe, killed and raped all those women, had accomplices. How anyone could be associated with that level of evil baffled Hayward.

"Alana, you and the kids go to the safe place. No, now—I need you to go now. I'll get some things for you and meet you there later. Yes, just leave his project there. I'll pick it up and bring it with me. Thank you, make sure you go now. Thanks, love you too. Bye."

"Fuck!" Pete said as he hung up the phone. "Fucker said he would be sending someone after my family and the love of my life. I'd like to get ahold of him. There wouldn't be any need for a trial."

***

"There's someone now," Craig said.

Cy jumped awake after just starting to doze off. They watched as a car pulled into the driveway and a man got out and went into the house.

"That definitely ain't her," Craig said.

"No, but Tommy said there may be an obstacle. Guess that's him."

Cy reached behind the seat and pulled out a hunting knife.

"You comin'?" he asked Craig.

"Might as well, at this point. If we get caught, I'm gonna fry witcha, anyway."

"That's the fucking spirit." Cy tucked the knife into his jacket. "I knew I was friends witcha for something other than your piss-poor rolling abilities."

Craig laughed.

"Let's go," Cy said as both boys jumped out of the truck into the oncoming darkness.

Chapter 20

Not This Time

"Listen, Hayward. I need to tell you something that I've been carrying around with me for the past seventeen years." Hayward listened intently, knowing nothing good came out of that time seventeen years ago. "You remember when Davey died?"

Hayward looked at him. *Do I remember! Are you fucking kidding? I never forgot. I think about it every day.*

Pete continued, "Davey didn't fall off the ledge."

Hayward looked at him, confused.

"What are you talking about? I was there. I saw him fall."

"You saw him falling. He was pushed."

"What?" Hayward said.

Pete began to sob.

"What?" Hayward said again, trying to comprehend.

"You . . ." Hayward said. "You . . ." He was having trouble getting the words out. "You pushed him?"

Pete nodded as he sobbed.

"You pushed him," he said again, sounding like he was telling his mind to believe it.

"I've never told anyone; I've been living with it for so long."

"You fucking pushed him!"

"I wanted to scare him. I didn't want him to die."

"You fucking bastard."

"He was my best friend, Hayward. I didn't want him to die. I just . . . I just . . ."

"You fucking murdered our friend," Hayward said, "and you didn't tell anyone."

"It wouldn't have changed anything; it wouldn't have brought him back."

"He wouldn't have fallen if you hadn't pushed him!" Hayward screamed. "Joe threw his life away because he couldn't get over it."

"I know, I know," Pete said as he sobbed.

"You fucking killed him too. Hell, we're all fucked up. You killed us all!" Hayward screamed. "You gutless fucking coward! Not one boy came up from the brook that day, you know."

"I know," Pete sobbed, sniffling.

"Not one of us has a childhood memory that doesn't involve that day. You killed Davey. You killed Davey. He was a little kid, and you killed him."

Pete sobbed uncontrollably.

Hayward screamed in his face, "And you kept it a secret all these years! While we spent our lives wondering why! You were okay, though, because you had the fucking answer!"

Hayward turned away, disgusted with Pete, and looked out at the harbour.

"I didn't want him to die. I miss him so much," Pete said.

"Shut up!" Hayward screamed.

"I didn't want—"

"Shut up!" Hayward screamed again. He stood directly in front of Pete and stuck his finger in his face. "Listen to me. Shut the fuck up and listen to me. I never, ever want to hear anything come out of your mouth again. Not a fucking word. You are dead now. You are dead like us, you fucking bastard. I'm dead to you. Do you understand? You killed us all that day, and now you live with that, you murdering son of a bitch."

Pete continued to sob as Hayward walked back to his car, got in, and drove away.

***

"What's the plan?" Craig asked as they walked up the driveway.

"Don't know," Cy replied. "Just follow my lead."

Cy rang the doorbell. He looked up at the canopy that overhung the front step. There was a fancy light there. A man opened the door and looked at the two boys quizzically before speaking.

"What can I do for you?" he asked, unimpressed that they were on his porch and taking up his time.

Cy hated him in the ten seconds he had been in his presence. This would be easy.

"Hi, we were just walking by, and we noticed that there were sparks coming out of the light fixture you got there. I have never seen anything like that before, so figured I better let you know."

The man looked up at the light fixture, concerned. He totally fell for it as he walked out onto the porch, looking up at the light.

"Sparks? Coming from where?"

Cy brought out the knife from his jacket. The man didn't even notice, just stood in front of him staring straight up. Cy plunged the knife into the man's gut. He let out a painful gargling noise.

"Get him inside," Cy said.

Craig and Cy pushed the man inside his house and closed the door. The man fell to the floor.

"What the fuck?" the man said. "What do you want? There's money in my wallet," he gasped.

"Oh, we're gonna take your money."

Cy grabbed his wallet, took the cash out, and glanced at the guy's ID. Daniel Green. Well, this was the right place. It would have been unfortunate for someone if it wasn't, Cy thought with a smirk. He positioned himself behind Daniel's head.

"You got the money, now leave me alone," Daniel said.

Who the fuck does this guy think he is? I'm in control here. It felt right, like it was in his DNA. He reached around with the knife and cut the guy's throat. Daniel screamed as Cy cut and then fell silent as his body fell to the floor with a thud. Blood began to spill from the neck, making a large puddle in the foyer.

"Go check the rest of the house. Make sure no one is here," he said to Craig.

Craig stood motionless, staring at the body.

"Go!" Cy yelled. Craig snapped out of it and began to run from room to room.

Cy looked at the front door; his mission was the bitch. The obstacle just became a bigger bloody mess of an obstacle. *Can't clean something like this up. Have to go to Plan B.* He laughed. There was no plan to begin with. He was doing what came . . . *natural. Gonna have to get her from outside. This aisle needs a major clean-up.*

Craig came running back.

"No one here," Craig said, out of breath.

"Okay, let's go back outside."

"What? Why don't we just hide in here?"

"Can't, man. Look at this. She'll see this and run for the fucking hills. You wanna try and hide this before she gets home?"

Craig looked at the massive puddle of blood.

"We'll get her from outside," Craig said as if it were his idea.

***

"Are you all done with your chicken nuggets?" Beth asked Phillip.

Phillip nodded as he played with the robot toy from his Happy Meal.

Time to go home and face the music. She wished she could take Phillip somewhere while she talked to Daniel. Oh well, he'd be fine in the car for a few minutes. She'd ask Daniel to talk to her outside, by the car, so she could see him, but he wouldn't be able to hear their conversation. *This is the hardest thing I'm going to have to do in my life.* She dreaded it. She thought about Hayward and the nice time they had spent together and smiled a little. Maybe there could be something there. *Maybe there already is.*

"Okay, time to go, Phillip."

Phillip shoved another half a nugget in his mouth and climbed down from his chair.

***

Hayward walked into his apartment and threw his coat on the chair. This was officially the worst day of his life. *They could write a script about my life, but no one would ever believe it*, he thought bitterly to himself. He opened the fridge, took out a beer, opened it, sat down in the chair, and turned on the television. He changed the channel to baseball. There, the Dodgers were playing—a nice baseball game. He took a couple gulps from the beer and started to play the day through in his head. The first talk with Pete. He wondered if Pete had done anything to try to help Joe's situation, but figured he hadn't. Then he had got suspended, because Daniel Greensnots was jealous. He took another couple gulps of beer. *That's the fucking kicker—jealous of me.*

Then that sick fuck killed Joe, and then told Pete he'd send someone after his family and the love of his life. That was an odd way to put it, he thought as he swigged the beer. Why wouldn't he just say Pete's family? His wife and kids were obviously the love of his life. Unless he was talking about someone else that wasn't his family. Did Pete have someone else in his life? Joe must have told him Pete's whole life story. He thought about the way Kelch had said it, with his head down, not looking at Pete. Joe had probably babbled to Kelch all their life stories. Hayward jumped up. A shiver shot up his back.

He was talking to me. The love of my life. Joe told him about Beth.

***

Pete pulled his car into the driveway of his house. He'd decided he would put in for a transfer. He needed to move, get a fresh start. *You're not going to get away with it this time*, he thought miserably. The hum in his head had gotten louder and had now started to sound like running water. He hoped in time the guilt for Joe would fade . . . *Now it's double.* The running-water sound in his head seemed to get louder. He had to pull it together—he was a father to two boys. *What kind of a father kills someone and keeps it a secret?* He wished his conscience would stop. He walked into the house. It was like his conscience had been hiding for years, but growing stronger, working out every day, and here it was today, a muscle-bound, repeating freak pounding the life out of him. *Like Davey's life, like Joe's life, like Hayward's.* He pulled a suitcase out of the closet and started stuffing some of his wife's clothes in it. He grabbed a few of his own things and threw them in.

Just get it together, get to Aunt May's, the safe house, and be with your family. It will be okay. He paused. *Why don't the other boys have families? Because of you.*

He thought of Hayward saying how they had spent their lives looking for the answers that he had. He started to sob again as he went into his sons' room and started grabbing some of their clothes.

The others have no children. You did that, and took their childhood.

"I lost my childhood, too!" he yelled at the empty room.

You killed it.

He stuffed the clothes in the suitcase. That's enough, he thought, and zipped it up.

You're not going to get away with this.

That's it. I am going to ignore you from now on.

Not this time.

The sound of the running water was getting louder. He placed the suitcase down by the door.

"What else do I need?" he said aloud and looked around the room.

***

Beth pulled into the driveway and saw Daniel's car.

"Okay, sweetheart," she said to Phillip, "I'm going to go talk to Daddy in that doorway, okay? You can see me right there. I need you to stay here, okay. Just stay in the car."

"Why can't I go up to my room?"

"Because, sweetie, we're going to go to a hotel for a sleepover tonight." She could tell Phillip was having a hard time processing the information. "Just wait right here, okay? And I'll explain when I come back."

Phillip looked at her, confused. "Okay, Mom," he said.

Beth leaned over and kissed his forehead. She opened the door, got out of the car, took a deep breath, and started walking toward the door. *Daniel must know this is coming, he has to know, he must know that you can't treat your wife like that.* She heard something and started to turn toward it when she was pushed to the ground with massive force. She slammed partly into the grass at the edge of the sidewalk and part of her bladder let go.

Daniel's going to kill me!

"Grab her feet," a voice said.

Oh my god! That's not Daniel. Terror took over her body, and the rest of her bladder let go. Someone pinned her shoulder blades with their weight.

"Grab her feet, I said."

Beth heard a crack and a thud.

"Fuck!" a voice yelled.

The person was off her back. She rolled over and looked up. A young man faced Hayward. He had a bat and he swung it hard, cracking the young man in the arm as he tried to block it. The young man held his arm, and Hayward swung the bat back the other way, so quickly that the young man couldn't block it and it caught him in the side of the head. Beth watched his knees give out and he dropped to the ground. Hayward held his hand out. Beth quickly grabbed it and he pulled her up.

"Let's go," Hayward said.

"Phillip," Beth muttered, "he's still in the car."

They ran to the car. As they did, Beth saw another man lying on the ground, rolling around in serious pain. Hayward opened the back door and she jumped in.

"Phillip," she said.

"Mommy."

Hayward jumped in the front. "Keys," he said, holding out his hand.

"They're in the ignition."

Hayward started the car and screeched the tires as he backed out of the driveway.

"Who were they?" she asked.

"I'll explain later." He sped away from the house.

"I'm so scared," she said.

"You're safe now," he said. "You're safe now."

And she knew she was.

***

Pete looked around the room. What else did she say to get? *You're not going to get away with it this time.* He saw some things on the table, Andrew's project. He walked over to the table and extended his arm to pick it up. He froze, staring down at the project. The water sound was getting louder and sounded like more water, *more like a rushing brook. You're not going to get away with it this time.*

He couldn't believe what he was seeing. On the table facing him was the cover of his son's project. It was a project on the ruffed grouse. He stared at the picture. *You didn't tell Hayward about that part.* The brook was getting louder. Pete felt as if all the blood had drained right out of his body. *You didn't tell him. Why?*

Pete turned and ran out of the kitchen and out of the house, leaving the suitcase. The sound of the brook got louder. He jumped into his car. *You didn't tell him why you pushed him, did you?* He backed out and drove down the street. *You're not going to get away with it this time.* He drove a couple of blocks and then pulled the car behind a strip mall and parked. The sound of the brook was deafening now. *You didn't tell him why, did you?* He took his revolver from its holster.

"I'm sorry!" he screamed. But all he heard was the rushing brook. Pete brought the gun up to his mouth.

"I'm sorry, boys," he said, and pulled the trigger.

About the Author

Kansas Bradbury was born and raised in North Sydney, Nova Scotia. He graduated from Saint Mary's University with a Bachelor of Commerce and subsequently became a drug store manager. In 2008, he moved from the retail business and began working as a heavy equipment operator in Alberta's oil sands. He started creative writing as a hobby, composing film scripts and short stories for fun. After receiving encouragement from his family and friends, he wrote The Rushing of the Brook, his first full-length novel. He currently resides in Fort McMurray with his wife Colleen and their two children.

CPSIA information can be obtained
at www.ICGtesting.com
Printed in the USA
LVOW12*0710071017
551575LV00007B/37/P

9 781525 501944